10/9

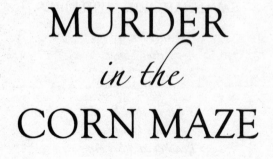

MURDER
in the
CORN MAZE

Books by G.A. McKevett

SAVANNAH REID MYSTERIES

Just Desserts
Bitter Sweets
Killer Calories
Cooked Goose
Sugar and Spite
Sour Grapes
Peaches and Screams
Death by Chocolate
Cereal Killer
Murder à la Mode
Corpse Suzette
Fat Free and Fatal
Poisoned Tarts
A Body to Die For
Wicked Craving
A Decadent Way to Die
Buried in Buttercream
Killer Honeymoon
Killer Physique
Killer Gourmet
Killer Reunion
Every Body on Deck
Hide and Sneak
Bitter Brew

GRANNY REID MYSTERIES

Murder in Her Stocking
Murder in the Corn Maze

Published by Kensington Publishing Corporation

G.A. McKEVETT

MURDER
in the
CORN MAZE

A GRANNY REID MYSTERY

KENSINGTON BOOKS
www.kensingtonbooks.com

KENSINGTON BOOKS are published by

Kensington Publishing Corp.
119 West 40th Street
New York, NY 10018

All Kensington titles, imprints and distributed lines are available at special quantity discounts for bulk purchases for sales promotion, premiums, fundraising, educational or institutional use. Special book excerpts or customized printings can also be created to fit specific needs. For details, write or phone the office of the Kensington Special Sales Manager: Kensington Publishing Corp., 119 West 40th Street, New York, NY, 10018. Attn. Special Sales Department. Phone: 1-800-221-2647.

Library of Congress Card Catalogue Number: 2019940171

Kensington and the K logo Reg. U.S. Pat. & TM Off.

ISBN-13: 978-1-4967-1629-3
ISBN-10: 1-4967-1629-9
First Kensington Hardcover Edition: October 2019

ISBN-13: 978-1-4967-1631-6 (e-book)
ISBN-10: 1-4967-1631-0 (e-book)

10 9 8 7 6 5 4 3 2 1

Printed in the United States of America

Lovingly dedicated to mothers everywhere:
those who bear children,
those who raise ones born to others,
and those who, by necessity, have mothered themselves.

Acknowledgments

I wish to thank all the fans who write to me, sharing their thoughts and offering endless encouragement. Your stories touch my heart, and I enjoy your letters more than you know. I can be reached at:

sonja@sonjamassie.com

and

facebook.com/gwendolynnarden.mckevett

Chapter 1

"Who woulda thought a shaggy ol' brown rug could change a nice little boy into a snarlin', spittin'-mad grizzly bear?"

Stella Reid stuck her needle into her pin cushion, sat back in her recliner, and admired her handiwork. Taking her praise to heart, her nine-year-old grandson, Waycross, cranked up the drama by lunging at his oldest sister, paper claws "shredding" the air a few inches from her nose.

"Watch yourself there, Mr. Grizzly Bear," Savannah warned him with all the authority of a precocious sixth-grader. "*I'm* the one carryin' the gun, and I'm death on soup cans on a fence. I could take you down with one shot."

"Could not neither!" Waycross stood on tiptoes in a vain attempt to be eyeball-to-eyeball with his sister. "That's nothin' but a silly BB gun you got there, and it ain't loaded! Even if it was, it couldn't bring down a rabbit, let alone a snarlin', spittin'-mad grizzly bear like me."

He turned to his grandmother, his freckled face almost as red as his mop of curly hair, which was sticking out from under the cap with round bear ears—also made from what had formerly been Stella's kitchen sink rug. "She couldn't take down no grizzly bear with a dumb ol' BB gun, huh, Gran?"

Some days, Stella felt like 90 percent of her time and energy were spent acting as judge and jury to settle disputes between her grandchildren. With all seven of them living beneath her roof, there was seldom a moment when there wasn't some sort of "trial" underway.

She liked to tell herself that she was "growing in understanding" along the way. She figured by the time she got to the Pearly Gates, she'd be able to give King Solomon himself a run for his money in the wisdom department.

"It's Halloween, Mr. Waycross," she said with a tired sigh. "So, your sister's as much of a real hunter as you are a real grizzly bear." She reached over and tucked some of his copper curls back beneath the cap. "And I reckon her gun's about as deadly as your claws. You both better show each other some heartfelt respect, if you intend to get through that parade tonight still alive and kickin', let alone with the prize!"

Both kids giggled, and the argument was ended, at least for the time being. Stella savored the momentary peace.

But her golden silence was short-lived.

A few seconds later, a series of bloodcurdling shrieks erupted from the children's bedroom. It sounded like someone's hide was being removed, inch by inch, with red-hot pinchers.

Or perhaps, one of the girls had grabbed eleven-year-old Marietta's favorite hair bow. With Miss Mari it was often hard to tell if she was being tortured or just pitching a hissy fit.

Stella jumped to her feet and ran from the living room into the bedroom, ready to apply a tourniquet, fetch the fire extinguisher, or remove sharp objects that had been manually inserted into a kid—who might or might not themselves be innocent—by a malicious, mischievous sibling.

Fortunately, the latter didn't happen often, but it wasn't exactly unheard of in the Reid household.

The last incident was when ten-year-old Vidalia had snuck beneath the bed and stabbed the sleeping Marietta in the rear with a hat pin.

The injury was worse than what Stella could treat with her bottle of Merthiolate and had required a trip to the doctor's office for a tetanus shot. Then there was a follow-up visit for antibiotics when the wound got infected.

Vidalia had spent some meaningful, educational time with her grandmother behind the henhouse for that infraction.

As Stella charged into the bedroom, she hoped that whatever the crisis might be, it would prove less expensive this time. Doctor visits, shots, and penicillin didn't come cheap these days, and she did well to afford oatmeal, bologna, and potatoes.

The vision that greeted her inside the tiny bedroom was one of mayhem. She had arrived not a moment too soon, because Marietta was trying to pull Vidalia off the top berth of one of the three sets of bunk beds. Only a year younger than Marietta and nearly as large, Vidalia wasn't making it easy for her.

Although she was completely off the bed, Vidalia's arms and legs were wrapped around the railing, and she was hanging on for dear life.

To make the scene even more bizarre, Marietta was attired in a red, chiffon evening dress and Vidalia a tropical-print, satin sarong. Both dresses had been borrowed from Stella's next-door neighbor, whose extensive wardrobe was far fancier than her own.

The girls also wore paper crowns spangled with glitter and the occasional rhinestone.

In the four seconds it took Stella to rush across the room, pull Marietta off her sister, and lower Vidalia safely to the floor, Stella had plenty of time to wonder how those crowns had managed to stay on during the fight that would have put a St. Paddy's Day, Irish donnybrook to shame.

"That stupid-face, contrary Mari was trying to snatch my crown," Vidalia wailed. "She was fixin' to rip it right off my head after me spendin' all day long gluin' glitter and diamonds on it!"

"I need it more than she does!" Marietta yelled. "She's just a *princess*, and I'm a *queen*. I need to wear the bigger crown, or we'll both look dumb as gutter dirt, and folks will laugh at us tonight at the parade."

Stella stood for a moment, staring at her granddaughter, whose audacity never failed to amaze and alarm her. Not to mention the girl's vocabulary.

"Do you have any idea what 'gutter dirt' is, Miss Marietta?"

The child thought it over for a while, then shrugged. "No, but it's what Vidalia's made of. And rat tails and slug slime and maggot poop and—"

"Okay! That'll be *quite* enough out of you, young lady. Apologize to your sister for manhandlin' her, sayin' ugly things about her, and tryin' to snatch the crown off her that she worked so hard on, just because you like it better than the one you made."

"But—!"

"No buts! Apologize and mean it, or you and me's gonna continue this discussion behind the woodshed."

"We ain't got no woodshed!"

"As you know, the henhouse does fine in a pinch. You sass me one more time, young lady, I'll be takin' you out there and introducin' you to Miss Hickory Switch. And believe you me, you won't like her one bit!"

Marietta weighed the pros and cons far longer than Stella would have liked.

I'm gonna have to find new ways to instill fear and trembling, or at least a smidgeon of respect, in that young'un or we're both doomed, she thought.

Finally, Marietta mumbled a lackluster, one-syllabled "Sorry," in her sister's general direction.

"That was one of the puniest apologies ever uttered in the history of the world," Stella told her. "Try again. Harder."

"S-o-o-o-r! R-e-e-e-e!" Marietta shouted in her sister's face. "I'm so, so, so sorry, Vidalia Reid . . . that your face looks like a skunk's rear end!"

"That's it!" Stella grabbed Marietta by the hand and escorted her out of the bedroom, through Stella's own bedroom and the living room, where Savannah and Waycross watched, eyes wide and mouths open.

"Wait! Granny! Wait a cotton-pickin' minute! Where're you takin' me? Are you gonna give me a beatin'?" Marietta asked when Stella pulled her out the front door and slammed it behind them.

Stella looked down at Marietta and saw traces of genuine fear in the child's eyes. She thought of the times she had seen her daughter-in-law raise her hand to the children. Violence and cursing were the only tools in Shirley Reid's parenting kit. They were all the children had known until the courts had removed them from their mother and placed them in Stella's custody.

"No, child," Stella told her granddaughter. "I would never beat you, and this time I'm not even gonna spank you, though sometimes you do stand on my last nerve and dance a jig. I'm fixin' to sit you down over here in a place of repose."

She led her to the large porch swing and settled her onto it.

"What's 'a place of repose'?" Marietta asked, flouncing about like a hen sitting on a nest made of barbed wire.

"A peaceful spot where you can rest and—"

"I ain't tired."

"You should be. After all that hullabaloo, you should be plumb wore to a frazzle. Rest, like I said, and compose yourself, and reconsider your ways."

5

"What's that?"

"Think about what you did wrong."

"I didn't do a blamed thing wrong! It's Vi who did wrong! She's the one you should be pushin' down on swings. She's too dumb to know that a queen needs a bigger crown than—"

"Hush, Marietta Reid. Just 'cause you're reposin' on the porch, don't mean that marchin' you off behind the henhouse ain't still a consideration if you keep smarting off to me. I am your *grandmother*, and I won't abide it!"

They glared at each other for what seemed, at least to Stella, a miserably long time before the child finally looked away and sighed. Her shoulders and her chin dropped a notch.

Stella had a feeling that was as much of a sign of contrition as she was likely to get this go-around.

"That's right. You sit there and think about how you could've handled the last ten minutes differently and had a better outcome."

Marietta opened her mouth to retort but seemed to think better of it and shut it.

As Stella walked back to the door, she added, "Don't you dare lift your hind end off that swing till I come back to fetch you."

As she walked inside the old shotgun house and closed the screen door behind her, Stella whispered a heartfelt prayer. "Lord, please fill my heart with patience for that child. Otherwise, I'm afraid that one of these days me and her's gonna tangle, and I'm not sure who'd win."

Chapter 2

A few hours later, as Stella stood with the crowd on Main Street in McGill, Georgia, watching the tiny town's annual Halloween parade go by, she couldn't help beaming with pride at the Reid children.

Her family was well represented, if she did say so herself. Unlike many of the other costumes that had been purchased through catalogues and on out-of-town shopping expeditions, her grandchildren's outfits were homemade. Gathering whatever they could find around the house and yard, they had used their imagination, thread, glue, and nails to transform themselves into characters they loved and admired.

The youngest, little first-grader Jesup, had chosen to be Tinkerbell for a night, in an old olive T-shirt, cut with a jagged hem. Cotton balls had been glued together to create large pom-poms that were then stuck to the tops of green flip-flops. Some coat hangers and panty hose had been transformed into translucent wings that bobbed nicely as she marched along, carrying a wand made of a broken broomstick, its tip dipped in glue, then glitter.

She was prancing down the street, dousing bystanders with her leftover "fairy dust."

But only the females.

Stella had warned her before the parade had begun that, "Menfolk don't cotton to gettin' glitterfied."

Between Jesup flinging magic here and there with wild abandon, and the two older girls' crowns, the glitter bill alone had laid waste to Stella's meager Halloween budget. But seeing the smile of pure happiness on little Tinkerbell's face, Stella decided it was money well spent.

Someone squeezed closer to Stella, then poked her in the ribs with a fingertip. She turned and saw it was her next-door neighbor, Florence. As always, Stella had mixed feelings about seeing her childhood friend. Flo was a good person—when it suited her purposes. She was always happy to do a neighbor a favor and was equally passionate about reminding them and everyone else in town about it from that day forward.

"Those two granddaughters of yours look mighty pretty wearing my dresses," Florence observed, pointing at Queen Marietta, dressed in the red chiffon number with a zillion yards of net petticoats, and Princess Vidalia, in the brilliant tropical sarong that Florence had bought last summer for a wannabe luau at Judge Patterson's antebellum mansion.

"They do," Stella said. "Thank you for the use of them outfits. It meant the world to the girls. They feel mighty glamorous in them."

"Well," Florence sniffed. "I knew the fanciest thing in your closet was your funeral dress, the one I bought for you when your Arthur passed away, all unexpected like."

Stella winced. Good ol' Flo had a way of finding a person's deepest, most painful wound, sticking her finger right in the middle of it, and twisting.

Discarding the first five possible retorts that ran through her mind, Stella settled on, "Thank goodness for you and your fancy dresses, Flo. Queen Marietta woulda hightailed it to Timbuktu if I'd suggested she wear my funeral dress. It's not exactly regal."

"No, but you're one of the best-dressed women at every funeral this town has, year after year."

Stella thought, *She's leavin' off the "Thanks to me" part. Reckon it's just understood.*

"Thanks to me," Flo added.

Or not.

"Hey, look who's walking over here," Florence said, jabbing her in the ribs again. "He's got a way of showing up wherever you are. Ever notice that?"

Stella looked around to see who Florence was referring to . . . although she had a pretty good idea. As a result of those suspicions, her pulse rate went up at least ten points.

Yes. There he was, strolling along the edge of the street, patrolling the parade, making sure no parent was too full of hard apple cider to keep their little ones out of the road and away from the floats and vehicles.

"Sheriff Gilford," Stella said when he stopped next to her and gave her a warm smile that caused her knees to weaken. "I see you're dressed in your usual Halloween costume."

Manny Gilford's celebratory attire was a running joke in the small town. Since he had joined law enforcement at the age of twenty-two, few McGillians had ever seen him in anything but his khaki uniform.

However, on major holidays he would exchange his mundane, chocolate-brown tie for some sort of colorful, outlandish monstrosity, befitting the occasion. Tonight, he was wearing one with glow-in-the-dark skeletons whose bony hands were outstretched, grasping for victims. At the bottom the word *Gotcha!* was dripping with "blood."

"Your clan's sure putting on a show," he said, pointing to the Reid kids, marching by. "They do you proud, Miss Stella."

"Mari and Vi are wearing *my* dresses," Flo interjected. "Heaven knows, they needed something fancy to wear if they were going to be royalty."

Stella couldn't help but be pleased when Sheriff Gilford chose to completely ignore Florence's declaration. In fact, she found it more deeply soul satisfying, on numerous levels, than she wanted to admit.

"Your little Alma's a cutie in that wig," he said. "She's Little Orphan Annie, right?"

"Reckon so. We worked on that headpiece for ages. Took three skeins of orange yarn and a ton of curlin' and sprayin' with starch. The worst part was, she kept sayin' 'Gee whiskers' and 'Leapin' lizards' the whole time. You'd be surprised how quick hearin' that gets old."

He chuckled, and Stella couldn't help being aware, as she had been for years, of what an attractive man the sheriff was—tall, tanned, strong-jawed, and muscular, with intense, gray eyes that missed nothing. Only his thick silver hair betrayed his fifty-plus years.

Stella had known him since they were both skinny, knob-kneed teenagers. He had grown more handsome with each passing decade. She wasn't sure if she had grown more or less attractive over time, but Manny still seemed to approve of her looks. He'd had a crush on her when they were kids, and she had reason to believe, now that he was a widower and she a widow, that flame might have been rekindled.

Since her husband's passing, Sheriff Gilford had stayed close, offering friendship, help, and protection to her and her brood of grandkids.

Stella spoke a prayer of thankfulness every night for the gift of a friend like Sheriff Manny Gilford.

He looked puzzled when he saw Cordelia pass, wearing an old white shirt that had *Dr. Cordelia Reid* scrawled above the pocket with a black marker. Around her neck hung an old stethoscope she had borrowed from their family physician, Dr. Hynson.

"Cordelia doesn't look so scary," he remarked. "Who's she supposed to be?"

Stella grinned. "She said she just wanted to be herself, only a doctor, so she could boss everybody around and tell them what to do."

"Now *that's* a frightening thought."

"Yes. I'm afraid she's already known around town for bein' a bit overbearing and opinionated."

Florence snickered. "Runs in the family."

"Shush, Florence Bagley," Stella told her, "or you won't be getting any of my Halloween carrot cake later tonight."

Manny quirked an eyebrow, suddenly alert. "Carrot cake? I think I'll come trick-or-treat *your* house."

"You're more'n welcome to." Stella felt yet another jab in the ribs.

Having reached her tolerance level with Florence, she turned to her friend and whispered, "The next finger you poke me with, gal, you ain't gettin' back."

"The bear and the hunter are my favorites, though," Manny added, watching the marchers and unaware of the women's exchange. "Your Savannah looks mighty stern, carting that BB gun on her shoulder. It's not loaded, right?"

"Of course not. We'd run outta BBs," Stella assured him with a smirk. "I debated the wisdom of lettin' the child march in a parade with an empty BB gun, but I'd run plumb outta rock salt for my shotgun."

He laughed. "Good call. Don't worry. If he gets too outta hand, I'll cuff him. I've taken worse grizzlies than that one into custody.

I bled some in the process, but so did they, and the job got done."

Stella laughed and watched her grandson's antics as he struggled to get away from his captor. She had to admit that she might have created a monster when she'd cut up her rug and fashioned that costume for the child. He was taking his role quite seriously. She had tied a large, thick rope around his waist, and Savannah was leading him by it—or was at least trying to—the chore made more difficult by the BB rifle propped on her shoulder.

Meanwhile, the boy growled, snarled, and clawed the air as he fought against the rope that held him, and occasionally lunged at those sitting on the curb.

Some of the onlookers appeared to be genuinely afraid... much to the ferocious bear's delight.

With pride, Stella noticed that her softhearted grandson didn't unleash his ferocity on the smallest members of the audience, but saved it for their older siblings and parents.

Nodding toward Grizzly Waycross, Manny said, "The way that boy's hamming it up, I figure he's a shoo-in for first prize. Not only that, but he would've given Mr. Michael Douglas a run for his money for that 'Best Actor' Oscar."

Something farther up the street caught Manny's eye. A group of teenage boys was darting across the street. They only narrowly missed being struck by the McGill fire engine with a gigantic tarantula and webs on its hood. Astride the spider was the fire chief, wearing a Ronald Reagan mask and an enormous cowboy hat. Waving vigorously to the bystanders, he shouted, "Mr. Gorbachev, tear down this wall!"

"Gotta go. Good luck with the judging," the sheriff said as he hurried away to deal with the miscreants.

"That Manny's downright sweet on you," Florence said in her ear. "He's carried a torch for you since third grade."

Stella felt another sharp poke in her ribs.

Half a second later, Stella grabbed the offending finger and gave it a considerable twist.

Florence yelped and pushed away from her. "O-o-w! Dadgum, Stella May, that *hurt*!"

"Good. I was intendin' for it to." Stella pointed to Cordelia. "Go tell it to my doctor granddaughter there. She'll listen to that finger with her stethoscope, give you a diagnosis, then offer you some good medical advice, like, 'Don't go pokin' my granny no more. Next time your finger might get broke!'"

Chapter 3

Ten minutes later, the parade had ended at the town gazebo, where the judges sat, preparing to grapple with their monumental decision: Who would win the contest for best costume in the McGill's Chills-and-Thrills Halloween Parade?

Pastor O'Reilly, Judge Patterson, and the town librarian, Miss Rose Clingingsmith, took their duties quite seriously. Not only was the cash prize of ten dollars a considerable amount of money to a child in their small, rural town, but the bragging rights to such an honor lasted a lifetime.

It wasn't unusual to hear people introduced or described years later with an appellation attached to their names that harkened back to their victory, as in: "Did you hear Sally Wilton's marryin' ol' Harv Brown, the Chills-and-Thrills winner of 1977? Yeah, he was the Fred Flintstone that liked-to-never got that glued-on black hair stuff off his chest, arms, and legs. I heard his wife had to shave him all over and scrub him down with Ajax to set him right again."

So, it was with a sense of apprehension and rapt attention that the townsfolk stood silently around the gazebo, straining to hear the whispered discussion between the three judges that would determine who would receive the coveted award.

Stella's grandchildren were gathered close around her, Savannah holding her right hand, and Waycross her left. Their friends and neighbors were sending admiring, amused looks their way, particularly at Waycross, who—overheated as he was from all of his bear duties—had pulled his shaggy cap off, releasing his wild array of red curls. It was, indeed, the first sighting of a ginger grizzly in McGill history.

It seemed a done deal, this contest. Obviously, he had been the star of the show, and Stella was happy for him. Not only would the money be a major lottery hit for him, but for the first time in his short life, he seemed to be on the town's good side.

Waycross was a bright, mischievous kid, and a few of his antics had earned him a reputation as a bit of a rascal. As a result, many parents encouraged their offspring to "steer clear o' that carrottop, Reid boy."

It took less time than usual for the trio of judges to reach their decision. After only half a minute, Pastor O'Reilly stood, a big smile on his face, and picked up a large blue award ribbon from the folding card table in front of them.

"We judges have made our decision," he began.

Both Waycross and Savannah gave Stella's hands tight squeezes. They looked up at her with eager, happy eyes, and she gave them encouraging nods.

"It is with great pleasure that we present the blue ribbon and cash prize to this year's winners of McGill's Chills-and-Thrills Halloween Parade. Drum roll, please!"

The librarian, Rose Clingingsmith, playfully used her fingers as "drumsticks" on the card table top, heightening the suspense.

Judge Patterson remained stoic and silent, as befitted his position as the richest and most powerful man in town.

"This bright blue, first-prize ribbon goes to"—Pastor O'Reilly turned and smiled at Waycross, then Savannah—"the bear and the hunter!"

Cheers erupted! Applause thundered! Stella heard her grandchildren shriek with delight.

But she heard a couple of other happy screams from the far side of the crowd. Turning, she saw two preschool-age boys pushing their way through the crowd, running toward the judges.

The smallest was wearing a dime-store, plastic costume that might have been a teddy bear at one time, before the face mask had become so worn that the features were almost indistinguishable.

The oldest looked like an elderly fellow in slouchy attire. He was dressed in a grown man's work clothes, with the sleeves and legs rolled into thick cuffs. A tie belt held up the pants, which were so large he and his brother could have both fit inside at the same time with plenty of room to spare.

Stella quickly surmised the child was wearing his grandfather's clothes.

She wasn't the only grandparent in town who was raising their grandchildren. So was Dave Houchin. His single-parent daughter had run away to Atlanta last year, leaving the boys with him. She hadn't been seen or heard from since.

Everyone in town knew that Dave, a widower with a kind and generous heart, was doing his best to raise the boys. Sadly, everyone also knew that, in spite of his good intentions, Dave wasn't up to the task. With arthritic knees, a failing farm, and a ramshackle house, he was struggling just to keep them fed and dressed. Clean and tidy were out of the question.

But they were sweet boys, with their grandpa's kindly disposition, and the family—minus the wayward daughter—was a favorite in the town.

The boys' joy and excitement were obvious as they scrambled up onto the gazebo, eager to collect the ribbon and cash prize.

She glanced down at her own grandchildren and saw the looks of shock and indignation on their faces. The crowd had stopped cheering and begun to mumble among themselves, questioning this turn of events.

Waycross tugged at Stella's hand. "He meant us," the boy told her. "Pastor O'Reilly meant us when he said 'the bear and hunter.' Not them."

One look at the minister's face told Stella that her grandson was right. He looked as confused and upset as Waycross.

"But the Houchin boys think *they* won," Savannah said softly. "Look at them. At their little faces. They're so happy."

"Of course they're happy!" Waycross replied indignantly. "They think *they're* gonna take *our* blue ribbon! But they can't! It's *ours*!"

Stella looked up at the boys on the stage, literally hopping up and down with glee. She thought of their mother, driving off and leaving them behind without a word, and the unknown fathers who had never claimed them in the first place.

Stella looked down at her own grandchildren, so in need of a blessing like this. She didn't know what to do.

Neither did Pastor O'Reilly. He was giving her a look of helplessness that mirrored what she was feeling.

Then she heard Savannah say, "Let's let them have it, Waycross. They've had a really hard time here lately. They need it more than we do."

"There ain't no red ribbon, no second place," Waycross argued. "It's blue and first place or nothin'. We won it!"

"And we know that," Savannah replied gently. "We'll always know we won. I reckon that's enough for me. Is it enough for you?"

Stella glanced around and saw that the whole town was watching and waiting, well aware of what was happening.

Waycross looked up at the gazebo, where the younger boys were hugging each other tightly and laughing.

His face softened, and he nodded. "They *have* had a bad time of it with their mom runnin' off, and then they caught the measles. Didn't git to play outside all summer."

Stella leaned down and put an arm around each child. "Is that what you've decided then?" she asked. "Are you gonna let them little guys have it?"

"It's the right thing to do," Savannah said most emphatically.

"Yeah, I guess," Waycross replied with far less enthusiasm.

Stella stood up, caught the pastor's eye, and gave him an acquiescent nod.

He smiled at her, Savannah, and Waycross in turn. Then went about his duties of bestowing the ribbon on the jubilant "winners."

"You did a good thing, children," Stella told the generous twosome as they watched the boys beam, accepting their prize. "I'm so proud of you both. You should feel a heap o' satisfaction, knowin' you were kind to those in need."

"Can't stick satisfaction in a frame and hang it on the wall though," Waycross grumbled.

"No, you can't. But better than that, you can keep it right here"—she tapped his chest with her finger—"and it'll warm your heart and give you comfort every single time you think about it for the rest of your born days."

Waycross looked up at her doubtfully. "That's better than a blue ribbon?"

"A sight better. Trust me."

"Okay. I hope you're right."

Stella laughed, kissed the top of his sweat-damp, copper curls, and sent a prayer of gratitude heavenward, giving thanks for her sweetest blessings . . . the best grandchildren in the world.

But, as usual, her moment of bliss was short-lived.

Hearing a loud shriek of familiar pitch and intensity coming from behind her, she whirled just in time to see Vidalia grab a large handful of Marietta's hair and give it a vigorous yank.

Observant as Stella was, it didn't take her long to discern the reason for the younger girl's attack. Marietta was holding her sister's oversized, queenly crown in her hand.

Managing to extricate herself and her locks from her sibling's grip, Marietta jammed the larger crown onto her head and attempted an escape.

Unfortunately, she chose a path directly through the McGill High School marching band. She had underestimated her own size—enhanced by the height of her sister's crown and the copious fluffy petticoats beneath Florence's evening dress. When she tried to dart between the tuba player's legs, she became hopelessly entangled and knocked him off his feet.

They landed on the asphalt in a crumpled heap that consisted of red petticoats, a well-shined tuba, the glittery crown, a squalling Marietta, and a now-dusty green uniform with white trim, gold braid, and a highly indignant band member inside it.

Stella rolled her eyes heavenward and amended her prayer about having the world's best grandkids.

"Except that 'un," she whispered. "I don't mean no disrespect, Lord, but you best give *me* patience or *her* some fleet feet, 'cause if I lay hands on that young'un, I swear, I'll—"

Chapter 4

Stella did manage to lay hands on Marietta, but as fate would have it—or as heaven had arranged it—Stella's best friend, Elsie Dingle, strolled by at that moment, decked out in a sequin spangled dress, fake fur, and oversized earrings. Though it might not have been obvious to all, Stella knew the glamorous attire was Elsie's way of paying homage to her favorite singer. Stella couldn't recall ever being so happy to see Miss Aretha Franklin—or Elsie in any shape or form—suddenly appear from out of nowhere and take matters in hand.

In her own gracious, peaceful way, Elsie intervened by gently removing Marietta's arm from Stella's grasp and pulling the child into her embrace.

Elsie had many talents, which included: baking the town's best coconut cakes, having the strongest, clearest alto voice in the church choir, creating peace where there was chaos, and hugging folks who needed it.

The deliciously plump, beautiful, black lady with a halo of silver hair had an exceedingly ample bosom, and its size was surpassed only by her enormous heart. As a result, when Elsie wrapped her arms around one of her fellow McGillians, who was hurt, anxious, or lonely, and invited them to lay their weary head on her chest, their troubles seemed to just melt away on the cushion of love she provided.

Although, at the moment, Marietta was doing a lot more wriggling and protesting than melting.

"Lemme go! Lemme go!" the child hollered, struggling. "Hell's afire, I can't catch a breath! You're smotherin' me to death here!"

Stella stifled a giggle as she plucked Vidalia's crown off Marietta's head and said, "Watch your language there, Miss Mari, or I'll tell Elsie to hug you till your eyes bug out. You better believe she can do it, too."

Handing the crown back to Vidalia, she gave Elsie a wink and a grin. "Thank you, Sister Elsie, for comfortin' my granddaughter in her time of need."

"My pleasure." Elsie released her captive and gave her a kiss on the top of her now-bare head. "Y'all headed out to the plantation for the hayride?" she asked Stella.

The question that hadn't been asked—that didn't need to be asked—was whether Stella would be treating her grandchildren to a trip to Judge Patterson's giant corn maze. Other than the lighting of the town Christmas tree, the unveiling of McGill's revered, life-sized nativity scene, and the singing of carols by candlelight, the corn maze was McGill's most celebrated annual event.

Every year, Judge Patterson invited the townspeople to a Halloween extravaganza at his majestic mansion, situated on the outskirts of town, among the cotton and cornfields. For as many generations as anyone could remember and longer still, the Patterson family had owned the largest swath of land, the most productive farm, and the grandest home in the county.

Not even the American Civil War had been able to destroy the Patterson family or their plantation. While most of the South's antebellum mansions had not survived the conflict, the Pattersons' had been spared and transformed into a military hospital by northern troops.

Many suspected the elegant old structure was haunted by the countless sick and wounded soldiers who had perished within its silk-covered walls.

Although Elsie Dingle didn't suspect.

She was sure of it.

Like generations of her family before her, slaves and free, Elsie had worked on the estate since she was a child. First, she had picked and chopped cotton, then performed menial duties in the kitchen. Finally, she had become head cook. More than once, Elsie had told Stella that she'd heard noises and seen apparitions within the main house that couldn't be explained, other than to ascribe them to the supernatural.

Often, Elsie had expressed her joy at having an apartment of her own above the garage, the carriage house in days of yore, and not a room in the grand old mansion itself.

"It's bad enough bein' there in the daytime," she frequently told Stella, "but come sundown, once them supper dishes are done, I hightail it outta there and don't look back. There just ain't room for Miss Elsie Dingle *and* a passel o' soldier boy ghosts under one roof."

Stella, on the other hand, was less impressed with such matters. Long ago, she'd decided she had enough trouble dealing with folks who were still above ground and sucking air, to waste time worrying about those who had passed on.

There were only two souls on the other side she was truly aching to see—her momma and her Arthur—and she had a gaggle of children yet to raise before she could look forward to joining them in Paradise.

Elsie leaned close to Stella and whispered in her ear, "If y'all wanna go through the maze and money's tight . . ."

"When ain't it?" Stella sighed. "These young'uns eat more with each passing day."

"That's what I figured." Elsie gave Stella one of her sweetest, most understanding smiles. "So, I worked a little something out with the judge. I told him I was gonna need some extra help, straightening up the kitchen afterward, what with all that punch I'm gonna have to make, and I asked him if I could hire you and the kids as assistants."

"Hire us?" Stella brightened.

"That's what I asked him, but he turned me down. You know what a tightwad the judge is. They say he's still got the first nickel that was ever given to him as a child."

Stella's heart sank a bit as she looked down at the happy faces of her grandchildren. Soon they would have to be told that, once again, they weren't going to the maze with the rest of the town's children. She had so hoped Savannah and Waycross would win the cash prize and offer to pay the one-dollar-per-person fee to enter.

"That's okay. At least you tried, Sister Elsie," she said, patting her friend's shoulder. "Bless your heart for thinkin' of us like that."

Elsie's grin widened. "I ain't told you the best part! When he said he didn't wanna spend the money, I told him he could pay you in maze tickets, one for each of you. He said he'd rather have the entry money you'd pay than some kitchen help for me, and I made sure he understood he wouldn't be gettin' no cash outta you. I told him you had too many grandkids and too many mouths to feed to waste money on a corn maze, so if he didn't fork over the tickets, he still wouldn't get no money, *and* he'd have a cranky cook on his hands, 'cause she'd have to clean up all that punch mess on her own."

Stella laughed, knowing exactly what the twinkle in Elsie's eyes meant. Although Elsie had a well-deserved reputation for being the best cook in town, she was also known for burning a dish now and again if she was in a bad mood and believed somebody had it coming to them.

"Judge Patterson might be a skinflint, when it comes to his wallet," Elsie continued, "but he ain't fool enough to get on the bad side of the woman who cooks his supper."

Stella laughed. "And breakfast and dinner. You mentioned he hates them tough ruffles around his fried eggs, not to mention biscuits with scorched, black bottoms."

Discreetly, Elsie slipped her hand into her coat pocket and pulled out an envelope, which she slid into Stella's purse. "There ya go, sugar. Y'all enjoy yourselves."

Stella hugged her friend, close and tight, and gave her a kiss on the forehead. "You are the *best*, Sister Elsie. And we won't let you down with that punch cleanup business, neither. You just let us know when you need us there in the kitchen, and we'll be there with bells on."

"Oh, don't be silly. I put out Thanksgiving and Christmas dinners for more'n fifty of the judge's guests every year and an Easter buffet that would've fed Sherman's army. I don't need help makin' a bit o' Halloween punch for the town children."

Stella gasped and whispered, "Why, Sister Elsie, you done *lied* to your employer!"

"Ain't the worst sin I ever committed," she replied with a snicker. "I done meaner this mornin' before I even hauled my bones outta bed, thinkin' about that lop-eared mule-of-a-boss of mine and what I'd like to do to him some days."

"Well, you must be doin' enough good in the world to offset it, 'cause you ain't been struck by lightnin' yet."

Stella looked over at Jesup, who was attempting to bestow her fairy dust on the judge's persnickety wife, and meeting hearty resistance.

"I better go round up my grandbabies," she told Elsie. "Looks like Mrs. Patterson ain't in the mood to go flyin' over London."

"Not everybody has a heart for the fanciful," Elsie said. "And that's just sad."

Stella hurried away to gather Tinkerbell, Savannah the hunter, Waycross the grizzly, Dr. Cordelia, Little Orphan Alma, Queen Marietta, and Princess Vidalia. As she herded them toward her old Mercury panel truck and loaded them inside, she thought how grateful she was to have these blessings. Every single one of them.

Yes, she thought, *even Marietta.*

They kept her heart fanciful. Sometimes they even made her feel like *she* was flying over merry ol' London town in the moonlight, glistening from head to toe with fairy dust.

Chapter 5

"Last year I got to go to the plantation in the school bus," Savannah said, peering out the windshield of Stella's panel truck at the two-lane highway that led to the Patterson estate. "Wonder why it is that the judge and his missus favor the fifth-grade classes like they do every year, giving them a special trip up here and a glass of punch each?"

"Don't forget the punkin!" Marietta piped up from the back. "They gave us a free punkin. Even if it *was* for the whole class. It wasn't a particularly big one either. Just an itty-bitty little thang with some bird pecks and poops on the bottom of it."

The six kids in the back collapsed into giggles at the word *poops.*

Savannah rolled her eyes and said, "You mustn't look a gift horse in the mouth, Mari."

"Or a gift punkin' on the butt!" Marietta shot back, causing a new round of guffaws.

"Okay, okay," Stella said, suppressing a grin of her own. "That'll be enough about punkin bottoms, bird droppin's, and the Pattersons. They do a lotta good for the folks of this town. Our family included."

She didn't add that, without the intervention of Judge Patterson and the insistence of Sheriff Gilford, she never would have been awarded custody of her grandchildren. To mention it would have opened a family wound that everyone in the truck felt, but tried not to discuss too often.

Having a mother in prison wasn't something the children were proud of, as it made them a frequent subject of McGill gossip.

One sideways glance at Savannah, and the serious look on the child's face told Stella that she was thinking the same thing.

Savannah lowered her voice and said to her grandmother, "The judge and his wife getting all generous once a year like they do . . . I think it has something to do with the election. When they hand you the punch, they give you a big old toothy grin and tell you to be sure your parents vote for the judge and his friends the next week."

"Graft and corruption," Stella said. "Bribin' innocent children with a half a cup of artificial-flavor fruit punch. That man and his kind's got a lot to answer for. And they will, one o' these days."

"You mean, when they get to the Pearly Gates?" Savannah asked.

"Long before that, child. A whole heap of comeuppance gets dished out this side of the grave. A body can't run round sowin' sticker burrs and expect to reap a crop of creamed corn casserole."

Savannah grinned. "I *love* creamed corn casserole."

"I know," Stella told her. "That's why I didn't say mustard greens."

"Bleeck. One of these days they're going to figure out that awful stuff's not even good for you, but that chocolate is. Donuts too."

"We can dream and hope, child. Dream and hope."

Stella could tell Savannah was mulling the idea over in that highly efficient brain of hers, because she was uncharacteristically silent—until Stella passed the main entrance of the Patterson estate and the long line of cars waiting to enter the property.

"Hey, Gran! Where're you going?" the girl asked. "You sailed right past it!"

"I'm following Miss Elsie. She's takin' us in the back way," Stella told her, pointing to the bright red, 1965 Mustang ahead of them. "And I hope she don't cause us both to get a ticket. When it comes to pushin' down a gas pedal, that girl's got a lead foot."

Savannah giggled. "Naw. It's just 'cause she's got a spunky red car. Red cars go faster. I'm going to get myself a red car just like that one when I grow up and be a police lady and drive it fast to catch bad guys."

"Hm. Somethin' else to think about that'll turn my hair gray. Even grayer than it already is."

"By the time I get to be a police officer, every single one of your hairs will already be gray, thanks to Marietta's shenanigans."

"Sh-h-h. Don't say things like that about your sister. Young'uns feel the need to live up to whatever reputation others assign to 'em."

Savannah gave a snort. "So, *that's* what happened to her. Somebody said something about how cranky she was the minute she was born, and she's been living up to it ever since."

"Savannah . . ."

"I can hear you, Savannah Banana-Nose," came a retort from one of the specially installed seats that lined the sides of the old truck. "Somebody with a nose the size of a gi-*gan*-tos banana shouldn't talk about nobody else."

"Marietta!" Stella groaned and shook her head. "That's enough outta both of you. Savannah's nose ain't no bigger or littler than nobody else's, and it wouldn't matter if it was. When it comes to noses and ears and eyes and such, we take what the good Lord gives us.

Long as they do their jobs, we consider ourselves blessed and find somethin' else to fret about."

Ahead, Elsie had turned right, off the highway, and was headed down a hard-packed dirt road that led through some cotton fields, toward the rear of the great house. Stella hurried after her, reminding herself—not for the first time—to never follow Elsie anywhere again. Neither the old panel truck, nor the woman driving it, was as perky as Sister Dingle and her "spunky" red Mustang.

"How come we're goin' in this way?" Waycross wanted to know.

"It's a special way," Stella replied.

"It's the *servant's* entrance," Marietta explained, disgruntled. "Us Reids ain't allowed to go in the regular way like regular folks, 'cause we're poor and our momma's a jailbird."

Stella pulled to the side of the road and brought the truck to an abrupt stop. She shifted it into park and whirled around in her seat to face her second oldest grandchild.

"Marietta Reid, I've enjoyed your company about as much as I can tolerate for one day. I'll thank you to be very careful about what comes out of your mouth for the rest of this evenin', or you and me are gonna be mixin' it up somethin' fierce."

In the semidarkness, Stella couldn't see the child's face very well, but she could hear the huffing and puffing of her breath and knew she was angry.

With Stella's other grandchildren, the mere suspicion that their precious grandmother might be ever-so-slightly annoyed with them was enough to bring tears to their eyes and trembling to their lower lips.

Then there was Little Miss Marietta, who seemed to revel in the joy of twanging her granny's last taut nerve like it was an overtightened banjo string, just to see if she could make it snap.

"If I hear one more unkind word out of any of you," Stella

said, looking around in the dim light at the truck's precious cargo, "the person who speaks it will not be going into the maze with the rest of us. Instead, you can sit under the giant oak tree and listen to Miss Rose read."

"And die of puredee boredom," Marietta mumbled. "Miss Rose's older than dirt and reads so slow, when she stops at a period, you think she's never gonna get herself goin' again."

Savannah erupted with fury. "Don't you say that about Miss Rose! She's a *librarian*! Other than being a police officer or a nurse, that's about the best thing you can ever be, so—"

"Okay. Okay." Stella laid a calming hand on Savannah's arm. "We know how much you love Miss Rose. She's a wonderful lady." Turning to Marietta, she said, "And you're going to be very, very kind and nice and quiet when you're sitting under the tree, listening to her read, instead of visitin' the maze with the rest of us."

"I don't care. I didn't wanna go into that stupid ol' maze anyway. Not after that terrible, awful, ferocious thing that happened last year."

"What awful thing that happened last year?" asked Jesup, her baby-soft voice tremulous.

Before Stella could intervene, Marietta told her little sister, "One of those zombie guys that jumps out and scares you was *real*. When they weren't lookin', he snuck in with the rest of the fake ones. He just waited his chance and then he jumped on a little girl and ate her right up! Her brains and *everything*!"

"Marietta, stop that lyin' or I swear I'll—" Stella reached for the girl, but she was just out of snatching range.

"O-o-o! That's plumb awful!" Alma whined. "I'm scared. I don't wanna go in the maze!"

"Me neither," Cordelia said. "I'd rather hear Miss Rose read. That's better than gettin' your brains ate up any day!"

"I hear she's readin' *The Legend of Sleepy Hollow* this year," Vidalia announced, sounding as shaky as her younger sisters. "It ain't that bad of a story, compared to gettin' chewed on by a zombie."

Stella felt her last ounce of patience circle the drain and go down with a *blurp-blurp*-ing sound. "Dadgum it, young'uns! Everybody's goin' into that maze if I have to drag the whole bunch o' you in, kickin' and screamin'. Except you, Marietta. You're gonna listen to Miss Rose, 'cause you just made that story up for pure spite. There ain't no such thing as zombies! Never was! Never will be!"

She turned back around in her seat, took a deep breath, and put the truck in gear, hoping she'd sufficiently made her point and would be able to catch up with Elsie's Mustang, which was now completely out of sight.

That was when she saw them.

A virtual herd of her townsfolk decked out in copiously applied zombie makeup and ragged, filthy, "blood"-stained clothes, crossing the road right in front of her truck. They were going from a large, impromptu parking area on the left, toward the fields in the distance, where the maze had been set up.

Two seconds later, the younger grandchildren saw them, too, and the truck erupted with heart-stopping, blood-chilling screams.

Mixed with the diabolical laughter of Marietta, the Mistress of Darkness and Naughtiness.

Chapter 6

Stella couldn't find Elsie or her red Mustang, so she decided to pull her truck into the line of other vehicles that had arrived at the plantation to join the festivities.

Just ahead, the queue split in half. The left led to an area where a couple of tractors were hooked to trailers, stacked with bales of hay. Those tractors would pull the trailers, laden with merry, dauntless adventurers, into the fields where the maze had been laid out a week earlier, before torrential rains had hit the region and turned every square foot of dirt into red, clay mud.

The right queue led to the mansion itself, where the less intrepid entertainment seekers were gathering under the supposedly haunted oak tree with its ancient, gnarled limbs, to sit on the damp grass and listen to Rose Clingingsmith read *The Legend of Sleepy Hollow* in her best, spooky, Halloween voice.

In the back of Stella's truck, the six children, other than Savannah, were discussing the pros and cons of having their maze visit canceled.

"I'm glad I don't have to sit there and listen to that same ol' story again," Waycross proclaimed. "I heard it too many times already, and I know how it ends, so—"

"That ain't true, Waycross Reid," Marietta shouted. "You're just too scared to listen to it. You cried last year when Miss Rose got to the part where ol' Ichabod Crane got hisself murdered."

"I don't wanna hear no story about nobody getting murdered," little Jesup whimpered. "But I don't wanna go into that maze and get my brains ate neither. So, I don't know what to do-o-o!"

"You gotta do something, you scaredy cat," Marietta told her. "You can't sit on the hay wagon the whole night, or people'll know that you're a chicken sh—"

"Sh-h! That's enough back there," Stella told them. "I done told y'all how it's gonna be."

She turned the truck into the line that was headed for the great house. "We're gonna stop at the old oak tree, and ever'body but Savannah and Waycross is gonna pile out and go listen to Miss Rose read the story. And Jesup, sugar, don't worry about hearing a murder, 'cause that Ichabod fella don't get kilt, just scared off by a nasty guy name o' Brom Bones, who pretends to be the ghost of a guy who's misplaced his head. You know, like I do sometimes when I've got too much on my mind. It just happens once in a while. You can't always help such things."

Savannah shot Stella a puzzled and disapproving look. "I thought the ending of that story was open to interpretation, Gran."

"Not tonight, it ain't," Stella whispered. "For this evenin', as far as these little 'uns are concerned, that innocent, peaceful ending's set in stone."

Savannah gave her a solemn nod. "Gotcha."

"But what if some of us don't wanna listen to that dumb ol' story again. What if we decide we wanna go in the maze?" Marietta asked with a whining tone that grated on Stella's nerves.

"The teenagers we saw crossin' the road back a piece, the ones the judge hires to dress up and scare people inside the maze, I hear they can get a bit rowdy sometimes," Stella told her. "I've rethought it and decided that anybody who's scared about hearing a little ghost story with a happy ending probably shouldn't venture inside there. I want ever'body to have fun tonight."

"That's good," Vidalia said. "I don't wanna get grabbed or tussled with."

"Me neither!" Cordelia said. "I'm not big on tusslin' with guys who'd as soon eat ya as look at ya. I'll just listen to the story."

Stella pulled the truck into the area where Miss Rose's audience was gathering and stopped. She opened her own door, looked around to make sure there were no other vehicles headed their way, rushed around to the rear of the truck, and opened the double doors.

Within seconds, eager children began to spill forth.

She offered a helping hand to the two youngest, Alma and Jesup, then pointed toward the massive oak tree that graced the mansion's side yard. She could see a crowd had already gathered beneath its branches that, due to the recent storm, had lost many of their leaves.

"Run along now and get yourselves settled before the story starts," she told them. "Mari, you and Vi will be the oldest in the group, so you're in charge. Put the youngest ones in a bunch between you and you two look out for 'em. If I hear there was even one cross word spoken among you, let alone any licks landed, you'll be in more trouble with me tomorrow than you'll know what to do with. But if I hear everybody was good, I'll pick up a bag o' candy corn at the store, and y'all can divided it up amongst you. Hear me?"

Egos inflated by their newly acquired positions of authority, Marietta and Vidalia nodded, grabbed the hands of their three youngest sisters, and marched them toward the tree.

Stella watched proudly as the larger part of her brood was greeted by the friendly librarian, who was handing out black, plastic trash bags for them to sit upon, so their clothing wouldn't get wet from the rain-soaked grass.

Once they were all settled in place, and Stella could see that they were behaving—at least for the moment—she got back into the truck.

"That was smart, making sure Marietta and Vidalia weren't sitting right next to each other," Savannah told Stella. With a chuckle she added, "You're pretty good at this grandma stuff."

Stella reached over and patted her granddaughter's arm. "I'm mighty glad you think so, Savannah girl. But you mustn't say that too loud. Lord knows, the night's still young."

In the back, Waycross snickered. "That's for sure. On Halloween night, 'bout anything can happen."

For some reason that Stella couldn't explain, she felt a shiver deep in her soul that she couldn't even name.

Later, when she would recall the moment and the feeling, she would describe it as "a dark and heavy sense of downright forebodin'."

Having ridden on a wagon to and from many fields to pick cotton as a child and young woman, Stella was less enthralled with the experience than her two oldest grandkids.

"Woo-hoo! This is fun!" Waycross announced just as the tractor that was pulling them belched a particularly thick, sooty cloud of smoke. It floated back to the wagon, where they sat on bales of hay, and sent all the riders crowded there into fits of coughing.

Once they'd recovered, Savannah looked down at her Grandpa Arthur's overalls that comprised the better part of her "hunting attire," and said, "I've gotten Pa's clothes muddy already, and we haven't even gotten started yet."

"Don't worry 'bout that, sugar," Stella told her. "He got 'em a sight messier than that back when he wore em. He was a hard-working farmer, your grandpa. Wasn't afraid to get his hands dirty. His clothes neither, for that matter."

For a moment, Stella felt the familiar pain cut through her spirit. Oh, how she missed Art. Even six years into her widow-hood, she still suffered the loss of the kind, sweet man who had been her true and devoted love, for so long.

Try as she might, she had found no cure for the pain of losing him. Although her duties as a sole caretaker of seven children kept her mind busy and her days full of hard work, she found there was still time to grieve. The sorrow ebbed and flowed daily, hourly. And sometimes, when she least expected it, a sudden tidal wave of sadness would catch her unprepared and over-whelm her, triggered by something unexpected.

Like the tractor in front of them.

It was newer and larger, but otherwise, not so unlike the one he had been driving that afternoon, when his life had been lost, and hers had been torn into pieces that she now believed would never be knit together again. At least, not in any sweet sem-blance of what it had been before that terrible day.

"Your grandpa wouldn't want you worrying about such things, Savannah girl," she told the child. "He'd just want you to have a barrel of fun inside that maze and get them clothes as dirty as you can. That's why the good Lord created washing machines."

"I thought that was Mr. Maytag," Savannah said with a grin.

"Okay, Miss Smarty Pants. But I do believe an invention as handy as that must've been inspired by the Divine!"

As the tractor slowed, then stopped, at the maze entrance, the excitement inside the wagon rose. Among the riders, the more stalwart of spirit laughed and leapt off without waiting for a makeshift set of steps to be dragged into place by a pirate with an aluminum foil sword and a Frankenstein with red yarn stitches and giant bolts glued to his face and neck.

As Stella turned to help her grandchildren down from the wagon, she realized they had already descended the steps and were waiting at the bottom, their hands out to assist her.

"Watch your step, Gran," Waycross said with a gravity that belied his tender years as he reached up and grabbed her hand and forearm. "Just hold on tight to me. I'll getcha down in one piece."

Smiling, Savannah lowered her own hands, stepped back, and allowed her brother to play the chevalier.

As Stella clung to the small hands—far more tightly than she needed to—she realized this was the first time in any of her interactions with her grandchildren that she had been considered the one who needed assistance, rather than the stronger, more able one, providing help. The recognition of their role reversal filled her with pride and joy at her grandson's newfound maturity, but also, a tiny sense of sadness to be the one considered the "weaker" in the relationship.

Life seemed to offer a new surprise with every hour. More than once it had occurred to Stella that the only thing that never changed was the fact that, sooner or later, absolutely everything changed. The only thing you could count on was the fact that you couldn't count on anything.

The uncertainty of it all, this living on ever-shifting quicksand, might have struck fear in her heart were it not for her belief that all pathways—even those with lots of twists and turns, pitfalls, and the occasional rock slide—took a traveler to a better place in the end. No matter how far down the road that happy ending might be.

Chapter 7

Stella continued to hold Savannah's and Waycross's hands as she guided them toward the entrance, marked with a large banner that read: WORLD FAMOUS PATTERSON MAZE.

Beneath the banner was a smaller sign that challenged visitors to: ENTER AT YOUR OWN RISK!

Their neighbors jostled around them, each group eager to enter the giant puzzle first. They were nearly knocked off their feet by a Marge Simpson, who was holding hands with the Phantom of the Opera.

Stella couldn't help thinking that Halloween shenanigans seem to bring out the worst in the townspeople. Folks who wouldn't dream of cutting in front of you in line at the grocery store were elbowing their way through the crowd like Mr. Steve Bartkowski of the Atlanta Falcons. They behaved as if they had precious little regard for life and limb. Their own or anyone else's.

"Let em go," Stella told her grandchildren. "No point in getting squashed flatter than a flitter just to be the first inside. The maze ain't going nowhere, and it's open till midnight."

Waycross tugged at her hand, as he watched a couple of particularly unattractive ghosts with gray faces, black lipstick, and dark smudging beneath their eyes stroll by. "But we ain't gonna stay in there till midnight, are we, Gran? I don't cotton to being in a place like that late at night. I'll probably get my fill in an hour."

One of the ghosts fixed him with a sinister gaze and let out an unearthly howl. "Maybe less," he quickly added.

Stella chuckled. "An hour sounds about right to me, too, puddin'. I know Miss Elsie said we didn't have to, but I figure we should at least show up and offer to help her with that punch fixin', her bein' kind enough to provide us with these free tickets."

No sooner had Stella uttered the words than she spotted the Honorable Judge Patterson himself, standing beside the entrance of the maze, his hand out, collecting tickets.

His Dracula costume, like his mansion and his estate, was far more luxurious than those of his fellow townsmen. The black suit he wore looked suspiciously similar to the tuxedo he commonly donned when attending any sort of even semiformal events in the area. Patterson was well aware that his was the only tux in town—except for, perhaps, the occasional wedding or prom rental. But the judge didn't mind standing out in a crowd. In fact, he worked hard at it.

His ancestors might have lost most of their fortune during the Civil War, but as far as Judge Patterson was concerned, owning the biggest house in McGill made him the Lord of the Manor, and he wasn't shy about dressing for the part.

"I wish I had that cape of his," Savannah whispered as they approached the haute couture vampire. "That red silk lining is pretty. I'd turn the whole thing inside out, carry a basket full of goodies, and pretend to be Little Red Riding Hood."

When Stella and the children were about ten feet from him, the judge recognized them. Stella cringed to see the disgusted, disgruntled look that crossed his face—as though he had just taken a swig of what he thought was wine and had gotten a mouthful of vinegar instead.

They were white trash. At least in Judge Patterson's less-than-generous estimation. Of that, Stella had no doubt. He had never bothered to hide his opinion of her family, and it hurt. She didn't mind so much that he held her in low esteem, or even her son and daughter-in-law for that matter.

But her grandangels . . .

She knew them far better than the judge did and, she knew their souls were precious and pure, shining just as brightly as any the Lord had ever breathed into being.

Stella couldn't help feeling a mite angry that anybody would consider those children beneath them just because that uppity person lived in a mansion on a plantation that had been given to them by their rich ancestors and because they could afford to fork over an obscene amount of money for a fancy bloodsucker costume.

With quite an effort, Stella shoved those contentious thoughts aside, reminding herself that, if it hadn't been for this man with the eyebrow-penciled widow's peak and lipstick "blood" running down his chin, she would not have custody of her grandchildren. She would not be able to sleep with them under her roof every night, knowing that they were well fed, warm, happy, and safe.

Count your blessings, Stella May Reid, she told herself. *The Lord uses all kinds to fulfill His purposes. Even ornery, stuck-up cusses like ol' Judge Patterson.*

He thrust his open hand in the vicinity of Stella's face, nearly striking her on the nose. For just a moment she entertained the notion of what she might have done had he actually made contact. Since it involved a rather high degree of violence and mayhem, she decided it was a good thing that he'd missed. That way she could sleep in her own bed tonight instead of stretching out on a cot in one of Sheriff Gilford's cells.

When Stella placed the tickets onto his outstretched palm, he gave her a nasty little smirk and said, "I'm sure glad that everybody ain't like y'all, their hands out, expecting charity. I'd go broke, now, wouldn't I?"

Before Stella could respond, Savannah stepped forward. She waved her hand, indicating his fancy costume, the surrounding farmland that stretched as far as the eye could see, and the mansion in the distance. Then she fixed the judge with a cold, steady gaze and said, "Well now, you going broke . . . that'd take a while, wouldn't it? You're not exactly living on Poor Street, Your Honor."

Suppressing a giggle, Stella said, "Sorry, Judge. My granddaughter meant no disrespect. We thank you for your generosity, and we aim to work our tail feathers off later on, helping Miss Elsie make up them gallons of punch."

He grunted and gave Waycross a push toward the entrance. "Get on in there then and don't tell anybody I let you in for free. If word of it gets out, they'll all want something for nothing. Don't hurt yourself in there neither. I ain't paying off no lawsuits to the relatives of knuckleheads who go in and never come out."

As Stella led them into the first stretch of the maze, Waycross tugged at her hand again. "He didn't mean that, did he?" the boy asked, a quaver in his voice.

"Of course he meant it," Savannah told him. "He's tight as a tick on a bloodhound's ear."

"No," Waycross replied. "I mean, he was just pullin' our legs about folks goin' in there, gettin' lost, and never coming back out, right?"

"They get lost," his sister said, a twinkle in her eyes, "but not forever. After the maze closes down, the farmhands plow the stalks under, and that's when most of the missing ones turn up."

Waycross snickered, but there was a note of nervousness in his laughter as he poked his sister in the ribs with his forefinger.

"You're just funnin' me, I know," he told her. "Ain't that many people in McGill, and everybody knows your business. If anybody'd kicked the bucket in a cornfield maze, we'd have heard all about it."

Savannah laughed with him and rubbed the top of his head roughly, mussing his already unruly curls. "I see I'll have to rise early in the morning to get one over on you, brother," she told him. "You're right. It would've been the talk of the town, and the dead person's family would've sued the bloomers off Judge Patterson and what a stink *that* would've made!"

As they reached the first abrupt turn in the path, Stella put a hand on her granddaughter's shoulder and said, "Savannah, sweetie, that man may have a stingy streak a mile wide, but he changed our lives for the better. We can't ever lose sight o' that."

Savannah stopped, looked up at Stella, and nodded solemnly. "Sorry, Gran. You're right. He did. I swear, I won't never, ever say another unkind word about him."

"Never, ever's a long time, sugar." Stella brushed the dark curls out of the child's eyes. "Don't go makin' promises you might not be able to keep."

"From now on, I'll try as hard as I can to speak to him and about him with respect," Savannah said.

"That's a fine ambition if ever I heard one," Stella assured her. "Always remember, we try our best to treat others with kindness and respect. Not because—"

"—of who they are," Waycross piped up, "but because it's the right thing to do, and we wanna look in the mirror and see a person who chooses to do the right thing . . . at least most of the time."

"That's right, grandson. Being able to like that person in the mirror—or at least understand 'em—that's one of the most important things in life."

Chapter 8

For a couple of minutes, Stella, Waycross, and Savannah walked quietly through the twists and turns of the maze, and the three of them absorbed the sights, sounds, and feel of the experience.

Above them, a full moon lit the way, painting the green cornstalks with its silver patina, turning them a ghostly gray. The honey-floral scent of the ripening corn, mixed with the smell of the rich, freshly rain-soaked earth at their feet, stirred Stella's childhood memories, reminding her of the many difficult days she had spent in these fields—working, not having fun.

She took a moment to say a quick, silent prayer of thanksgiving that her grandchildren's childhoods, challenging as they had been, were still easier than her own and those of many others back in those troubled times.

A chilly wind swept through the field, rustling the stalks around them, and for a moment, the moon slid behind a cloud.

"Are you two warm enough?" Stella asked the children. "Looks like the wind's pickin' up."

"After tussling with my ferocious bear brother from one end of

Main Street to the other," Savannah said, "I don't reckon I'll ever be cold again."

"Me either," Waycross added. "Who woulda thought bein' a grizzly'd be so much work? 'Bout wore myself out! And didn't even get nothin' for it."

He glanced up at his grandmother and quickly added, "Except a helping of self-satisfaction that's supposed to be better than a pretty blue ribbon to hang on your wall and a whoppin' ten dollars that'd keep you in candy bars for a year. Maybe two."

As Stella considered the various ways to answer that thinly veiled complaint, they rounded another corner in the path and nearly collided with two of Savannah's classmates. Tommy Stafford and Jeanette Parker, both the ripe old age of thirteen, were locked in an embrace so tight one would have been hard-put to slide a potato chip between them.

Worse yet, they appeared to be devouring each other as voraciously as a starving child would consume the head of a chocolate Easter bunny, having eaten nothing since Christmas.

"Stop that!" Stella heard herself shout, before she had time to consider the particulars of the situation. "Quit it! Right now!"

The startled barely-teenagers jumped apart and instantly donned less-than-convincing "What the heck? We weren't doing anything!" looks.

Jeanette appeared mortified to be caught having her virtue compromised. She cleared her throat, then stared down at her feet, as though suddenly fascinated by the amount of mud that had collected on her bright yellow galoshes.

Even by the dim light of the partly cloud-covered moon, Stella could see the girl was blushing.

Tommy Stafford . . . not so much.

Stella was surprised and a bit perturbed by the lack of remorse registering on his young face—a face that was far too mature and handsome for the boy's own good.

So striking was the blond, green-eyed lad that most females in McGill had taken notice and had shared predictions about whether, "with looks like those," Master Thomas Stafford would grow up to be president of the United States or, better still, a movie star.

Stella's concern heightened considerably when she saw that, although he had stepped back from Jeanette, putting a bit of distance between them, he was giving Savannah a flirty grin that bordered on a salacious smirk.

To Stella's dismay, she watched her granddaughter flutter her eyelashes, then return the smile.

Uh, oh, Stella told herself. *Gonna have to keep a sharp eye on that situation. If worse comes to worse, I might have to jerk a knot in that young man's tail and lock that gal in her room till she comes to her senses.*

Of course, having been a young lady of thirteen herself, Stella knew that no amount of tail-knotting or locked doors could put an end to that sort of tomfoolery, if the love bug had already bitten the young'uns in question.

Stella put her hands on Jeanette's shoulders, turned her around until she was facing the path that led right. Giving the girl a gentle push, she said, "Get along, sweetie, before you wind up doin' somethin' you wouldn't want your momma to know about."

She reached for Tommy, grasped him firmly by the back of the neck, like a mother dog with a wayward pup. "And you, young fella, better remember what a fierce daddy that Jeanette's got. Big too! A smart boy should know better than to get overly friendly with a gal who's got ferocious relatives!"

She glared at him for what seemed like an eternity, watching his expression for evidence that he had caught her meaning.

Unfortunately, she saw not even a smidgeon of remorse or fear.

She gave him a shove, far harder than the gentle push she'd given the girl, and sent him scrambling down the path to the left.

When he had to grab some nearby cornstalks to keep from falling on his face in the mud, she added, "Next time I catch you playin' fast and loose with any of the girls in this town, it'll be my foot on your backside."

When she turned back to her grandchildren, she saw that Waycross was giggling and Savannah had an expression of pure horror and embarrassment on her face.

"Gran!" she said. "You had no call to do that! They were just . . . you know . . . kissing a little and—"

"I reckon I know a bit more about that sorta thing than you, Miss Savannah," Stella replied. "And that weren't a *little* kissin'."

"It sure weren't!" Waycross piped up. "What they was doin' was dead-serious slobber swappin' if ever I saw it! Ew-w-w, gross!"

Savannah groaned and rolled her eyes.

Stella grabbed Waycross by the back of his grizzly rug "shirt" and directed him toward the path straight ahead. "All right. All right. That'll be quite enough on this topic. Savannah, you got them lights I asked you to bring?"

"They're right here, Gran," Savannah replied, pulling three flashlights from the generous pockets of Grandpa Art's overalls and handing one to her grandmother, then her brother. A bit too brightly, as though happy to change the subject, she added, "I brought one for each of us, like you told me. No telling how dark it'll be by the time we make it to the middle."

"That's true, kiddo. We'd better get gettin'. We got us a maze to get into and then back out of."

No sooner had they resumed their journey and rounded the next corner than an ugly zombie with a deathly gray face and "blood" running down his chin jumped out of the stalks, lunged at Waycross, and grabbed him by the arm.

The boy shrieked, wriggled away, and ducked behind the first object he could find, seeking safety.

His sister.

When the walking dead man tried to reach around her to grab the younger child, Savannah smacked the aggressor on the forehead. "You quit that right now!" she shouted at the grungy offender. "I can tell it's you, Joe Barkley, and you oughta know better, picking on a little kid like that. I'll tell your momma on you, and you'll be in a mess of trouble! Scaring the pee-diddle outta somebody way smaller than you. Shame! She taught you better!"

"But that's the job," Joe whined. "The judge's payin' us a quarter an hour to shake folks up in here."

"Then concentrate on the older people," Stella told him, "and use your voice to do the frightenin'. Don't go layin' hands on nobody, or you might get your clock cleaned."

As they watched the vanquished Zombie Joe disappear down the path, Stella shook her head and said, "Lord've mercy. It's a good thing the littlest ones ain't along for this mess. They'd be scared as a deviled egg at a church picnic!"

"Hey, look!" Savannah cried as she and her now mollified little brother rounded the next corner. "We made it! It's the middle!"

When Stella caught up to them, she saw the large sign, painted with dripping red paint on a plank of plywood and propped against a bundle of cornstalks tied together with twine. It said simply, THE MIDDLE. Beneath that curt message was a slightly more informative one, also painted sloppily in crimson, GOOD LUCK GETTING OUT!

Savannah gave Stella a wry half smile and said, "Old Judge Patterson didn't exactly knock himself out on this maze, did he?"

"That's for sure," Waycross agreed. "I heard the one over in Harvey Hollow had maps and clues and puzzles and creepy music and cats and wolves howling and a lot spookier stuff. More zombies, too. Ones that didn't snatch atcha!"

"His Honor probably blew his whole Halloween budget on that satin cape," Savannah suggested.

"I thought we were only gonna say nice things about the judge," Stella said.

Savannah rolled her eyes. "Okay. Judge Patterson's got himself a nice cape. And this is a great maze. It's worth every penny we didn't pay for it."

The trio turned around and began the trek back to the entrance—or at least, they chose the path they thought would lead them out. But it didn't take long for them to realize they had made a wrong turn at some point.

The area they had entered wasn't at all familiar. Even more concerning, unlike before, they couldn't hear their fellow explorers chattering away on nearby paths.

"I think we blew it, Gran," Savannah said, shining her flashlight above the cornstalks at a thick copse of trees a bit farther down the path.

"I'm afraid you're right, Savannah girl. From where we first started out, you could see that woods, and it was on the far side of the maze."

"Leave it to us to go the exact wrong way," Waycross complained. "Ain't nobody else out here with us neither. We're lost and on our own."

At that moment an owl hooted loudly in the trees ahead. Startled, the boy jumped and said, "'Cept for that fella there. It's spooky enough out here without him addin' his two cents' worth to the situation."

Stella noticed that Savannah was heading down the path toward the woods. "Hey, sugar, whatcha up to there? Reckon we should be headin' the opposite direction."

"I have an idea," Savannah replied over her shoulder. "A good one."

Stella chuckled. As the oldest of the seven Reid siblings, Savannah was accustomed to taking charge whenever a problem presented itself.

Since the children had come to live with her grandmother, Stella had tried to impress upon Savannah that she was no longer responsible for the horde of energetic children that her parents had brought into the world but habitually neglected to nurture.

Daily, sometimes hourly, Stella attempted to set her eldest grandangel's mind to rest and to show her that a responsible adult was now in charge. But no amount of reassurance seemed to convince the child that she had now been permanently relieved of her duties as primary caregiver to her brothers and sisters. Apparently, things like maternal responsibility became deeply engrained early in life.

However, Stella had to admit that, occasionally, the girl came up with a good solution that she, the grandmother, would never have considered.

Stella had decided long ago that it never hurt to ask before pooh-poohing one of Savannah's ideas.

"Whatcha got in mind, sweetie?" she asked, following Savannah toward the trees.

"That old owl can see a lot from where he's perched up there in those branches," the girl observed. "I was thinking that—"

"No!" Stella said. "If what you're thinkin' about is what I think you're thinkin' about, don't even *think* about it."

Savannah stopped, turned around, and gave her grandmother a playful, quizzical look. "I'll bet you can't say *that* five times fast."

"You know what I mean. You ain't shinnyin' up no tree out here in the dark wilderness with medical help miles away. It's not like I keep bandages and Merthiolate in my pocket, you know . . . although that's not such a bad idea."

Savannah laughed and scurried down the path toward the trees, faster than Stella could keep up with her. Although Stella could see, from the beam of the girl's flashlight, where she was at every moment.

"I mean it! You climb one of those trees, after me telling you not to, and you'll wish you hadn't!"

"Yeah!" Waycross yelled, running along at Stella's heels. "Granny's li'ble to pull a switch off one of them branches and tan your hide with it, Savannah Sue!"

"A pine tree switch?" Savannah shouted back, laughing. "Granny's gonna beat me with a *log* covered with pine needles—?"

"And pinecones, too!" Waycross replied. "Gran's fierce. She don't abide outright rebellion!"

"I'm not rebelling! First, I'm just going to check the lay of the land. Then, if there is a good tree that's fit for climbing, and Gran says it's okay, maybe I can . . ."

Savannah's voice trailed away, and at the same time, Stella lost sight of the feeble flashlight beam.

A sense of apprehension—dark, evil, and deeply upsetting in its intensity—trickled through Stella's spirit and body, causing her limbs to tremble and her pulse to quicken.

Something was wrong. Badly wrong.

Stella knew it.

Even before she heard her granddaughter scream.

Chapter 9

"Savannah! Savannah! What's the matter? Where're you at, girl?" Stella shouted, as she raced to the spot at the edge of the trees where she had last seen her granddaughter's flashlight beam. The spot where she just heard her scream.

Savannah wasn't a child given to hysterics, and as much as Stella tried to tell herself that nothing terrible had happened, she couldn't. She had never heard her granddaughter cry out like that.

From terror? Pain? Or both?

Stella couldn't tell.

The path that created the maze ended abruptly, just before the forest began, and she could see a space between the cornstalks that appeared large enough for the child to have passed through it.

"In there, Granny," Waycross said, pointing to the parting of the stalks. "She might've ducked in through there!"

He tried to get around Stella to go through himself, but she caught him by the back of his bear shirt. "Hold on there," she said. "You ain't goin' in till I see if it's safe first."

"But Savannah—"

"She's okay, grandson. Your big sis's all right."

"She didn't sound like she was just funnin' us. She sounded—"

"I know. Calm down. All will be well."

Stella wished she could believe her own words as she shone her own flashlight's beam along the edge of the woods, looking for her grandchild and seeing nothing. No movement of any kind.

"Savannah!" she shouted again. "Answer me! Right now! Where are you?"

"Yeah, Miss Savannah Reid! You speak up this very minute!" Waycross added, his childish voice trembling despite his authoritative words. "If you're pulling our legs just so's we'll be in a dither, all worried 'bout you, I swear I'm gonna help Granny whup you myself! Twice! Just to make sure we've got your attention!"

"Sh-h-h, Waycross," Stella told him. "I don't think she's joking around. I think somethin's bad wrong and—"

That was when Stella heard it, a distinct rustling off to her left. She yanked Waycross behind her with one hand and turned her flashlight beam toward the direction of the sound.

At first, she thought it was an animal, crawling on the ground. Then she realized it was her granddaughter on her hands and knees, scrambling through a particularly thick patch of mud at the base of a giant pine tree.

It was an eerie sight, the child's long curly hair hanging down around her dirty face, both covered with the black sludge of rotting forest debris and litterfall.

Savannah's eyes were wide as she scrambled toward her grandmother, making small, incoherent cries, like that of a creature who was badly wounded.

Stella ran to her, dropped to her knees, and gathered her in her arms. Savannah grabbed her around the waist and held her so tightly that Stella could hardly breathe.

"I've got you, sweetheart," Stella told her. "I've got you. Whatever happened . . . it's all done now. You're safe."

Stella could feel the girl shaking violently as she ran her hands over her, searching for injuries.

At the same moment, Waycross was shining his own flashlight up and down his sister's filthy form, though little was revealed beyond the mud and grime covering her.

Stella glanced around them, looking for what object or being might have caused Savannah's terror. But the thick trees blotted out the moonlight and little could be seen beyond the forest's edge.

"Are you hurt, honey?" she asked Savannah. "Did you fall or—"

The girl nodded vigorously.

"You fell?"

Again, Savannah nodded, then pointed to the base of a nearby tree. "There."

"And you hurt yourself?"

Savannah looked confused for a moment, then looked down at her muddy clothes and hands and said, "No. I don't think so."

"You sure hollered awful loud," Waycross said, "for somebody who wasn't even hurt. You screamed so bad, we thought a bear had ripped your leg off and was eatin' it right in front of you."

"Waycross! That'll be quite enough of that! Can't you see your sister's in a state?"

She turned her attention back to Savannah, who still looked just as frightened as when Stella had first spotted her, crawling out of the mire.

Stella used the hem of her sweater to wipe the grime off the child's face. "If you ain't hurt bad, then you must've been scared bad," she said. "Tell me what scared you, sugar. Did you see an animal or—"

"No. A person."

Stella snapped to attention. They weren't alone after all! Some-one had just frightened her grandchild half to death. What else might they be capable of?

Her mind raced, trying to think what she might use for a weapon if she needed to defend her grandangels. But all she had at her disposal was the flashlight in her hand. Although it was metal, it wasn't more than ten inches long and weighed next to nothing.

It would be hard to wage much of a battle with so little.

"Where were they?" she asked Savannah, shining the light into the dense forest brush. "Where did you see them?"

"Right over there." Savannah pointed to the tree where she said she had fallen.

Stella saw nothing but a prominent tree root, protruding from the wet ground. She wasn't surprised that Savannah had tripped over it.

"Did you get a good look at 'em?" she asked her granddaughter.

Savannah started to cry. Her sobs were deep and harsh, caus-ing her entire body to heave. "Yes. I shone my light right on her face."

Time slowed for Stella, long enough for her to process the fact that it had been a female who had scared her granddaughter so badly.

While Stella didn't exactly relax, her fear did lessen a little, thinking that, should she have to defend herself and the children, at least it would be against another woman and not a grown man.

Although she figured, to save her grandkids, she could fight off all of the women in town and most of the men if necessary.

"Did you recognize her?" Stella asked.

Savannah wouldn't meet her eyes as she whispered, "I think so."

"Who do you think it was?"

There was no reply. Only a long, tense silence that Stella finally decided to break.

"Well, she's gone now," she told Savannah as she stood and helped the child to her feet. "There's no need to worry about nothin', except getting you home and into a warm bathtub."

She shone her light onto her granddaughter's face, but didn't see a trace of relief there. Only terror.

"She's not gone, Gran," Savannah said. "She's right there."

"Where?"

"I don't see nobody," Waycross said, flashing his light left, then right, among the dark trees. "She probably hightailed it outta here, soon as she heard that scream of yours. I tell ya; it was a doozy! It darned near curled my ears!"

"She's right there, I tell you," Savannah repeated, pointing to the forest floor beyond the giant root. "On the ground. Looks to me like she's been there for a mighty long time, too."

The relief Stella had felt at finding her granddaughter alive and uninjured vanished as she grasped the significance of the girl's words.

Suddenly, like pieces of a gruesome puzzle, her observations began to come together and make sense.

Even as she told her grandchildren to stay where they were, then began to walk to the area Savannah had indicated, Stella knew what she would find.

Not whom.

But what.

Her mind tried to come up with a less horrific explanation: *It's one of the zombies that the judge hired, overplaying her part. Or it's an especially realistic Halloween decoration that somebody threw away. It's gotta be. Savannah's mistaken. It can't be a—*

Dead body.

A real person. A really dead person.

As Stella walked up to it and played her beam of light up and down the corpse, there was no way she could explain this other than the hard, horrid truth of it.

This was no joke, no discarded decoration.

This was a now-dead human being who had been lying there, at the base of that tree, for a very long time.

Long enough for their flesh to decompose and mingle with the other, natural litter on the forest floor.

All that was fully visible was the skull, and even it was turned on its side and half buried in mud. Further down, Stella saw a bit of the torso area, which was partially covered with a torn and muddy dress that had once been a festive, floral print. The hands were exposed, sticking out of the rotten debris and together in front of her, as though she were praying. But a closer look sent a shiver of horror through Stella's spirit, evoking a dark, haunting memory of her own.

The woman's hands were bound with a man's necktie that, like the dress and the woman herself, had once been colorful and vibrant, but was now a faded, ruined version of its former self.

Some of the dead woman's dark, curly hair remained, matted and filthy, but still held in a bun at the nape of the neck with a distinctive leather barrette. The sharp pain that Stella felt in her chest at seeing it caused her to fall to her knees.

She didn't have to look closely to know that there was a symbol cut into the leather of that barrette.

Two arrows crossing each other.

The Cherokee sign of friendship.

"No, no, no," she whispered, so as not to further traumatize her grandchildren, as her heart screamed its horror and sorrow. "Please, dear Lord, no."

Of course, Stella knew it was a prayer that could never be answered. There was no point in begging God to return the dead to their loved ones. If that request, daily and fervently pleaded all over the earth, could be granted, the world's streets and homes would be filled with those whom love had resurrected. Her own sweet Arthur would be beside her and not lying in the ancient graveyard at the edge of town.

Tears filled her eyes, mercifully diffusing and softening the harsh, brutal image before her.

"I wanna see." She heard Waycross's voice, as though from far away, not the spot only twelve feet away where she had told him to wait. "Can I come see, Granny? Can I? I ain't never seen a dead body, 'cept in the funeral home, all dressed up nice and in a fancy coffin."

"No. You stay right where you are." Stella struggled to her feet, wiped her tears on her sweater sleeve, and drew a deep, shuddering breath. Then she forced herself to leave the woman on the ground and return to her grandchildren.

When she reached Waycross, she placed her hand on top of his wild, copper curls, looked into his sweet face, so soft and inno-cent in the silver moonlight, and said, "If you ain't seen such a sight, then you've been blessed, Master Waycross Reid. Blessed right and proper. I pray you remain so for the rest of your born days."

"That's for sure," Savannah whispered, moving closer to her grandmother and clasping her hand with both of hers. "Believe me, tripping over an honest-to-goodness dead body out in the open like this here . . . it ain't all it's cracked up to be."

Chapter 10

They were a quiet trio—Stella, Savannah, and Waycross—as they plodded through the muddy paths of the maze, trying to find their way back to the entrance or one of the other two exits.

It wasn't long before they could hear the voices of the other visitors, laughing, arguing with their companions about the best turns to make. They even encountered a few who didn't seem to notice that they weren't as jovial as the rest.

Stella was grateful that the journey back had seemed much easier than it had appeared just before they'd found the body. She could hardly form a coherent thought in her mind, which was all but paralyzed by grief.

Since they had left the forest's edge, Savannah hadn't let go of her grandmother's hand. She was squeezing it so tightly that Stella's fingers were numb.

Once they had passed a particularly rowdy group of revelers, Savannah leaned closer to Stella and, lowering her voice so that Waycross, who was walking a few feet behind them, couldn't hear, she said, "You know her, don't you? You know who she is. I mean, was."

Stella nodded. "Yes. Reckon I do."

"She's the lady in the old, crinkled up, yellow picture. The one in the wood frame on your dresser, next to your hairbrush and comb set."

"Yes, sweetheart."

They walked on a bit farther. A cold wind swept across the field, causing the stalks to rattle. For some reason, it sounded to Stella like ancient, dried bones, clanging against each other in some sort of macabre wind chime.

Once again, Savannah tugged at her hand. "I asked you one time who she was . . . and who the little girls were, standing on either side of her."

"I recollect you asking me that. 'Twas a long time ago."

"Yes, I was just a kid then."

"Not the young lady you are now," Stella added with a sad, wry smile.

"Yes. But I remember what you said. You told me she was your second momma. I was little and didn't know much. I thought that was strange because, how can one person have two mommas?"

Stella considered postponing this conversation to a later time, when she had less on her mind and could do the explanation justice. But she realized things were going to get a lot busier, sadder, and more complicated before they got better.

Might as well get 'er done and over with, she told herself. *It ain't like there's ever a good time to talk about the heartbreaking stuff.*

"You remember how Farmer Buskirk's milk cow got sick after she had her calf?"

Savannah nodded. "And she wouldn't let the calf near her?"

"That's the one. The vet figured out what was wrong with her and fixed her up, but even once she got to feelin' better, she wouldn't take to her new calf."

"That was mean of her, not accepting her own baby."

Stella shrugged. "Who knows why an animal does what it does—or a person either, for that matter? Anyway, Farmer Buskirk had another momma cow with a calf of her own. And when he introduced that orphaned calf to that momma cow, she fed it just like it was hers."

"That was nice of her."

"Yes, it was. Some mothers get sick and can't take care of their young'uns. Some seem healthy, but they don't appear to know how. Others are gone entirely."

"And sometimes they're healthy and they know how, but they just don't give a hoot," Savannah said with a note of bitterness in her voice that added to the despair Stella was feeling already.

She glanced down at her granddaughter, and even by the dim moonlight, she could see the anger on the girl's face.

That much bitterness—it's too great a burden for even a grown-up to carry, let alone a little one, she thought. *Rage makes a lousy travel companion. Even a child needs to learn how to shed it as soon as they can.*

"It can sure seem that way sometimes," Stella told her. "But human beings are complicated critters. It's hard to know why they do what they do. There's only one thing you can be sure of. . . ."

"What's that, Gran?"

"A cow who don't take care of her baby—that's about the cow, not about the calf."

"So, it's the cow's fault?"

"Might be. Might not be anybody's fault. But it's never, never, ever the calf's fault."

Stella looked down, studying her granddaughter's face. She felt a bit of relief to see some of the anger and resentment fade from the girl's otherwise innocent, sweet features.

A few minutes later, Savannah spoke again, her voice soft and thoughtful. "That lady in the picture . . . she was your momma when your own couldn't or didn't take care of you anymore?"

"Yes. For a short time, she was. God bless her."

"And you were one of the little girls in that picture on the dresser?"

"I was. The one on the left."

"Who was the one on the right?"

Stella felt the tears she had been holding back rush into her eyes, hot and blinding. Her throat felt as though she had just swallowed something hard and unforgiving that was ripping its way downward, far too slowly.

"Don't you know?" she asked Savannah, who was staring up at her, upset to see her grandmother cry.

"I think I do."

"You're a pretty good detective. Who do you think that other young'un in the picture is, Savannah?"

"Well, the girl is black, like the woman."

"Yes."

"She's got a big, nice, friendly smile—like the woman."

"Yes. And . . . ?"

"I think the other little girl in the picture is Miss Elsie."

Stella lost the battle with her tears. They flowed freely down her face as the knot in her throat choked her. She couldn't speak as she thought of her dear friend, serving punch at the mansion to the town's children, giving healing hugs to everyone who needed them, baking the best coconut cakes in the county, and quietly, humbly, gifting them to her neighbors whose spirits were heavy-laden, who needed to be reminded that someone cared and loved them.

Stella just nodded. And kept walking.

Stella, Savannah, and Waycross rounded a final corner and saw, to their great relief, that they were back at the maze entrance. Although Stella received little satisfaction from it, considering what heartbreak the night was yet to bring.

She stopped them a few feet from the entrance, where the judge was still standing, collecting tickets and cash from those who had arrived late. Pulling them to the side of the path and close to her, she leaned down and whispered, "Not one word to anybody about anything. You hear me? Not a word."

They looked up at her questioningly, and she knew what they were thinking. This was a big deal. The most momentous occurrence in either of their young lives. No doubt, they were aching to share their earthshaking news with everyone they met.

"But, Granny—" Waycross began.

"No *buts* about it, grandson. I ain't funnin' about this. You're gonna have to trust me when I tell you that we have to keep everything we just saw under our hats. Not one word till we can tell it to the right people."

"Like Sheriff Gilford," Savannah said with a somber tone. "We have to tell the law before anybody else finds out about it. Otherwise, the whole town will hightail it out there to those woods and walk all around the body and ruin the crime scene before it gets investigated properly. Right, Gran?"

Stella stared at her precocious granddaughter and briefly wondered, not for the first time, if a steady diet of Nancy Drew and Hardy Boys books might not be the best for a young girl.

On the other hand, Savannah made no bones about the fact that she intended to be a police officer when she grew up someday. If, indeed, she held fast to that dream, Stella reckoned she was halfway to a detective's gold shield already, thanks to the McGill Public Library and Rose Clingingsmith.

"That's right, sugar," Stella told her. "Justice needs to be got for that woman layin' out there and for those who loved and lost her. We don't want to ruin the chances of that happening by flappin' our jaws to the wrong people."

She looked down at the boy's woebegone face and added, "But I know you'll want to talk about it, grandson. You'll need to talk about it to get it settled in your mind. You might need to talk about it for years. The time will come when you can. It just ain't time yet. Understand? The wrong words . . . or even the right words, spoken at the wrong time, can hurt folks worse than rocks. We don't want to hurt people with our words, do we?"

He thought it over for a few moments, then shook his head and said, "No. We sure don't. I won't say nothin' outta turn, Granny. But as soon as the coast's clear, and I can let 'er rip, you let me know. Right then. Not a minute later. Okay?"

Stella kissed his sweaty forehead, loving the little-boy smell of him. "I most certainly will, sugar plum. I know you're bustin' at the seams. It's just human nature to wanna tell all ya know."

Having led Savannah and Waycross to the listeners' circle beneath the old oak tree and quietly seated them at the edge of the group, Stella couldn't help noticing that Marietta was sitting only inches away from Miss Rose. The girl was wearing a grumpy expression. Several degrees more sullen than usual.

The younger Reid children were still sitting in their original places, listening to the story with rapt attention. Stella could only surmise that the librarian, who was known for her ability to keep law and order in whatever environment she found herself, had moved Marietta closer. Within arm's reach.

Although embarrassed, Stella wasn't surprised. Marietta required a short leash at all times, because at any moment she might pitch a fit that would lead to violence—either her dishing it out or receiving an equal helping of retribution.

But Stella pushed it from her mind. She would deal with it later, if at all. Long ago she had learned that a body had only enough energy to deal with one true crisis per day. If that. Anything more could cause you to blow a fuse, and then you wouldn't be much good to yourself or mankind.

As she left Miss Rose and her audience, Stella noted that the librarian was barely halfway through the story of the hapless schoolmaster, Ichabod Crane, and his archrival, Brom Bones. She had at least another hour to go, which provided Stella with an opportune babysitter. If she wasted no time in fulfilling her unpleasant duties, it should be long enough.

Hurrying around the side of the mansion, toward the servants' entrance in the rear, Stella whispered a quick prayer. "Please, Lord, don't let me run into Elsie. I know I'll have to talk to her sooner or later, but not yet. Not until I find the words."

She could feel the tears forming in her eyes again. But she quickly wiped them away. There were more important matters at the moment than her own sadness. Much later tonight she might have the luxury of breaking down in the privacy of her own bed. Until then, she had to think of others and try to figure out the best course of action.

More than anything, she just wanted to put her hands on a telephone. She wanted to get in touch with Sheriff Manny Gilford.

She wanted to hear his deep man's voice telling her that it was going to be okay. That he was going to make everything right— or at least, as right as anything could be made when one human being had taken the life of another.

Just for a moment, Stella thought of that necktie, wrapped around the dead woman's wrists. The memory of what she had seen that night melded with a long-ago remembrance of another night, and was almost more than she could bear.

A scream, born of horror and unspeakable grief, welled up inside her, and it was all she could do to stay upright, put one foot in front of the other, and make her way across the judge's wet lawn.

When she reached the rear of the house, Stella slowed her pace and carefully, quietly climbed the stairs that led to the back door. If she could just get inside and through the kitchen area, she might be able to sneak down the hallway and into the judge's library.

As she opened the creaking, old door and stepped into the mud-room, her lips moved, sending yet another supplication heaven-ward, silent though it might be.

"Clear the way for me, Lord. Please let me get in there and back out again, sight unseen, by anybody. One look at me and a blind man wearing a football helmet on backwards could see something was wrong with me. You know I ain't good at fakin'. Never was."

Her prayer was answered.

Although she could hear someone, probably Elsie, moving about in the kitchen, Stella managed to slip through that area and into the hallway without seeing anyone or being observed.

She found the hallway just as empty and whispered a grateful, "Thank you, Lord. I owe you one. And while I've got your atten-tion, if you could arrange for that office to be unoccupied, too, I'll be scroungin' for ways to pay you back, once the dust settles around here."

Having visited the house at other times—usually when the judge and his wife were out of town and Elsie craved company—Stella knew that the first door on the right was the judge's study, formerly the mansion's library.

She had spent pleasant moments in that beautiful room over the years. With the master and mistress of the estate out of town, Elsie had invited Stella over and given her a mini-tour of the grand, old house.

In the judge's study, Elsie had shown her the mahogany, wain-scoted walls with their antique paintings, tintypes, and Civil War memorabilia. With tremendous pride, Elsie had guided Stella around the room, explaining the history behind every item of furniture—not a single piece of which had been changed in over a century.

Stella hadn't seen the study for a long time, and under happier circumstances, she would have been excited to see it again.

But for now, she would settle for just getting in and out, doing her business, and not getting caught.

She glanced up and down the empty hallway, walked to the doorway, leaned forward, and placed her ear against it. After listening intently for what seemed like forever, she determined it was empty.

To her relief, when she turned the knob, she also found it unlocked.

So far, so good.

Easing it open, she found the lights in the brass sconces on the walls were on and casting a warm glow onto the mahogany paneling and bookshelves.

As Stella had hoped, that room, too, was unoccupied.

Quickly, she slipped inside and closed the door behind her.

She debated about locking the door but decided not to. If confronted, she could simply tell the truth and say she had come inside to make an important phone call. But if the door were locked, she would appear even more suspicious.

She glanced around the lovely room and thought it looked just the way she remembered it. Diamond-tucked, wingback chairs with matching footstools invited visitors to take one of the leather-bound books from a nearby shelf and sit in front of the fireplace to read for a few hours.

She couldn't imagine enjoying her evening Bible study or her morning tabloid newspaper in such an opulent setting.

The rug on the floor had seen better days; its reds and blues had faded and the main traffic areas were well worn. But it lent the same air of long-past opulence to the surroundings as did the stained-glass lamps with beaded, fringed shades and the judge's massive mahogany desk, whose legs were hand-carved, snarling lions, rearing on their haunches.

The only modern features in the space were the telephone on the desk and a radio on a nearby wall shelf.

Stella wasted no further time or thought on the room, but hurried to the phone and lifted it from its cradle.

She dialed the sheriff's station and cringed when she heard the twangy, lazy-slow voice of Deputy Mervin Jarvis.

"Yeah," was his lackluster greeting.

It was no secret around town that Deputy Merv lived in constant terror that he might overextend himself with things like common courtesies.

You knucklehead, Stella thought. *You sure as shootin' wouldn't answer the phone like that if the sheriff was in the room with you.*

But she saved her time and energy for more important things than trying to teach a mule to bray on key and with a bit of vibrato.

She'd decided long ago that some folks were just a lost cause, and Mervin Jarvis was one of them.

"This is Stella Reid," she said, trying to keep her voice low. "I'm at the Patterson plantation, and I have an emergency."

"What?"

"I said . . . This is Stella Reid and—"

"Whuzzamatter?"

Stella opened her mouth to tell him that they had found a murdered woman, but remembered that when in possession of a juicy tidbit of gossip, he suddenly dropped the one-syllable responses and became a babbling fount of colorful conversation.

If she told him what they'd found, the news would be all over town before Manny could even make an appearance at the crime scene.

"I need to talk to Sheriff Gilford," she told him. "Is he there?"

"Nope."

Stella's last drop of patience evaporated. "Mervin Jarvis, this here is an honest-to-goodness emergency I got here, and I need the sheriff to get out here to the plantation *pronto*! I'm gonna be waiting for him by the back gate, the servants' entrance, and if he don't show in the next twenty minutes, I'll know it's because *you* were too dadgum lazy to get on that radio and tell him I need him. *Bad!*"

She took a deep breath and paused, giving her words a chance to sink through Mervin's thick skull.

When she heard him give a little groan, she figured he'd gotten it.

She plunged ahead. "I don't think I have to tell you that Sheriff Manny's pretty fond of me and mine, and if he finds out you took this situation lightly, he'll skin you alive, tan your hide, and hang it on one of them big billboards at the edge of town, so's everybody can see it comin' and goin'. You want that, Deputy Jarvis? You reckon your mangy carcass is gonna be a fine sight nailed up there, stretched out on top of a cigarette ad?"

"Nope."

"Me neither. So, are you gonna hop on that radio and send him out here right now?"

"Yeah."

"Good. I'll be waitin' at that rear gate with bated breath, and you best not let me down."

Stella hung up and shook her head. "I swear, that boy's as useful as a pogo stick in quicksand."

Chapter 11

Deputy Merv must have taken her seriously, Stella decided, when she saw Sheriff Manny Gilford's big, black and white cruiser pull off the road and stop a few feet from where she stood beside the gate.

She had waited only two minutes at most. He must have left wherever he was and whatever he was doing the moment he received word.

That didn't surprise her. Manny Gilford had been sweet on her since grade school and—other than the period of time when they had both been married to other people—he hadn't bothered to hide the fact.

Neither of them had fully recovered from losing their mates. Those unresolved issues, Stella's commitment to raising her seven grandchildren, and Manny's efforts to serve and protect the community all kept them from acting on their long-held affections.

But Stella couldn't help noticing and appreciating how quickly he appeared anytime she or her family needed him.

The moment the vehicle came to a stop, he jumped out and ran over to her.

"What is it, Stella?" he asked. "Merv said it's an emergency. I could hardly understand a word he was saying on the radio. Babbling on about somebody hanging from a billboard?"

Stella nearly laughed, in spite of the seriousness of the situation. "Nobody's hangin' from nothin'," she said. "It's worse than that."

She looked around and, although she could hear noises from the festivities and see the lights of the house in the distance, they appeared to be alone.

A particularly cold wind swept down the road. She shivered and pulled her old cardigan—Art's old cardigan—tighter around her.

He reached out and placed his hand on her forearm. "What is it, Stella May? What's wrong?"

"It's bad," she managed to say, though her throat felt like it was closing again.

"I gathered." His fingers tightened around her arm. "Take a deep breath and tell me about it."

She did as he said. In fact, she took several deep breaths, until the horrible, dark sensation began to ease a bit. Then she said, "Do you remember, when we were kids . . . hearing about Elsie's momma?"

He scowled, as though searching his memory. "I think so. Wasn't her name Becky?"

"It was."

"And didn't she take off, leave her family behind?"

"That's the story what was told at the time."

"She ran off with another man, I believe."

"That's what that no-good husband of hers, Edom Dingle, told ever'body. He spread that story far and wide to anybody willing to listen to it and even some who'd rather taken a beatin' than hear it again and again and again."

"Okay."

"She didn't run off. Least ways, if she did, the poor thing didn't get far."

"How do you know this?"

"We found her."

"Who's *we*?"

"Savannah and Waycross and me."

"When?"

"'Bout an hour ago."

"Where?"

"There in the corn maze." Stella reconsidered. "Well, not actually in the maze, but just outside it, at the edge of that woods that borders the north side of the property."

"I know the spot." He reached up and brushed a few of her wayward curls back from her face, then gave her a sad, searching look. "I'm assuming, since you're so upset, that she's not alive and well."

Tears filled Stella's eyes once again, as they had more times than she could count in the past hour. She shook her head. "No. She's not, Manny. She's dead. Has been a long time from the looks of her. She's just a skeleton, half-buried in the mud at the bottom of one of the trees there."

"Do you know for sure it's her?"

"Yes. She's wearing that pink and purple flowered dress that she wore to church and on special occasions. I believe Elsie told me she bought it when her and Edom tied the knot. And . . . .."

Stella thought of the dark, curly hair that had once been the woman's crowning glory, now a filthy, matted mess, and she couldn't speak.

"And what, darlin'?" Manny asked. "What else?"

"Her hair. It's got that leather barrette holding it back."

"Are you sure it was Mrs. Dingle's?"

"I'm sure." She swallowed hard. "I gave it to her."

"Oh. I'm sorry."

"It was made for me special by Magi Red Crow."

"Magi . . . Do you mean that old Cherokee fellow who lives near me on the river?"

"Yes. My daddy got mad when he saw it and threw it away. But I rescued it and cleaned it up and gave it to Miss Becky, 'cause of all she did for me after my own momma died."

Memories washed through Stella, hot and bitter, as a tsunami of fresh tears flowed, adding to the countless old ones that had been shed over the previous decades.

Stella felt her knees going weak again, and if Manny hadn't caught her and pulled her to him, his arms around her waist, supporting her, she would have fallen to the cold, muddy ground a second time.

She felt him kiss the top of her hair, softly, lingeringly. His breath was warm and comforting on her forehead.

"There, there," he said, as though reassuring a troubled child. "I know, honey. I know. It must have been awful for you . . . finding her that way."

"It was." She nodded and continued to sob against his chest. "And I couldn't let on that it hurt as much as it did with the children there. They were already half scared to death. It was poor Savannah who found her. Practically fell right smack on top of her."

His arms tightened around her. "I'll talk to her," he said.

"That'd help. You know how much she looks up to you."

"Still wants to be a cop when she grows up?"

"More'n ever."

She pulled back just enough to look up at him. Even in the most troubled times, she couldn't help noticing what a handsome man he was. His thick, silver hair shown in the cruiser's headlights. His expression was filled with concern and affection for her.

"I'm sorry you went through that, Stella. It shouldn't have been you who found her. It's not right with all you went through before. It must've been like having somebody poke a sharp knife into the worst wound you ever had, huh?"

"That's exactly what it felt like. Feels like, still." She hugged him closer and steeled herself for what she had to say next. "And that ain't all," she added. "That ain't the worst of it."

"Okay," he said, looking grim, as though he guessed what was coming. "Tell me the worst."

"Miss Becky's hands are tied . . . in front of her."

He looked as though she had just slugged him in the solar plexus. It took a few moments before he seemed to find his voice and say, "Don't tell me she was restrained with . . . Not with . . . ?"

She nodded. "Yes. She's bound with a tie. A man's necktie."

"The same way that . . . ?"

"Yes."

"Oh, Stella." He pulled her to him again, so tightly that she could hardly breathe, but she didn't care, didn't even notice, because the waves of grief were crashing over her so hard that breath was impossible anyway.

"Yes," she gasped between sobs. "Her hands, they're just exactly like my momma's were . . . when I found her."

Chapter 12

As Stella and the sheriff agreed, she left him, waiting for her in his cruiser, and returned to the party on the mansion's lawns just long enough to deal with the children.

The librarian had nearly reached the end of her story, so Stella crept to the back of the audience, where Savannah and Waycross were seated. She squatted beside them, whispered the latest developments, and asked them if they wanted to come along with her and the sheriff back to the woods.

Waycross had declined instantly and in no uncertain terms. "No way! I don't ever want to be that close to a dead body again in my life. Especially one that I ain't allowed to even look at and can't talk about!"

"I do," Savannah had replied, far more solemnly. "I don't necessarily want to see her again, but I want to help Sheriff Gilford any way I can."

"Okay," Stella told her. "I've gotta find a babysitter to look after the other six of you while we're out there with him. I'll come back to fetch you just as soon as I got somebody lined up."

She left them to listen to the rest of the story as she searched for reliable, and if at all possible, free, child care.

Normally, she would have asked Elsie, who had never been blessed with children of her own and loved to babysit every chance she got. But under the circumstances, Stella knew that she could never look into her friend's beautiful, trusting eyes and pretend that everything was fine. Before the night was over, Elsie Dingle's life would change forever—not for the best.

While Elsie might consider it good news to know that her mother hadn't deserted her as she had been told so many years ago, to hear that one's mother had been a victim of murder would rend any heart, let alone one as tender as Elsie's.

Stella searched the crowd until she found Florence, chatting with some other women near the gazebo. She pulled her away from the group and carefully weighed her options before asking Florence for the favor. While Stella might have been the nosiest woman in town, she knew when to keep a secret. Florence possessed no such talent. She might have been the richest woman in town, owning McGill's only grocery store, pool hall, and one of its three taverns. But money didn't buy discretion, or if it did, Flo hadn't spent a penny on that particular virtue.

Stella knew she had to watch what she told her and be careful not to arouse her suspicions. Stella needed her neighbor friend to watch her grandchildren for the rest of the day, not stalk her, trying to find out what was going on that had absolutely nothing to do with her.

"I got myself in a bit of a bind," Stella began. "And I know it's a really big favor to ask. But could you possibly watch the young'uns for me for a couple of hours. Maybe just a little bit more?"

Instantly, Florence perked up. Any deviation from anyone's routine in the small town was grist for the gossip mill. "How come?" she asked. "How come you need yourself a babysitter on the spur of the moment like this?"

Stella knew, if she was going to have any peace at all, she would have to give Florence something to hang her hat on. And the juicier, the better. It didn't have to actually be juicy, as long as Flo thought it was. Since her mind tended to lean in that direction anyway, it wasn't difficult to mislead her.

To her shame, Stella had to admit she was pretty good at that sort of thing. Especially with someone like Florence, who wasn't quite as bright as she thought she was. Flo's two years in college might have given her a bit more education than the average McGillian. But more than one of her neighbors had been heard to remark, "Florence Bagley's got more money than Campbell's got soup cans, but she ain't the sharpest sandwich in the drawer."

In spite of Florence's reputation for having diminished good sense and Stella's confidence that she could deceive her in most situations, Stella tried to use her powers for good, not evil, and keep those occasions to a minimum.

Tonight, however, she was going to have to make an exception.

She looked her lifelong friend in the eye and said with a perfectly straight face and even tone, "I need to spend some quality time with a handsome man, and I can't do it in the presence of my seven grandchildren."

Flo's mouth fell open for a moment, then closed into a sly smirk. "This handsome man wouldn't happen to be the county sheriff, now would he?"

Stella glanced around, lowered her voice, and whispered, "He just might be at that. But of course, I'm relying on you to say absolutely nothing to anybody about it. I got a reputation to uphold in this town, and I don't want to be known as a fallen floozy of a grandma."

"Even if you're fixing to become one?"

"*Especially* if I'm fixin' to become one."

"Okay, I'll watch them for you, but only if you promise to give me all the dirty details when you get back home after your night of carousing."

For a moment, Stella could feel the mask on her face slip away as she thought of what those "dirty details" would consist of. They most certainly would not be the salacious sort that Florence was eagerly anticipating.

Her evening, spent with the deliciously handsome and devastatingly sexy Sheriff Manny Gilford, would be far removed from anything written in those books that Florence bought by the boxful—their covers graced with muscular, bare-chested men gazing lustily at women whose clothing was fast sliding south.

No, Florence was bound to be disappointed and maybe even figure out that she had been duped.

As Stella walked away, heading for the oak tree and her eagerly waiting eldest granddaughter, she knew that, after this, she was going to have to crank out a batch of cherry pecan fudge to get back on Florence's good side. Maybe even a double batch.

Stella collected Savannah from under the old tree and led her around the side of the mansion and toward the rear where, farther down the road, Manny was waiting for them.

"Thank you for letting me come along, Gran," the girl told her, as soon as they were beyond the crowds. "I was fit to be tied, wondering what was going on without me there to see it."

"You didn't miss much, sweetie," Stella assured her. "I just told the sheriff what we found, and that was about it."

Stella was already starting to worry about how much of her dark family history was going to come out during the process of investigating this killing. Over the years, talk in town had died down, and she had been grateful that her grandchildren hadn't heard it.

She figured they had enough to handle already, considering their wayward parents. They didn't need to know what had happened to their great-grandmother and what role their great-grandfather might have played in it.

Stella hoped she could continue to keep them blissfully ignorant, but she doubted that would happen.

A quick, sideways glance at her granddaughter told Stella that the child, who had been beside herself with horror earlier, appeared to be more excited than frightened now. Stella suspected that was because Savannah knew Sheriff Manny Gilford was on the case. Savannah had always idolized Manny, and Stella couldn't blame her.

Gilford was the sort of larger-than-life figure who inspired respect in the town's do-gooders and fear in the no-gooders.

"What did the sheriff say when you told him?" Savannah asked as they neared the end of the road and could see the cruiser sitting on the side of the highway and Manny right where Stella had left him, standing next to the vehicle, his arms crossed, looking in their direction. "Did you tell him that I was the one who actually found her? Was he impressed with us?" the girl babbled on.

Stella chuckled and put her arm around her granddaughter's shoulders as they hurried along the old, dirt road and the highway, where Gilford waited. "I told him you were, indeed, the one who found her, and he mentioned how much he thinks of you and what a fine policewoman you're gonna be one day."

"Really?" Savannah flushed, ducked her head, then gave the sheriff a wave, which he returned. "That's cool. I guess you told him who it is. Does he know who did it? Has he got it all figured out?"

"You got a mighty high opinion of our sheriff there, kiddo. He's a wonder, to be sure, but even Mr. Sherlock Holmes himself would have to mull it over for at least a minute or two to figure out this stumper."

Savannah's forehead crinkled as her young face took on the look of someone far older and more somber than the average thirteen-year-old. "First he'll have to process the crime scene," she said. "Although, we don't know for sure it's the actual crime scene. The victim might have been killed elsewhere and then moved to that spot. Murderers do that sort of thing a lot, you know. It's not convenient to keep a dead body in your kitchen or wherever it was that you did them in."

"No, I don't reckon it is," Stella replied with a sigh . . . and a reminder to herself to ask Rose Clingingsmith to guide Savannah away from the mystery section at the library and maybe toward the romances.

Then she remembered the covers on the books that Florence had stashed in the basket of reading materials in her bathroom next to the commode.

She recalled the gleam in both Tommy Stafford's eyes and the flirty smirk her granddaughter had shot back at him.

No, she decided. *Reckon we'd better let "well enough" alone.*

Chapter 13

A few minutes later, Stella and Savannah were riding along in Sheriff Gilford's car, heading down the highway toward a road that he claimed led directly to the forest where they had made their distressing discovery.

Stella had suggested that Savannah have the privilege of sitting up front in the passenger's seat, next to Manny. The look of rapture on her granddaughter's face when she did so was payment enough for Stella having to sit in the rear "cage."

Thankfully, the backseat was clean.

Stella knew what an effort the sheriff made to keep it so, considering the state of the McGillians who were forced to ride back there. To say the least, they were seldom at their Sunday morning best.

On more than one occasion, she had seen him behind the station house, literally hosing down that backseat and the rear floorboards.

No sooner had they gotten into the cruiser than Savannah had begun a barrage of questions. Stella considered intervening to spare Manny the experience of being grilled more intently than a prosecuting attorney with a resistant defendant on the stand. But seeing that he was holding his own with the girl without her help, Stella decided to let the "interview" run its course.

"Do you figure the killer used this road here to dump the body?" Savannah's face glowed with excitement and the green and blue lights of the vehicle's copious dashboard and console equipment. "It would make a lot more sense than dragging her through the fields—if that land was planted in those days. We're going to have to question people who were alive back then and spent time here on the plantation. They'd be most likely to know that sort of thing. Huh, Sheriff?"

Stella glanced up at the car's rearview mirror and saw Manny looking at her, a patient grin on his face. She was relieved to see that he was appreciating the child's enthusiasm, rather than finding her and her questions a nuisance.

He gave Stella a wink, and she returned a grateful smile.

"You're absolutely right. Those are excellent observations, Savannah," he told his eager passenger. "Thank you. I'll certainly take your suggestions under advisement."

Stella watched as he pulled the cruiser off the highway onto a tiny, weed-infested, dirt road that she had driven by, countless times, and never noticed.

She could see the plantation house in the distance, off to the right, and between the mansion and the road they traveled was the maze itself. Dozens of hearty souls were still inside. She could tell from the beams of their flashlights that shone first one way, then the other, as they walked the twists and turns of the puzzle.

It was an eerie sight, made even more so by what she knew lay nearby.

"There's the woods!" Savannah exclaimed, pointing off to their left. "It's not as big as it looked. Not more than a dozen trees or so."

Stella agreed that it had seemed larger when standing at its edge with her frightened grandchildren. But then, she had discovered that most things in life that scared a body were far less large than they appeared at first glance.

"Of course," Savannah continued, "it's not how big the forest is, but what's in it that matters."

"That's true, Miss Savannah," Manny replied. "I'm so grateful that you and your family made this discovery. Sad as it may be, I've found that the truth—especially in matters as important as this—can set a lot of people free. You've done a good deed."

"I'll remember that when I become a cop someday," Savannah said with the solemnity of a Supreme Court judge taking an oath of office. "I'll find out every truth I can and set a bunch of people free."

"I believe you will," Manny told her. "You're extremely smart and determined and strong and brave. Any one of those things would make you a good police officer, let alone all of them. Once you're grown and have a badge of your own, this world will be a safer, better place. I've no doubt about it."

Savannah wriggled with delight, and Stella silently blessed Manny for doing what her own son had never taken the time or effort to do—instilling the precious gift of male approval in her granddaughter in such a positive, wholesome way.

Telling a young female that she was smart and strong, not just pretty and sexy, gave the child at least a little protection against the Tommy Staffords of the world.

Manny slowed the cruiser as they approached the copse of trees and turned off his lights. "We don't want those folks in the maze to notice we're here," he said, "so we've got to keep our voices down and not use our flashlights any more than we have to."

"We don't want them traipsing all over the scene before you get to investigate it thoroughly," Savannah said.

"True. Though I'm not optimistic that after forty years or so, there's going to be a lot of evidence. Especially on the surface."

"Why do you figure nobody's found her before this?" Stella asked as he parked the car and cut the engine. "Folks had to be out here to plant this cornfield and groom the maze. Seems like somebody would've seen her."

The three of them got out of the vehicle and quietly closed their doors behind them. Manny produced a flashlight and shone it over the ground at their feet and leading up to the trees.

"It rained a lot here last week," he reminded them. "Way more than usual. You can see there was a mud flow right through here. That might have uncovered her."

"It's real muddy where she's at," Savannah said.

"Okay, take me to her," Manny told her, "if you want to. If not, I totally understand. Your grandmother can take me there and you can wait right here. Or in the cruiser if you like."

Stella could tell Savannah was having an internal battle—her desire to be as actively involved as possible versus the emotional upset of returning to the grisly sight that had scared her so badly before.

She knew her granddaughter. Therefore, Stella wasn't surprised when Savannah squared her shoulders, lifted her chin, and said, "I want to take you. I want to help you find the truth and set people free."

"Okay," Manny told her. "Let's get at it."

As Stella followed along behind them, she couldn't help thinking of her dear friend and wondering, *When Elsie finds out about this, will she consider herself "set free"? Or will she wish this day had never come?*

Savannah led the sheriff straight to the spot, pointed to the ground, then stepped back and watched as he squatted next to the body and ran his light over it.

For what seemed like forever to Stella, he swept the beam from one end of the remains, slowly to the other and back, focusing on some areas more than others.

He spent an especially long time looking at the skull.

Finally, Savannah broke the silence by asking, "Do you see anything, Sheriff? Can you determine a cause of death?"

At first, he didn't reply. Then he stood and gave Stella a questioning look.

She nodded slightly, figuring that, if the girl was old enough to ask the question, she was mature enough to receive some sort of reply.

"I can't say for sure," he replied. "Herb Jameson will have to look her over good there at the mortuary. Being the coroner, he'll do a real autopsy. At least, as best he can with what's left here. He'll make the official determination. But considering the location and the fact that her hands are bound, it's obvious that the manner of death is homicide."

"And the *cause* of death?" Savannah asked.

"Mercy, girl," he said, "you do read a lot of murder mysteries, don't you? Nancy Drew?"

Savannah shook her head. "Not anymore. Last year, I graduated to Agatha Christie, P. D. James, and Tony Hillerman."

"Oh, well, no wonder." He trained his light again on the upper half of the body. "I do believe I see a fracture in the skull. At some point, she might have received a blow to the head. That could be the cause."

Stella felt a chill run through her that had nothing to do with the autumn wind that was now blowing harder and colder than before.

For a moment, her eyes and Manny's met, and she knew he was thinking the same thing she was, remembering with her, grieving for her.

She hoped he wouldn't say anything. If there was one family story her grandchildren could be spared, she hoped it would be that one.

He seemed to agree, because he quickly changed the subject.

"We're not going to be able to do much tonight," he told them, turning off his flashlight and tucking it into his duty belt. "While I was waiting for you ladies to join me, I called the head of the university's archeology department. They're going to send a team to excavate this whole area at first light. I talked to Herb, too, and he'll be here bright and early. We'll make sure it's done right."

"Can I come for that, too? Please, Gran!" Savannah asked.

"You've got school tomorrow, sweetheart," Stella told her. "And besides, the sheriff can't have people who aren't part of the investigation runnin' around here while they're searching. Wouldn't be proper."

Savannah turned to Manny, her eyes pleading. "Sheriff? Would me being here, even for a little while tomorrow, cause you a problem?"

He gave Stella a questioning look. She shrugged, unsure about how far to encourage this all-too-adult interest in a child.

He laid his hand on Savannah's shoulder and said, "Your grandmother and I will talk it over. Maybe we could arrange a quick trip here after school's out for a look-see?"

"That would be great! Just a short look. I want to see how they do it—the digging, that is. I've never seen anybody actually collecting evidence before. That must be about the most interesting thing to watch in the whole world."

He gave her a gentle smile. "Maybe not as fascinating as you might imagine. It's mostly just a lot of hard, sweaty, dirty work."

"But if it leads to the truth and sets people free . . ."

"Yes. Then it's worth it."

* * *

A few minutes later, Stella, Savannah, and Manny were back in his vehicle, gratefully soaking in the warmth from the car's heater and discussing their next courses of action.

"I'm going to stay here for the rest of the night, just in case somebody got wind of what's going on and decides to come by and check it out," he told them. "But first, I'll take you back to the plantation or your house, or wherever you like."

"Flo used my truck to haul the rest of the young'uns home and put 'em to bed," Stella told him.

"Then how are you going to get back?" he asked.

"I've got a spare key to her car. She's always losing hers, so she gave me one. I'll drive us back in that." She took a deep breath. "After . . ."

"After?" He studied her in the rearview mirror.

"After I tell Elsie," she said. "She's going to find out from somebody soon enough, and it ought to be a person who loves her. Somebody who loved her momma. With your blessing, I'd like to be the one."

"That's a tough job, Stella, informing the next of kin." The expression on his face as he looked at her in his mirror was one of profound sympathy and respect. "You sure you want to put yourself through that, darlin'? You've had a really rough night. You know better than anybody how she's gonna take the news. Maybe you should spare yourself that."

"Yes, I reckon I *do* know better than anyone else," Stella said, feeling the sense of dread rise in her. "That's all the more reason why I should be the one to tell her."

Chapter 14

"Once we find Elsie," Stella told Savannah as they entered the mansion through one of the rear doors, "you're going to need to occupy yourself for a little while elsewhere. We're going to need a bit of privacy, considering . . ."

"I understand," Savannah assured her. "Nobody would want an audience when getting told something awful like that."

"Thank you for understanding."

"No problem, Granny. I'll find something to do where I won't be in anybody's way."

Stella gave her a quick hug. "You ain't never in nobody's way, sugar. Far from it. I never saw anybody, child or grown-up, who was as quick to make themselves useful as you do."

"Thank you, Granny. You tell us to do things that give us good reason to like the person we see in the mirror. I don't want to look at myself in the bathroom cabinet glass every morning and see somebody worthless."

"That's right."

"I've got Marietta to look at if I wanna see 'worthless.' "

Stella gave her a scowl that was half a smirk. "And you were doing so-o-o well."

They found Elsie exactly where Stella expected they would— in the kitchen, tidying up the remains of the punch-preparation extravaganza.

Elsie's face lit up instantly when she saw them.

"There you are!" she said. "I was wondering where y'all got off to!"

"I'm sorry," Stella said. "We didn't turn out to be much help at all, did we?"

"Don't be silly. I told you I didn't need you anyway. This was nothing." She waved a hand around the spotless old kitchen with its gleaming white tiles and copper pans. Nothing was out of place or in need of washing or polishing.

Elsie hurried over to the refrigerator and brought out a pitcher of leftover red punch. "I did set this back for you and your grand-kids, though. Figured y'all would be thirsty after walking around in that maze. How was it, by the way?"

Stella and Savannah looked at each other, then down at the floor.

"What's this?" Elsie said. "If you're both all down in the mouth, it must've been quite a disappointment."

Stella turned to her granddaughter. "Savannah, could you please put that pitcher back in the icebox for us?" To Elsie, she said, "Are you off for the night now?"

"I sure am. Would you like to come to my apartment and visit for a spell?"

"Yes," Stella replied. "That's a very good idea. That's exactly what we should do."

"I'll go back out front," Savannah said, "and sit under the oak tree. There might still be some kids there who need to hear an-other story . . . or whatever."

"You can come with us, sweetie," Elsie said. "I think I got

some of those chocolate chip cookies in the jar. The ones you like so much. Maybe even some pecan sandies."

Savannah shot Stella a troubled look.

"That's okay. Thank you, Savannah," Stella told her. "I'll come fetch you there under the tree when Miss Dingle and I are done with our visit."

Savannah nodded and quickly disappeared out the back door.

Elsie turned to Stella, looking confused and a bit worried. "What's up with that girl?" she asked.

"What do you mean?"

"Something's seriously wrong with her! When did you ever, in all your born days, hear a Reid gal turn down anything with chocolate or pecans in it? I think you'd best get her to Dr. Hynson. Pronto!"

Stella had visited Elsie's apartment above the old carriage house many times before under happier circumstances. It was a luxurious accommodation, as befitted her station as head chef on the estate.

Now, as every time before when walking from the main house, past what had once been the barns to the large building with its three massive doors and dormered windows upstairs, Stella thought of Elsie's ancestors who had served generation after generation of the Patterson family on this property, since long before the Civil War.

She wondered how those who were enslaved would have felt if they'd known that someday, decades later, one of their descendants would live in the plantation overseer's apartment and not in the ramshackle slaves' quarters, where they had been born and would probably die. Would seeing into that brighter future have brought them any sense of optimism, any relief at all? Or were their burdens too oppressive to allow even a glimmer of hope?

As the two women walked up the stairs to the rooms above the carriage house, which now functioned as a garage for the judge's classic automobiles, Stella thought of the woman in the forest. Of how someone had used and abused her, robbing her of her life.

It occurred to Stella that maybe Elsie's family hadn't progressed all that far from those dark days. How could one be truly free if they had to fear for their life and lose it anyway?

Stella followed Elsie inside the large studio apartment, her thoughts churning. At least one hundred times already during the evening, she had mentally rehearsed how she would break the news to Elsie. And no matter what words she chose, they sounded harsh and cruel.

She tried to imagine how Manny would do it and wondered if maybe she should have left it up to him. No doubt, he would have been more polished about the process, since he had far more experience.

But then, experience or not, there was just some news that couldn't be broken gently.

Lord, help me, she prayed as she took a seat on Elsie's old but comfortable sofa. Its dark, royal blue velvet set off the snowy doilies that graced the center of its back and covered the arm rests.

Elsie herself had crocheted the lacy decorations on lonely nights when her work at the house was finished, having no husband or children with whom to pass her long evenings.

Colorful afghans were draped gracefully over accent chairs, and on the floor lay several hand-hooked wool rugs in rose patterns.

On the walls were pictures of long-ago family members, including a particularly lovely one of her mother, Becky, when she was in her early twenties.

Until that moment, Stella hadn't taken time to consider how beautiful Elsie's mother had been. A woman with bright eyes, high cheekbones, and a broad smile—much like her daughter's. She also had a curvaceous figure, full and womanly.

Her dress was simple and modest, the skirt reaching below her knees, a wide belt setting off her tiny waist.

She was standing next to a large farm horse. Her hand rested easily on its muzzle, as though she knew the animal well and was perfectly comfortable being so close to him.

"My mother always loved animals," Elsie said, as she draped her fake fur over a chair, then took off the long, rhinestone-studded earrings and placed them on the table. "And they sure loved her."

Stella hadn't realized that her friend was watching her. She felt as though she'd been caught doing something she shouldn't.

"You're good with animals, too," Stella finally said, after searching her brain for a reply. "You nursed that old barn cat back to health after he got in a fight with one of the judge's huntin' beagles and lost."

Elsie brought a plate of cookies from the kitchen area and set it on the coffee table before them. "There ya go. Dig in," she told Stella. "Unless you'd rather have some Halloween candy. I'm sure I could scare some up."

Stella found that she couldn't laugh. The time had come. There was nothing to be gained by putting it off any longer.

"What's the matter, Stella May?" Elsie said, sitting on the sofa next to her. "First your little Savannah turns down my cookies, and then you do, too. Something's amiss for sure."

"It is, Elsie," Stella admitted. "Bad amiss. And I'd give anything in this world not to have to tell you about it."

"Sounds like you'd better get to it right away."

Stella looked into her friend's sincere, coffee-colored eyes and felt time slow as it did at moments of high stress. She could hear Elsie's cuckoo clock ticking away on the wall, feel the intricate pattern of the doily at her fingertips, smell the cookies on the plate nearby.

She could sense the tension rising in both her own body and her friend's.

"When we were in the maze tonight . . ."

"Yes?"

"Well, not exactly in the maze but that edge of it . . ."

"Okay."

"We found something."

She waited for Elsie to ask, but she didn't. She just sat there, her soft eyes wide, her breath quickening by the moment.

"Elsie, we found a body."

The words seemed to hang in the air a long time, until Stella realized that, once again, Elsie didn't intend to reply.

"A person's body," Stella added. "A female."

The cuckoo clock door flew open and both women jumped. The tiny bluebird announced the top of the hour by chirping eleven times, its tiny beak opening and closing, its tail twitching.

Having finished, it popped back inside.

Stella continued, "I called the sheriff to come out, and he took a look at her. He seems to think she's been out there a long, long time. Say, forty years or so."

Stella didn't know what to make of her friend's silence. She wasn't sure how much more she would have to say before Elsie would begin to understand the truth of the situation, grim as it was.

"He doesn't think she had an accident," she added. "There were some pretty clear signs it was foul play."

Finally, Elsie opened her mouth to speak, choked, swallowed, then tried again. "Is it my momma?"

Stella was taken aback by the blunt question, but said as gently as she could, "Seems so, sugar. Seems so. I'm so, so sorry."

She waited for the flood of tears, maybe even shrieks and hysteria. Who could blame Elsie for any reaction she might have to such news?

Recalling how she herself had reacted when told that Art had been killed, Stella certainly wouldn't. Grief had a mind of its own and a way of spilling out at odd times and in uncomfortable situations, whether the bereaved approved or not.

Though some did, Stella would be the last to judge anyone for "falling apart at the seams" over losing a loved one.

But Elsie wasn't falling apart.

A couple of tears, one on each cheek. That was all.

"Are you okay, sweetie?" Stella asked. "Can I get you a glass or water or—"

"She warned me about this." Elsie took off the apron she had been wearing over her spangled dress and wiped her tears away with the hem. Then she straightened her back and turned to look Stella in the eyes. "Momma came to me. 'Twas about a week ago."

"She did?" Stella was confused.

"Yes. I was layin' there on that bed, half awake, half asleep, and I felt her touch my hair, right here, on the back of my neck. It about frightened me half to death. I thought somebody'd broke into my place here and had evil on their mind."

"I'm sure it must've scared the piddle outta you."

"You joke, but it did! Literally! When it was all over, I had to go take a shower and change my bed sheets!" She laughed feebly. "But once I got hold of myself, I realized it was her."

"How do you know it was her who touched you?"

"'Cause when she did, I came full awake and flipped on the lamp right away, and there wasn't nobody here but me. A burglar couldn't have gotten across the room and out the door that fast. Besides, it was October the twenty-fifth, my momma's birthday. And she was the only one who ever touched me like that, there on the back of my neck. When I was little and couldn't get to sleep, she'd play with my hair that way to get me to relax."

Stella could see by the expression on her friend's face that

Elsie believed every word she was saying. To her surprise, Stella found that she did, too. Elsie had always possessed a special sort of spiritual depth that Stella herself couldn't claim. Even though she didn't understand the connection her friend had with "the other side," Stella didn't dare scoff at it.

Elsie Dingle was a woman who was practically brimming with what their pastor called the "fruits of the spirit"—love, faith, gentleness, and peace. So Stella wasn't inclined to argue that Elsie couldn't also know a few things most folks weren't aware of when it came to the unseen world.

"You said your momma warned you about this," Stella said. "What do you mean by that?"

"The very next night, after she'd touched me, while I was half awake and half dreaming, I saw her. She didn't look exactly like I remember her. She was bigger and stronger looking and sorta full of light, but I knew it was her. I told her she'd scared me plumb to death, and she laughed. But then she got real serious and told me to prepare myself. That something was about to happen."

"Did she say what?"

"Not exactly, but she told me that I was going to find out, once and for all, what really happened to her. She swore she didn't leave me like they said she did. She didn't run off with no man and desert her family. She wasn't like that."

"Everybody who knew and loved Miss Becky knew what a good person she was, Elsie. We all knew she hadn't just run out on you. Even if she'd had to leave that husband of hers, she'd never have abandoned her child. You were her pride and joy."

"Thank you, Sister Stella," Elsie replied. "I know that was always your stand. You thought the world of her and her of you."

"That's true. Did she say anything else?"

"She told me not to grieve when I found out what happened. She said she didn't suffer too much. That it was all over quick, and she went straight from this mean ol' earth to a beautiful place. She says she's settled in there real nice and is looking forward to greeting me when it's my time to join her."

Stella didn't know what to say. She was afraid if she even tried to talk any more, she'd start crying. She told herself, *Since Elsie's taking this so well, you don't wanna be the bawl-baby who ruins the moment.*

Fortunately, it was Elsie who broke the long silence. "I'm glad she came to me like that, or this news about you finding her would be a whole lot harder to hear."

"Me too," Stella said. "For sure."

Elsie picked up the plate off the coffee table and offered it to her once again. Because she sensed that her friend wanted her to, Stella took one of the treats.

Although it was one of Elsie's specialties, the pecan sandie tasted like paper in her mouth. She chewed and chewed and eventually managed to swallow it.

"How do you reckon your momma knew that we were gonna find her tonight?" she asked, unable to help herself.

Elsie shrugged and set the plate back on the table. "I've no idea. They're privy to all sorts of things on the other side that we don't know. That'll probably be one of the nicest things about passing on. All of a sudden, you get so much smarter."

"That'd be nice. 'Twould sure come in handy from time to time."

Stella thought of the archeological team that would be assembling at the burial site at sunrise.

She thought of Herb Jameson, the town mortician. He would try his best, but he had next to no training as a true coroner.

She thought of Sheriff Manny Gilford and the forty-plus-year investigation he would be facing.

Physical evidence would have deteriorated. Witnesses would have relocated or died off. Those who remained and were available would have only stale, unreliable memories.

Yep, Manny's gonna have hisself a rough row to hoe tryin' to solve this thing, she thought. *No doubt about it.*

If only she could help him.

What she wouldn't give to have some of that "special knowledge" possessed by those who had already crossed over.

Stella knew she shouldn't ask, but she simply couldn't help herself. She was, after all, only human. . . .

"Elsie, when you and your momma were chattin' the other night . . . she didn't happen to mention who it was who hurt her, did she?"

"No. The subject didn't exactly come up."

The two women looked at each other for a long time, understanding dawning on their faces.

"If she happens to drop in on you for another visit," Stella heard herself saying, knowing how incredibly rude she was being, "you might wanna broach the topic."

"Oh, I will!" Elsie didn't seem to mind Stella's insensitivity at all. "I'd done decided ten minutes ago, if she shows up again, I ain't gonna let 'er go till she tells me!"

Chapter 15

Any other time, Stella would have enjoyed driving Florence Bagley's brand-new Lincoln Continental. It was certainly the fanciest car she had ever ridden in, let alone sat behind the wheel.

But just after midnight, when she pulled the luxury car off the main highway and onto the dirt road leading up to her humble, shotgun house, Stella was soul-deep happy just to be home. She would have been pleased if she had been driving a team of mules and sitting in a rickety wagon.

It seemed like hours since she had left that little house, where she had lived for more than forty years—first with her new husband, the love of her life, and then as his widow.

When she was tired to her marrow and weary of heart, no place on earth offered her the same soft, healing solace quite the way her home could. Its roof might be missing shingles, its paint peeling and porch sagging, but the memories contained inside those walls more than made up for its faults.

Much like any old and faithful friend.

Speaking of friends, she told herself, *this day and its tribulations ain't over yet. You still got Florence to contend with.*

"Oh, goody," she whispered. "Ain't that the way life is? Always some such thing to look forward to?"

But as she parked the Lincoln next to her old panel truck in front of the house, she reminded herself of what she had already endured during the past few hours.

You found a dead body, kept your grandchildren halfway calm and collected through the whole mess, informed law enforcement, and notified the next of kin—who just happened to be your very best friend in the world. And through all that you didn't crumble into a thousand pieces. You can probably handle the likes of Florence Bagley.

"Yes, I'm a tough old turkey. It'll take more than this to kill me," she whispered as she walked up the porch steps.

But the moment she opened the front door, Florence was on her like a flock of hens on a five-inch earthworm.

They nearly collided with each other as Stella stepped inside.

"Where in tarnation have you been, girl?" Florence demanded. "I've been worried sick. I figured you and the sheriff would have your business done and over with by ten o'clock at the latest."

Stella walked past her and tossed her purse onto the piecrust table next to the door. "What can I say, Flo? It took longer than I thought it would. These things happen. I hope you weren't too inconvenienced, stuck here with the kids for so long."

Florence had her hands propped on her hips and a fierce gleam in her eyes that told Stella this argument was not going to be put to bed as quickly as she wished it could be.

"Of course it was an inconvenience. You know full well that I like to be home in time to watch *Falcon Crest*. What happened? Are the two of you so old that you forgot how to do it?"

"Florence Bagley! Whatever are you suggesting? Am I to understand that you think the sheriff and I were off somewhere—fornicating?"

Suddenly, Florence shifted from indignant to embarrassed. Her angry expression disappeared and she dropped her arms to her sides. "Well, no. I wasn't suggesting nothing as nasty as all that. I just figured y'all had rented a hotel room and was fooling around a bit. Wouldn't be no harm in it, the two of you being widow and widower the way you are."

"I ain't so sure that Pastor O'Reilly would agree with you there, but it don't matter, 'cause that wasn't what was happening." Stella walked over to her favorite chair, her avocado leatherette recliner, and sank wearily onto it.

"No," Stella said. "What we were doin' was worse than that."

Flo laughed uneasily as she sat down on the sofa near Stella. "Worse than fooling around in a fleabag hotel with a man you're not married to?"

"Way worse."

"Then what were you two doing? Robbing a bank? Committing murder?"

Oh, brother. Here we go, Stella thought. *There'll be no rest for the weary tonight.*

But she had to tell Florence. She had no choice. Soon after daybreak, word of the discovery and archeology team would spread across town faster than warm butter on a hot biscuit.

Once Flo found out that Stella had held back the juiciest gossip to hit McGill since the Prissy Carr Massacre, she'd pitch a duck fit that would last into the next millennium.

It was easier just to get it over and done with now.

"No, Florence," Stella said as she pushed the side lever on her recliner, lifted her feet, and settled in for the long haul. "We didn't murder anybody. But we *did* find a body that somebody else murdered."

"*What!?* You did *what*? Lord have mercy! Tell me all about it, and don't you dare leave out a single thing!"

"I heard Mrs. Bagley jabbering on there in the living room until dawn-thirty," Savannah said the next morning as she and Stella stood at the kitchen sink, washing the breakfast dishes.

"Florence has many fine qualities." Stella handed her a freshly rinsed plate to dry, then added, "Unfortunately, knowing when to go home ain't among 'em."

Savannah dried the dish with an expertise uncommon in one so young. As she stacked it and its companions inside the cupboard, she said, "From what I could hear, it sounded like she was able to wring every itty-bitty detail out of you before she was done."

"Heaven knows, she tried, bless her heart. I told her most everything except that it's almost sure to be Becky Dingle. That ain't official till Herb Jameson makes his coroner's ruling, so she don't need to know it. I don't reckon poor Elsie would want that all over town before she even gets her morning coffee drunk."

"How did Miss Dingle take the news?"

"Better than you might think. She'd sorta been prepared for it."

"She knew that her mother wouldn't desert her like they said she did?"

Stella hesitated, wondering as she frequently did, how much to share with this child who seemed to have the mind of an adult. Stella had to constantly remind herself that, mature as Savannah might be, she was still young and needed to be protected, as much as possible, from the harshest aspects of life. At least for a few more years.

So, she decided not to share the spiritual aspects of Elsie's story.

"Yes," Stella replied, "she had never believed that her momma ran away, so maybe it wasn't such a shock to her after all. It might've even done her a little bit of good, just to have the matter settled, once and for all, after so many years."

"I'm glad," Savannah said. "Miss Dingle is one of my favorite people. She's so sweet, always doing nice things for other folks. No matter how bad you feel, when she gives you one of her big hugs, you can't help but cheer up."

Stella chuckled. "That's for sure. Elsie's famous for those hugs of hers. They're even better than her coconut cakes, and that's saying something."

Savannah folded the dish towel and hung it neatly on the oven handle. Her expression turned quite serious as she said, "When I hear people saying mean stuff about black folks, that they're all bad because of their color, I always think of Miss Dingle and her hugs."

"Me too, sugar. Her hugs are the first thing that crosses my mind when I hear that sort of nonsense."

"I guess it's easy to not like certain kinds of people, if you've never loved one of them."

"I reckon you're right about that. Love changes how people think about a lot of things."

Stella glanced up at the clock. "You and the others best get out to the truck right now. If you don't shake a leg, you're gonna be late for school."

Savannah gave her one of her woebegone puppy looks. "Are you really going to make me go to school today, Gran, what with all that's going on, and you knowing how interested I am in all that sort of thing?"

Stella sighed, feeling the lack of sleep and the trauma of the past twenty-four hours course through her exhausted body. Not to mention her dismay at having to disappoint her grandangel.

"I told you, sweetcheeks, that I'll come get you the minute school's out, and if Sheriff Gilford says it's okay, you can watch a bit of what they're doing there in the woods."

"But by then, they might have everything already done. I don't want to miss any of the important stuff. How often do I get a chance to see something like this?"

"Hopefully, not until you're completely grown up and doing that job yourself, like you've been looking forward to. I swear, Savannah Sue, I've never seen a child as fixated on a certain career as you are."

"That's not true. Marietta thinks she's going to downright die if she doesn't get to be queen of something one of these days."

They both laughed.

Stella looked into her granddaughter's bright blue eyes, so like her own. How could she blame the child, when she herself had an equally intense curiosity about all that would transpire out there in the woods today?

"I'll make a deal with you," she told the girl. "Instead of picking you up after school, I'll write a note to the principal and ask him to let you go at lunchtime. I'll say it's for a special, educational outing. How does that sound, kiddo?"

Savannah's cheeks flushed pink with joy. "That sounds wonderful, Gran. Thank you so much."

"Okay, but don't mention it to your brother and sisters. It'd be sure to start a war, and we don't need that on top of everything else."

"I understand. I'll keep it under my hat. I promise."

"I'll be waiting at straight-up noon, there on the corner where I pick you up after school."

"Okay. I'll run the whole way there."

Stella leaned close and whispered in her ear, "And once I've got you, the two of us will hurry over to the Burger Igloo and treat ourselves to a burger, fries, and a small shake before we traipse out there to the plantation. Do you like the sound of that?"

Savannah threw her arms around her grandma's neck, gave her

a tight squeeze, then raced off to collect her brother and her sisters.

"That may not turn out to be as fun as you think it's gonna be, young lady," Stella said as she removed her apron and hung it on the refrigerator's handle. "With any luck, once you get a good look at that body in the light of day, you'll be able to keep that hamburger and fixin's down."

Chapter 16

As soon as Stella had dropped the children off at their school, she turned the old panel truck around and headed for the Patterson farm. This time, she had no intention of sneaking on and off the property. Her best friend lived there, and if that didn't give her the right to come and go as she pleased, what did?

As long as she wasn't raising a ruckus, she figured the judge had no reason to complain.

But when she arrived and checked the apartment above the carriage house, Stella was surprised to discover that Elsie wasn't at home.

Stella thought, after receiving such disturbing news only hours before, Elsie would be in bed or at least, taking it easy today.

However, considering the judge's reputation was that of a man who placed great significance on a nickel, Stella didn't take long to figure out that her friend was probably "on the job." Family tragedies or not.

Sure enough, when Stella entered the rear of the mansion, she found Elsie in the kitchen, placing a tray of biscuits into the oven. On the stove, a pan of bacon sizzled and coffee perked, filling the place with their delicious mingled fragrance that marked the beginning of each day in many southern households.

Elsie closed the oven door, then saw Stella standing there, watching her.

Elsie's eyes, swollen though they were, lit up when she realized her friend had come to call. "Sister Stella!" she said, running over to embrace her. "You're a sight for sore eyes, girl." A bit less happily she added, "And today that's not just an expression."

Stella laid her hands on her friend's full cheeks and studied her closely, evaluating, understanding.

"It finally hit you," she said softly.

Elsie nodded. "It did. About dawn."

"I'm so sorry, sugar." Stella kissed her forehead. "I was afraid you might have one of them delayed reactions they talk about."

"Was probably bound to happen sooner or later," Elsie replied, squeezing her friend one more time, then pulling away. She scurried over to the refrigerator, chose four large eggs, then hurried to the stove and placed them in a nearby basket.

"Care to talk about it?" Stella asked her.

"Not much to talk about. 'Twas around sunup when I realized that I hadn't given up all hope after all. You know, of her being alive. Of her coming back someday and having a good explanation for why she'd been a no-show for forty years. Seems silly now that I hear myself saying it. But I guess a smidgeon of that hope remained. Enough to hurt somethin' fierce, when I realized I'd have to let it go, too. That hope was the last thing I had left of her."

"Aw-w, Elsie. I don't think it's silly at all to hope and pray a lost loved one will return to you. Who wouldn't do that if they was in your place?"

Elsie sniffed and turned away. She grabbed a fork and began to transfer the bacon strips onto a plate.

At that moment, the grease popped and splattered on her hand.

"Ow-w-w!" She jumped back from the stove, dropped the fork on the floor, and grabbed her fingers.

Stella rushed to her and surveyed the damage. She could see some small blisters already starting to rise on her skin.

Leading Elsie over to the sink, she turned on the faucet and shoved her friend's hand under the cold stream.

"You're in no fit shape to be working today," she told her. "You go back to your apartment right now and get into bed and stay there until you're good and ready to climb back out of it again. You hear me?"

"I can't! The judge and missus have gotta have their breakfast!"

Stella left Elsie with the water running over her hand and hurried to the stove. She grabbed a clean fork from the drawer and finished the job of transferring the bacon. Then she began to crack the eggs, one by one, and place them in the hot grease.

"How do they like their eggs?" she asked. "Sunny side up? Medium? Well done?"

"You can't make the judge's breakfast, Stella! That's my job!"

"Not today it ain't. Today you take care of *you* for a change. If he don't like my cookin', him and that hoity-toity wife of his can just learn how to boil an egg themselves or hightail it into town and get a plate of sausage and gravy at the Breakfast Hut."

Elsie turned off the faucet and dried her hand on her apron. "Really?" she asked, as though unable to imagine such a thing.

"Really! And if you ain't back by dinnertime, they can just break down and order a pizza like the rest of the rich folks in town do."

"He'll fire me for sure. Judge Patterson's real picky about what he eats."

"Don't you worry, sister. I got this covered."

"Well . . . It would be nice to go back to bed and get another hour or two of snoozin'. All right. I'll do it." She headed for the door, then said over her shoulder, "Mrs. Patterson likes her eggs sunny side up. He likes extra crispy bacon and his eggs medium, but he's death on ruffled edges on those eggs."

"Okay. Run along and don't fret. I'll make sure the judge understands the situation."

Once Elsie was gone, Stella took the egg turner out of the drawer, smiled, and whispered, "By the time I'm done with him, His Honor is gonna realize what a jewel of a cook he's got, and how he couldn't live without her. By the time I get done fryin' these suckers, their edges are gonna be so ruffled that his prissy wife could wear 'em for petticoats the next time she goes square dancin'. Or *he* could. Now wouldn't *that* be a fine sight to behold!"

Stella's plan unfolded exactly as she'd intended. The moment she slid the judge's breakfast plate in front of him, his much-celebrated temper exploded. His bulbous nose, which was usually red enough to suggest that he spent quite a lot of time with a bourbon bottle in hand, turned an even deeper shade of red.

His eyes widened and his large, bushy eyebrows shot upward like a couple of white peacocks spreading their tail feathers.

Stella couldn't help thinking that, with his silver hair standing practically on end and still wearing his red and blue striped pajamas, Patterson didn't exactly look like a fellow who put on a black robe, smacked a sounding block with a gavel, and changed the lives of countless people forever with his weighty judgments.

"What the hell is this?" he shouted, pointing to the overdone eggs. "And what are *you* doing in my house, let alone cooking my food? Where's Elsie?"

"Unfortunately, Your Honor, Elsie isn't fit to work today. She's in a state."

"Well, she'd better be in *this* state, or she's fired. She knows better than to take off without asking my permission first."

"What I meant, sir, is that she's in an emotional state," Stella replied. "Turns out, she's had a major family crisis."

"Elsie doesn't have a family," Mrs. Patterson replied, patting her enormous, platinum-blond updo and adjusting the lace cuff of her negligee. Daintily, she spread her napkin onto her lap, then dug into her perfect, sunny side up egg as though she hadn't seen food in a week. "Except for that worthless father of hers—if he's still alive," she added, munching away. "Last I heard, he was holed up in a cabin in the swamp, drinking himself to death." She dabbed her lips with her napkin and smiled at Stella. "By the way, my eggs are lovely. Absolutely perfect."

"What sort of family crisis is she supposed to be having?" Patterson demanded, even more annoyed as his wife made quite a show of enjoying her breakfast, closing her eyes and groaning with every bite. "Whatever it is, it can't be bad enough to justify her not showing up for work. If she has a real crisis, I would've been told about it."

A movement just outside the dining room window caught Stella's eye. It was Sheriff Gilford's cruiser pulling up to the front of the mansion.

She watched as he got out of the vehicle and walked to the house, holding a manila envelope in his hand and wearing a grim look on his face.

Turning back to the judge, she said, "Something tells me that, any minute now, you're gonna hear al-l-l about it."

Soon afterward, Stella was sitting in the passenger's seat of Manny's cruiser as he drove them down the highway and then the dirt road that led to the woods. Looking into the right-side mirror, she saw a cloud of dust behind them and Judge Patterson's big white Cadillac in the middle of the haze, as he followed, practically on the cruiser's bumper.

Manny glanced in his rearview mirror and chuckled. "I guess you heard what he said when I served him that search warrant."

"Not every word, but enough to catch his drift. He wasn't a happy whistler. Some of the mess I did hear wasn't nice. He was saying stuff that would've got his mouth washed out with soap right proper in my household."

"He didn't appreciate being on the receiving end of one of those. Figured he's above it, I suppose."

"Maybe he'll think of that the next time he's considering whether to issue one or not."

They looked at each other and said in unison, "I doubt it."

"How did your talk with Elsie go last night?" he asked her.

"Not too terrible. Though, after she had time to think it through, she was in worse shape today."

"Sometimes it takes a while for these things to sink in."

"It does."

They sat in silence a while, and Stella knew he was thinking of his wife, Lucy, just as she was remembering Art.

"When it's something as big as losing a parent . . . or a mate . . ." she said, "sometimes the heart has to be careful how much it lets in at a time. Or it might just break in two."

"That's true."

He reached over and placed his hand on top of hers, then gave it a squeeze. "I was thinking about you all night, Stella May, when I was sitting there, keeping an eye on that site. I was re-calling how many losses you've suffered, some at a tender age, and how you've just kept going."

His words touched her heart and brought tears to her eyes. But they were good tears. Healing tears. The kind that washed a bit of the pain from the heart.

"Sometimes you don't have much of a choice," she said, "but to keep on going. Life ain't like a merry-go-round. You can't just jump on and off when you've a mind to."

"Well, some folks jump off. Once. But I can't believe that solves much."

"Certainly not for those they leave behind."

Stella glanced again in the mirror and saw that the judge was even closer. "Don't make no sudden stops or His Honor'll be in your trunk."

"I know. You think I should pull him over and give him a ticket for tailgating?"

She squinted, looking at the dust cloud. "I do. He ain't above the law. While you're at it, I think his right blinker's out, too."

She giggled, then said, far more soberly, "I shouldn't say a bad word about the judge after what he did for me and mine."

"You don't need to be all that grateful," Manny replied. "Any judge in the land would've taken those kids away from Shirley, after her nearly killing them like that. He was just doing the right thing, and that's what he's paid to do."

Stella thought for a moment, then decided to ask a question that had been bothering her for a long time. "Have you heard anything about how Shirley's doin' there in prison?"

"Not much. But from what little I've gathered, she's not doing that great. Gets into arguments, sometimes worse, with her other inmates."

"That girl's always had a temper, and it doesn't serve her well."

"I hear you haven't taken the kids out there to see her."

"No. I haven't. I was debating about it, praying, trying to decide what was best for the young'uns. It's their welfare I care most about, not hers, I'm ashamed to say."

"Don't be ashamed, Stella. That's why she's in prison now . . . not putting her children before herself."

"True."

"Then you decided it'd be best if they didn't see her?"

"Actually, she made the decision for me. I was wrestlin' with it, night and day, when I got word that she didn't want no visitors at all. Not me, which I can certainly understand, but not even her own kids. Said she'd flat-out refuse to see them if I drove them there and brought 'em in. That'd plumb break their little hearts. So that was that."

"Did she refuse to see her husband, too?"

"I heard she wanted Macon to visit her, but when he found out she'd refused to see the kids, he wouldn't go neither."

"Does he ever come around, Stella? To see you or his children?"

"No. Too busy. Like he's been for the last ten years or more."

Stella stole a sideways glance at Manny and saw the grim look on his face. His jaw was tight, his brows knit, and she knew he was deeply angry.

He was also kind enough not to rub in the fact that her son had, for all practical purposes, abandoned his mother, leaving her to care for his children with no help from him—financially, physically, or emotionally.

Knowing Manny as she did, Stella predicted that if the sheriff ever had the chance to have a chat with her son, it would turn out to be a very serious conversation, indeed.

She decided to change the subject. Long ago, she had learned to protect her mind, spirit, and body from taking on too many burdens in one day. A person could only stand so much. She had discovered that even people, like her, who had a large percentage of vinegar running through their bloodstream had their limits.

"Did the judge look surprised when you told him about the body?" she asked.

Manny thought for a moment before answering, then said, "Not quite as much as you might expect."

"Did he ask you who you thought it might be? If it was a man or a woman? How they might've died? If you saw any signs of foul play?"

"Nope. Didn't seem the least bit curious. Just mad. Like I'd upset his apple cart or something."

"Hm . . ." She didn't think she should say what she was thinking—that Judge Patterson, patriarch of the county or not, had just been added to her mental suspect list.

"Yeah. Hm-m . . ." Manny replied. "Just between you and me, Stella May, I'm going to be watching Judge Patterson real close to see how he reacts when he first sets eyes on that body."

"My thoughts precisely."

Chapter 17

The moment the cruiser reached the burial site, Stella saw a van and a sedan parked near it. Both vehicles were white and their sides bore the insignia of the university's archeology department—a crest with a scroll and a trowel.

Several young men and a woman, wearing protective body suits, gloves, and masks, appeared to be stretching thick white cord back and forth across the grave in a grid of one-yard-wide squares.

"Wow, they're at it already?" she asked Manny as he brought the car to a stop and turned off the engine.

"They're an eager group. Showed up even before daybreak." He gave her a gentle smile. "Oh, to be young again."

She sniffed. "I wouldn't be young again for nothin' if it meant I'd have to give up some of the smarts I've collected along the way. Them dribs and drabs of wisdom don't come easy."

"That's for sure." He nodded toward the Cadillac that was pulling up beside them. "Speaking of folks with more energy than they've got coming to them, there's the judge."

They watched him bound out of the Cadillac and head for the

workers. "That's about as riled as I've ever seen him," she said. "Except for when I set them burnt eggs down in front of him."

Manny jumped out of the cruiser and headed after Patterson with Stella right behind him.

Like the sheriff, Stella wanted to see the judge's reaction when he saw the body. She didn't really believe His Honor had ever killed anybody, not to mention the fact that he would have been very young at the time Becky Dingle disappeared. But he did seem to be having a strange reaction to the circumstance.

To Stella's way of thinking, most people would have been horrified at the news that a murdered person had been found on their property, not get in a huff about it.

When Patterson saw the archeological team, he turned on Manny and shouted, "You've started already? What's the point in serving me a search warrant if you've already started searching?"

"No sir," Manny replied as calm as the judge was enraged. "We haven't started looking at anything yet. They've only just determined where the area of investigation will be. It'll stretch from"—he pointed toward the maze—"from where you plowed and planted the corn, all the way back there, past the grave and into the woods, another twelve feet or so. Then the same distance wide. That's a search grid that they're laying down right now, Your Honor. They're mapping the scene. No excavation's been done. Nothing's been touched yet."

Patterson grumbled something under his breath and started trudging through the mud toward the grave.

That was the first time that Stella noticed, much to her surprise, that he was still wearing his lamb's-wool and suede house slippers, and beneath his hunting jacket, she saw the same red and blue striped pajamas he'd had on at the breakfast table.

The slippers were goners for sure, she decided, and the pajamas would never be the same again.

She'd had the presence of mind to wear her galoshes, and

Manny was well booted, so they had no problem keeping up with him.

In fact, Manny moved ahead of him and stopped him before he reached the body. "I'm sorry, Judge," he said, putting a hand on his chest, "but this is as far as you go. Nobody but this team is going to step into that grid—not even me—till they've finished their work. If you want to have a look at the body, you're going to have to do it from here."

"Get your hand off me, Gilford. Who in tarnation do you think you are?"

"I'm just doing my job."

"You ain't gonna *have* a job if you don't move your hand this instant! You forget who you're messing with."

"I apologize, sir. I regret having to take a stand like this with you, but—"

"But nothing! This is my property and I'll step anywhere I want to on it!"

"That's true, Your Honor. It's your land, but it's also a crime scene, and we have to keep it as uncontaminated as possible."

Patterson tried to push Manny's hand away, but couldn't budge him. The sheriff was younger, far more fit, and apparently more determined.

Finally, Patterson settled for leaning to his right and looking around Manny's shoulder.

That was when Stella heard him gasp. And although she hadn't yet seen the corpse by day, she remembered all too well how the gruesome sight had appeared in the moonlight. She wasn't surprised to hear that sharp intake of air, followed by a slight groan as though someone had just given him a sucker punch to the gut.

The next thing she knew, Manny wasn't restraining the judge any longer. In fact, Manny appeared to be holding Patterson up, trying to keep him from falling to his knees in the mud.

She hurried forward to help, but before she could reach them, the judge had broken away from Manny and was stumbling back toward her.

He looked and acted like a man who had consumed far too much of his favorite bourbon. A highly intoxicated man with unfocused eyes and a pasty, white face.

"Get the hell outta my way," he mumbled as he passed her, his arms outstretched, as though feeling his way through the darkness.

She did so without hesitation. He certainly sounded like he meant it.

He pushed past her and wobbled on his ruined slippers to a thicket of brush, where he dropped to his knees.

A moment later, Judge Patterson, richest and most powerful man in the county, lost every morsel of the badly cooked breakfast she had prepared for him.

"Well, that was fun," Stella said dryly as she and Manny watched the judge and his Cadillac disappear down the dirt road, heading back to the highway in a cloud of dust.

"Wasn't it though?" Manny's arms were folded over his chest as he watched the massive vehicle's retreat. "Think he recognized her?"

"I don't see how. In the first place, he only looked at her for half a second before he skedaddled off into the weeds to up-chuck. Besides, I doubt the two of them ever made each other's acquaintance."

"But she worked for him here on the plantation, picking cotton, didn't she?"

"Yes, along with my mother. But they were just field hands. He wouldn't have paid them no never mind."

"Your mother and Mrs. Dingle were very pretty ladies. I was a kid, but even *I* noticed them. I'm sure he would've, too."

Stella shook her head. "A man as rich and powerful as the judge, known throughout the county . . . He'd had women throwin' themselves at him left and right. He wouldn't've had to sink down to cotton pickers. Especially ones who weren't, well, like him and his."

Manny looked confused, so she elaborated. "Mrs. Becky Dingle was a black woman. My momma was Cherokee, and she looked it. I don't think an uppity white man like Judge Patterson would have given them a second look."

"If you say so," Manny replied, obviously less convinced. "You might be surprised what uppity men will do, no matter their color . . . or that of the lady in question."

He glanced over at the grave, where the female archeologist was meticulously taking a photo of each individual square in the grid they had marked. "They're going to keep doing that all the way through the excavation," he told her, "taking pictures as they clear away layer after layer. It's part of the record they're creating. They're very thorough."

"I'll say they are. Here I just figured they'd traipse out here, pick her up on a stretcher, and carry her out."

"No. If there's a single piece of precious evidence left, they want to make sure they find it." He gave her a long, searching look. "How would you feel about walking over there and taking a close look now that the sun's up? I won't ask you to if you're not up to it, but if you are . . ."

Stella swallowed and cleared her throat. "I can do it, if you think it might help."

"It might. Sometimes things look a lot clearer in the light of day."

"That's what I'm afraid of," she muttered.

He reached for her arm and gently guided her toward the site. She was surprised when he stepped into the gridded area and encouraged her to do so, as well.

"But you told the judge . . ." she began.

"That's why you probably shouldn't mention that I let *you* in," he said with a grim smile. "Truth is, we need an official identification of the remains, or at least, as official as we can get. If you're not sure, I'll get her no-good husband, Dingle, to come look at her, once she's been moved to the funeral home. But I don't want to wait that long to find out if it's her for sure."

Stella could have told him that it was Becky Dingle for sure. She never would have broken the news to Elsie the night before if she hadn't been completely certain. But the sheriff seemed to think it was important for her to have a second look, and she wasn't inclined to disagree with him.

She took a deep breath and told herself, *It ain't Miss Becky. She's up in heaven. Leastways, when she ain't runnin' around here on earth, talking to Elsie and the like. These are just bones. Just bones.*

She didn't realize she had spoken the words aloud until Manny replied, "That's right. This isn't her. What's here is just nature, returning to nature. No life, no spirit left whatsoever. It's nothing to be afraid of."

"I ain't afraid," she said, gripping his hand far too tightly as he helped her step over the cord grid. "Just sad. And mad, *real* mad, that some lowlife would turn that sweet, pretty lady I knew into . . . this."

"I understand, darlin'. Me too."

One of the young men wearing the protective gear stepped forward and removed his mask. "Hello," he said. "I'm Charles Courtright. I hear you and your grandchildren stumbled upon, um, this, last night."

"You heard right," Stella replied, shaking his gloved hand.

"This is Mrs. Stella Reid," Manny said, "an old and dear friend of mine. She's got a good idea who this is, but I'd like her to take a second look and make sure. We'll be in and outta your hair as soon as possible."

"No problem. Take as long as you need." Charles stepped aside.

That was when Stella saw it . . . once again . . . without the silvery moonlight to soften the image.

What she had been dreading for hours turned out to be less horrifying than what she had viewed the night before.

The sunny autumn day left nothing to the imagination, and Stella found that was a good thing. Surveying the mortal remains of Rebecca Dingle in the unforgiving daylight, Stella realized that what Manny had just said was quite true. There was nothing left of the woman she loved here. Not in those bones. Not even in these woods.

Becky Dingle was truly . . . elsewhere.

Stella was glad to realize how much comfort and peace that knowledge gave her.

But what was here, lying in the mud, nature returning to nature, might tell them who had done this. And that made this patch of earth, and everything on it and in it, precious.

Stella stepped close to the body, closer than she had thought she could bear to be, and studied everything she had seen the night before by moonlight and the beams of their flashlights.

"Her hair looks just the same," she said, "thick and curly. She always complained that she couldn't do a thing with it. That's why I gave her that barrette."

"It's leather. Looks Native American," Charles said, squatting down to study the ornament.

"Cherokee," Stella told him. She turned to Manny. "Like I told you before, Magi Red Crow made it for me, gave it to me on my tenth birthday. But when my father found out, he pitched a fit and threw it in the fire barrel. I waited till he walked away, and I pulled it out. I hid it and then gave it to Miss Becky for Christmas. I told her it was strong enough to keep her hair in place even on a windy day."

She looked down at the neat bun at the nape of the neck, held tightly by the leather and the pointed, wooden dowel passed through it. "Reckon I was right," she added.

Her eyes traveled downward, and she saw a glint of silver in the neck area, then a pendant. It was a tiny bit of silver, set with an even smaller piece of turquoise.

"That's the necklace Elsie gave her on her last Mother's Day. Elsie picked cotton like a crazy girl for months, over a hundred pounds a day, to save up the money for that. I went with her to Woolworth's the day she bought it. 'Twas one of the proudest moments of Elsie's life."

"I'll make sure she gets it," Manny said, "later."

"Good. That would mean a lot to her, I'm sure."

Stella looked down at the pink and purple flowered dress and thought how pitiful it looked, all dirty and faded. "I saw her wear this dress more'n a hundred times," she said. "It was her 'other' dress, which tells you the size of her wardrobe. She told me one time it was the only new, store-bought dress she'd ever owned. Mr. Dingle treated her to it for their wedding day. She saved it for special occasions and church."

"I recall her wearing it," Manny said. "When this is all over, I'm determined that's how I'm going to remember her. Walking down the front steps of the church in this dress, wearing her fancy Sunday hat, and a big smile on her face. Not like this."

Stella decided then and there she would do the same. She had countless happy memories of Mrs. Becky Dingle. She felt she owed it to that dignified, elegant lady to remember her in one of those joyful recollections, not like this.

It wouldn't be easy, she knew, but, like Manny, she was determined to accomplish it, sooner or later.

Stella continued to study the body. At least, as much as she could see, with it still being half buried in mud. She saw the left hand, or what remained of it, and the thin, gold wedding band on the ring finger.

"Doesn't seem like her killer was out to rob her," she said, pointing to the ring. "It's not very big and doesn't have a diamond, but it's gold and would be worth something, surely."

"That's true," Manny agreed. "I doubt she ever had any money to speak of on her person. If the killer was out to rob someone, he probably wouldn't have picked one of the poorest women in town. A thief would have taken the necklace and ring for sure, rather than walk away with nothing."

The female in the team, a petite redhead, walked over and introduced herself as "Wanda Milton" in a soft voice. Then she asked, "Do we know what she was doing when she was last seen?"

"I don't think I ever heard," Manny replied.

"*I* heard," Stella said softly. "I recall it was in the winter, not long before Christmas. A Sunday. Miss Becky had attended the evening service at church."

Manny nodded. "Which would explain her wearing this dress."

"I reckon so. I wasn't there, but Elsie told me that, well, one thing led to another," Stella said, deliberately leaving out some more salacious details that she would share later, privately, with Manny. "Her husband, Edom, started to thump on her. As he frequently did for sport. Only that night, the whuppin' he gave her was even more fierce than usual. Elsie said the last time she saw her momma, she was running out the front door, fleeing for her life."

"Did Mr. Dingle go after her?" Manny asked.

"I don't know. Elsie didn't say. Though she did tell me that later, when he'd drunk some more and passed out, Elsie went out in the night, searching for her momma. Needless to say, she never found her."

"I'll talk to Elsie," Manny said. "She might've seen something that mattered but didn't realize it at the time. She was just a kid. What was she, Stella? About ten?"

She nodded.

"That's so sad," Wanda said. "I can't imagine anything worse than that . . . watching your mother run away from your father and then never return."

Manny shot Stella a concerned, compassionate look, then took her hand again. "We'll get out of your way," he told the team that had now surrounded them, listening to all that was being said.

He led her quickly from the grid and out of earshot of the others.

"I'm sorry, sugar," he said. "She doesn't know."

"Of course she doesn't. How could she? She's just a kid. Wasn't even born back when . . ."

Manny cleared his throat and glanced down at his watch. "I haven't slept or eaten anything for ages," he said. "I can go without sleep and skip some meals, but not both at the same time. If I don't go grab myself some dinner, I'm likely to fall down right in my tracks, and—"

"Oh! Lord have mercy!" Stella looked at her own watch. It was ten minutes until noon. "Savannah! I promised her faithfully that I'd pick her up at twelve sharp, take her for a burger, and then, with your blessing, bring her back here to watch the goings on! Can you take me back to the house so I can collect my truck?"

He slid his arm around her waist and hurried her toward the cruiser. "I've got a better idea. *You* let *me* drive you to the school to collect our little detective, then I can take my two favorite girls out for burgers."

"Really?" Stella thought of how pleased Savannah would be to see that shiny, big cruiser pull up to get her, instead of the battered old Mercury panel truck.

Lunch with the sheriff would be the cherry on the child's sundae!

"Really," he said, opening the car door for her. "You won't even be late. I've got lights and a siren!"

Chapter 18

When Sheriff Gilford and Stella rounded the corner in the cruiser and spotted Savannah standing on the sidewalk, waiting, Stella decided that she had probably seen a brighter smile blossom across her granddaughter's face at one time or another. But she couldn't recall when.

"Just look how happy you made her, Manny," she said, reaching over and patting his arm. "Thank you so much."

He flushed under his tan, brushed his hand over the lower part of his face to hide a broad smile, and chuckled.

She was pleased to see that such a small acknowledgment could mean so much to him.

"No big deal," he said. "You Reid females are easy to please."

"We are? I thought we had a reputation for being fearsome. Maybe even dangerous."

"Only to those who don't know you . . . or who've done something they shouldn't and are worried about you finding out about it. Personally, I consider 'fearsome' a virtue. Especially in a female. Not a fault."

"But then, you're not fixin' to knock over a bank when you get off work this evenin'."

"Well, I was, but I'll drop you and your granddaughter back at the Patterson place first."

He pulled the car up to the curb next to Savannah. Stella opened her door and got out, motioning for her to get into the front passenger seat.

The child had enjoyed sitting up front so much before, Stella thought she'd treat her to the honor once again.

"No, no," Savannah said, hurrying to the back door. "You're the grandma. I'll sit back here in the cage and pretend I'm arrested."

Manny unlocked the rear door for her. She climbed inside the back and, once again, Stella slid onto the front seat.

"Just so we can keep our stories straight when questioned," he said, grinning at the girl in his mirror, "what exactly did I arrest you for? Jaywalking?"

Savannah thought it over for a moment. "No. It should be something more serious than that. How about felonious overdue library fines?"

"Oh-h-h! You're a dangerous suspect. I should've searched and cuffed you before transporting you. I'm taking my life in my hands!"

They all three laughed, as he pulled back into the street.

"Sheriff Gilford invited us out to lunch with him at the Burger Igloo," Stella told her. "Are you hungry?"

"Does a one-legged duck swim in circles?"

There weren't that many eateries in McGill. But then, the town was only three blocks long, so fine French cuisine, an authentic Italian bistro, and a five-star steak house wouldn't have been expected.

The drugstore had an ice-cream counter. Next door to the laundromat there was a pizza joint, but their crust was so soggy that the only customers they seemed to attract were folks who were stuck, waiting for their washing to cycle, without a candy bar in their purses or pockets to tide them over.

The Breakfast Hut was on the edge of town, but they were only open until noon, and they weren't careful to keep things well-separated on their grill. More than one citizen of McGill had complained of finding chopped onions in their pancakes.

There was an A & W stand between the church and the pool hall, where waitresses delivered your order on roller skates. But the gals weren't such good skaters, and customers got tired of having their root beer floats hurled through the half-open windows and onto their laps. The waitresses tended to wobble sometimes when trying to attach the tray to the glass. And only the local body repair garage owner appreciated the fact that they frequently dented fenders when they misjudged the distances and couldn't get stopped in time.

Therefore, the Burger Igloo, right in the middle of town, with its 1950s charm—its black and white floor tiles, red and chrome booths, and old movie posters—was officially the "happening" place.

If Sheriff Manny Gilford had escorted Stella and Savannah into the finest Michelin-starred restaurant on Fifth Avenue in Manhattan, the occasion could not have been more auspicious in their eyes.

Or maybe even his, considering the smile on his face as he ushered them inside and seated them near the window, next to the jukebox.

The other midday diners turned to watch them closely as they took their places at the four-seat table. Stella and Manny sat across from each other with Savannah between them.

Stella couldn't help noticing the extra attention, but she was also aware that Manny appeared oblivious to the curious glances. She figured he was used to it.

Most folks kept track of their sheriff's comings and goings. Some wanted to know where he was if they needed some sort of assistance, while others hoped to avoid him when they were up to no-good.

A waitress, wearing a name tag that read *Jean Marie* and a pink and white striped uniform with a short, barely-past-her-butt skirt, sidled over to them, her attention fully trained on Manny. She looked quite young, hardly a couple of years older than Savannah. But the sashay in Jean Marie's walk suggested she was old in the ways of the world.

She moved so close to Manny that her rear was only an inch or so from his shoulder.

"Why, hello there, Sheriff Gilford," she said in a tone far too breathy and sultry for a family café. She patted her enormous hair, batted her mascara-caked eyelashes, and added, "How are *you* today?"

A wave of something that felt a lot like jealousy swept through Stella, catching her off-guard. Why would she have any objection to a waitress flirting with Manny? she asked herself.

No doubt, it happened all the time. He certainly didn't belong to her. She had no claim on him whatsoever.

So why did she feel the need to yank out a patch of Jean Marie's overprocessed, bigger than big hair?

Stella had to admit that she was pleased when Manny didn't even seem to notice the woman, hovering at his shoulder, trying so hard to be noticed. He just gave her a brief nod and said, "Fine, thanks. But these two lovely ladies are my guests, and they're about to starve to death. If you'd fetch them a couple of milkshakes right away, just to get them started, I'd be most grateful."

"Oh, okay." She turned to Stella. "Strawberry, chocolate, or vanilla?"

"Chocolate for both of us," Stella told her. "If you please."

Jean Marie turned back to Manny. Her eyes had lost their lustful glimmer. "You want anything?" she asked him.

"Coffee. Biggest mug you've got. Black."

She walked away, sashay-free.

Savannah had eaten her burger before Stella and Manny could finish theirs. Although Stella tried to stop him, Manny handed Savannah a handful of quarters, and she scurried away to the other side of the restaurant to play the *Pac-Man* machine.

"Them things are everywhere now," Stella said. "They gobble up quarters faster than those little ghost things gobble down those dots."

"I know. There's one at the service station now. I wouldn't be surprised if ol' Herb puts one in his mortuary."

"'Twould liven things up a bit around there."

They both laughed.

He leaned across the table, lowered his voice, and said, "I meant to ask you something on the way here, but it slipped my mind. So, now that we're alone for a minute . . ."

"Okay. Go ahead."

"Back there at the burial site, when we were talking to the team, you were telling us what Elsie had said about the night her mother disappeared."

Stella knew what was coming next. Nothing got past Sheriff Manny Gilford.

"I was. And?"

"I got the feeling you were holding something back. It might have been related to the big fight they had just before she ran out the door."

"Yes. It did. I don't know those young folks who are there doing that digging. I didn't want to tell them the worst of Elsie's family's business."

"I understand. But now that they aren't around, could you tell me?"

"I'd rather you ask Elsie for the particulars,' cause it's truly her story to tell. But the gist of it is—Edom was out drinking when she came home from church. By the time he finally made it back to his house, he found that his wife had, shall we say, company of another kind."

"A man?"

Stella nodded.

"Okay."

She could practically see Manny's mental wheels churning.

He looked over at Savannah, as though making sure she was still out of earshot. "Did he catch them, um . . . ?"

"No. Just sorta, well, inclined in that direction."

"Just how 'inclined' are we talking about?"

"Kissing."

"I see. Well, I gotta say that would put a crinkle in most men's britches, to come home and find his wife . . . so inclined."

"True."

"Did a fight ensue?"

"Yes. Apparently, Edom cleaned the fella's clock and threw him out the door."

"Do we have any idea who this guy was?"

"No. Elsie never told me, though I did get the feeling when she was sharing it with me that she knew."

Manny drained his coffee cup, then counted out some bills and left them under the sugar dispenser in the middle of the table.

"I assume the beating that Edom gave his wife, Becky, came after he tossed her lover out the door."

"That's the way Elsie told it."

"Then we have to find out, if we can, whether or not Edom ran out into the night after her, trying to find her."

"That might be difficult," Stella replied. "Because Elsie says she ran after her mom by herself and looked for a long time. Unless she crossed paths out there with her daddy, she probably don't know what he was, or wasn't, up to."

"That's true." Manny nodded toward Savannah, who had left the game and was returning to the table. "Either way, we'd best get back out there and see if they've dug up anything. Your granddaughter's chomping at the bit to get there and supervise the operation. I think we've delayed her about as long as she's gonna let us."

Chapter 19

When Stella and the sheriff returned to the dig with Savannah, the anthropology team appeared surprised to see a child on the scene. But within minutes, Wanda had taken the girl under her instruction and was showing her how they were slowly removing the soil that covered the area, bit by bit, and sifting it through a screen to remove anything of evidentiary value.

"This is how we check for any bones that might have been separated from the body," she patiently explained. "Or maybe bits of clothing or anything that doesn't look like it belongs to the woods itself."

"Have you found anything yet?" Manny asked.

"Three small scraps of fabric from the dress," Wanda replied, pointing to several small paper sacks that had been labeled, sealed, and placed in a nearby cardboard box. "They're already bagged, but if you'd like me to open them—"

"That's okay," he told her. "Carry on. Looks like you're making progress."

"We are, Sheriff," Charles said, joining them. "We've almost uncovered the entire body. When are you expecting your coroner to arrive?"

Manny looked at his watch. "Any minute now. He had a viewing there at the mortuary this morning, but he told me he'd head over as soon as it was done and he could get away."

Stella watched Savannah carefully to see how she was coping with the emotional, grim task.

She appeared to be doing as well as could be expected. Maybe even a bit better. Though solemn and respectful, she seemed to be concentrating on the various tasks at hand, rather than the more gruesome aspects of the situation. Stella thought, and not for the first time, that if any child she knew had what it took to grow up and become a police officer, her Savannah certainly seemed to.

Though Stella might have wished her granddaughter had chosen a safer dream to pursue, Stella had already decided that she would be happy for her and very proud someday to see her wear a badge as she protected and served her community.

She watched as Manny moved a bit closer to Charles, and although he lowered his voice, she could hear him ask the technician, "Did you find any more bones, you know, scattered around?"

"No, sir. Not one. Now that the entire skeleton is exposed, it appears to be intact. Of course, the coroner will be able to tell for sure, once he does his own examination back at the mortuary, but I don't see any signs at all of animal involvement."

"That's good." Manny looked relieved, and Stella understood why. It would mean one less heartache for Elsie to know that her mother had lain, undisturbed, in her makeshift grave all these years.

"Isn't that kind of unusual?" Manny asked. "Half exposed like that, you'd think it was vulnerable to animal involvement."

"We don't think it was above the soil all these years," Charles replied. "We suspect it was in a grave, maybe shallow, but covered."

"Then what happened?"

Charles pointed to one of the other team members, an older fellow who was methodically sticking rods in and out of the ground, measuring and writing down the various depths on a clipboard.

"That's Don over there," Charles said. "His field of expertise is soil compaction and the effect human beings have on it when they do things like dig graves or plow and plant cornfields."

"Like the maze?" Stella asked, walking closer to them and joining their conversation. "Is that the first time that area's been planted with some sort of crop?"

"Don seems to think so," Charles replied. "And he believes that after the virgin soil was tilled, it changed how excess rain water was channeled through this area."

"Like when we had that big storm this week?" Manny asked. "That was the most rain we've had all year."

Stella turned to Charles. "Since the judge had this field plowed and planted for the maze, disturbing the way things were . . . would that have led to a gully-washer like we had running over her grave and uncovering her?"

Charles nodded. "That's Don's theory, and I'd say it's a sound one."

"That would explain why no one spotted the body before now," Manny said. "Why the animals didn't get to her."

"Thank the Lord for small favors, I reckon," Stella said softly, pushing the awful thought from her mind before it could form horrible, unforgettable images that would haunt her dreams.

Hearing an automobile coming down the dirt road, the group turned to see Herb Jameson's big, black hearse heading toward them. He parked next to Manny's cruiser, got out, and hurried over to the gridded area.

"I'm sorry it took me so long to get here, Sheriff," he said, running his fingers through his thick, auburn hair whose waves were, as usual, rebelling against the copious amount of oil he applied to keep them in check. "That wake took longer than I anticipated, and I can't rush folks at a time like that," he added in a voice that some of the townspeople unkindly called "femmie." But Stella had always thought Herb Jameson just sounded sweet and gentle. And sweet and gentle men would always be those closest to her heart, who engendered her deepest respect.

"Of course, you can't rush grieving folks out of a funeral parlor, Herb," Manny told him, shaking the mortician's hand. "I'd never expect you to. No harm's been done. Your timing's just right."

"Mr. Charles Courtright here says they just took the last layer of mud off the lower part of the body," Stella told her old friend and fellow church choir member. "They're all ready for you."

For a moment she wondered how she could refer to Becky Dingle, a person she had known and loved, as "the body." Such a cold, clinical phrase for a warm, loving woman.

But Manny's words had sunk deeply into her, and she truly was seeing what was there on the ground as a source of possible answers, rather than her former friend.

It helped her remember that Miss Becky was gone.

Except in her daughter's dreams.

Stella glanced over at Savannah to see how she was doing and was happy to see the girl had a mask over her mouth and was scribbling on a clipboard in her hand. Her brow was knit in a grimace of deep concentration, an expression she had worn frequently as a kindergartner, when coloring with crayons or cutting out paper dolls.

Nearby, Wanda was using a small trowel to remove a bit of soil from around the body and place it onto a framed screen for sifting.

From time to time she would say something to Savannah, and the girl would scribble violently on the paper.

But when Herb Jameson stepped into the grid and made his way to the corpse, Wanda, Charles, the other workers, and Savannah moved aside to clear his path and give him room to work.

He donned a pair of surgical gloves, accepted an extra mask from Wanda, and began his work.

After an overall perusal of the body in general, he knelt beside the head and focused on the skull.

"Have you taken all the pictures you need?" he asked the team.

Wanda nodded. "Yes, sir. Of this layer anyway. We'll take more once the body's been moved."

"Okay. Thank you."

Carefully, he moved the skull a bit from side to side, studying what bone he could see through the hair. "The posterior cranial fossa has a depressed fracture," he told them.

"Sorry, Herb," Manny said, "but us lay folks only understand plain English. What does that mean?"

"She received a crushing blow to the lower back of the head. Enough to not only fracture her skull, but to push the broken bone fragments into her brain, causing severe damage to it," Jameson replied.

The brutality of his words hung in the air for a moment, then sank deep into the hearts of everyone present.

Stella tried to guard her heart but couldn't. No amount of pretty thoughts, like *She's in a better place now*, could quell her sorrow or her rage at the person who had done this.

"Reckon I don't have to ask if that was enough to kill her," Manny said with a sigh.

"No doubt about it," Herb replied. "Without even doing an autopsy, I can tell you, that's almost certainly the cause of death."

"Is there any chance," Manny asked, "that the break you see

there could have been caused postmortem, maybe by an animal, or something falling on the body here in the forest, some natural cause?"

Herb shook his head. "Sorry, Sheriff. That would be a bit more comforting, I know, but there's nothing natural about that head wound. Nothing at all."

"Okay. Thank you, Herb," Manny replied.

Stella stepped forward. "Herb, I have to ask you," she said, fighting back tears. "Would her death have been quick?"

The undertaker looked up at her, his sensitive eyes filled with sympathy.

Stella knew Herb, being a funeral director, had perfected the art of empathizing with the grief stricken. But she also knew that at heart he was a kind and caring man. He didn't need to fake it. McGill's favorite, and only, mortician had a loving nature.

"I'm not sure if it was quick or not, Sister Stella," he answered her honestly. "Could have been. Might have taken a while for her to pass. We can all pray that she didn't suffer undue misery when she left this world. She was a good woman. The people of this town won't soon forget her."

"Then you know who she is already?" Manny said, his eyes alert, searching the undertaker's face.

"Sure, I do. When I was a kid, sitting in church, I'd look up front at the choir and see Mrs. Becky Dingle, wearing that pink and purple flowered dress. And I recall very well the day after Christmas, when she showed up with that leather barrette holding back all those pretty black curls of hers, saying how proud she was of it, that it'd been given to her by a young girl she was more than fond of."

He offered Stella a gentle smile. "You and her Elsie were the stars in Becky's heaven. You can always take comfort in remembering that."

"Thank you, Brother Herb," Stella said, wishing she could

just turn away from all of them and leave this sad site. Maybe walk into the center of the woods and cry until she was all cried out.

But she knew how badly that would upset her granddaughter. Savannah was a strong child. She seemed to be able to handle almost anything—except seeing someone she loved in pain.

Besides, she had promised to help Manny. What help would she be in the middle of the woods, sobbing her face off?

She turned her attention back to the remains on the ground and asked herself several questions: Other than the obvious, the body of a murder victim, what was unusual about this scene? Was anything out of place or unexpected?

"She ain't wearing any shoes," Stella said, then asked, "Did anybody find them hereabouts?"

The search team members looked at each other, then to the sheriff. Everyone shook their head.

"People run around barefoot sometimes," Savannah offered. "But not usually when they're wearing their Sunday best dress."

Herb bent over and studied the feet carefully. "I do believe a couple of her toes are broken."

Manny turned to Stella. "You mentioned that, the night she disappeared, she ran out the door during an argument with Mr. Dingle. If she was desperate to get away from him, maybe she didn't have time to put on shoes."

Stella nodded. "And if she was running across fields and such in the dark, she could have banged her feet on most anything and broke a toe or two."

They all stood there for a moment, mentally picturing the beautiful young mother in her flowered Sunday best, trying to escape her attacker in the darkness.

"Did ol' Edom catch up to her?" Stella wondered aloud. "Or did she run straight into some devil who was even worse than him?"

"That's what I aim to find out." The grim, determined expression on the sheriff's face left no doubt as to his intentions. "First I'm going to go talk to Elsie and find out where Edom is and what he's up to these days. Once I find him, we're going to have a long, serious talk."

Turning to the archeological team and coroner, he added, "You all are doing just fine here without me. And you, Herb, I reckon you can stick around until they get the body ready for you to take to the mortuary, right?"

"Absolutely, Sheriff," Herb assured him. "Other than a burial tomorrow morning, this here is my first priority."

Manny walked over to Wanda and said, "If anything comes up, if you need me for anything at all, just call the station house. They can get in touch with me on the radio."

"Thank you, sir," Wanda replied. "We'll have a full report for you in forty-eight hours. But if we come across anything remarkable as we finish up here, we'll let you know right away."

"Can't ask for more than that." Manny leaned over Savannah's shoulder and glanced at the paper on her clipboard. "What's that you've got there, Miss Savannah? You've been working on it something fierce."

Stella watched as her granddaughter proudly showed the sheriff her workmanship. "I'm keeping a grid record, like Miss Wanda asked me to. See, it's just like what they marked off on the ground. And I'm writing in each square what they found there. Miss Wanda says they're going to put it into the official record."

Her blue eyes glistened with the joy of self-satisfaction as she showed him the paper with the various drawings and scribbles.

It occurred to Stella that Thomas Jefferson himself couldn't have been prouder of himself after he had penned the Declaration of Independence than her granddaughter was at that moment.

"That's mighty fine work there, young lady," Manny told her, placing his big hand on the top of her head and ruffling her thick, black curls. "We're mighty glad you were able to join us here today."

"My pleasure, sir. I wouldn't miss it for anything." She gave a quick, sad glance toward the makeshift grave and added, "As sad as it is. Still needs to be done."

"It does, indeed," he agreed, then turned to Stella. "Are you about ready to go, Stella May? I can take you back to the Patterson place to get your truck now. I need to go there anyway to see Miss Elsie."

"Sure," she said. "Whatever's convenient for you. We're ready when you are."

From the corner of her eye, she saw a look of disappointment cross Savannah's face. But it couldn't be helped. Stella figured this experience, the child's up-close view into the harsh, adult world, was more than enough for one day.

Savannah handed her clipboard to Wanda. "Thank you for letting me help you, Miss Wanda," she said, "I'm never going to forget this for as long as I live."

"You did a fine job, Savannah. It was an honor working with you," Wanda replied as she removed the paper from the board, folded it, and stuck it into her pocket.

"Run along now, Savannah girl," Stella told her. "Get in the sheriff's car. You can sit in the front. I'll be the caged criminal this time."

As Savannah scurried away, Stella whispered to Wanda, "Thank you so much." She pointed to the grave. "For what you're doing for my friend, and for being so kind to my grandchild."

"She's delightful. You seldom see such well-behaved children these days. The next time you see her parents, you tell them they're doing a wonderful job with her."

Stella saw Manny shoot her a quick glance. She swallowed, smiled, and nodded. "I sure will," she told the younger woman. "Thank you."

Manny glanced over at the cruiser and watched as Savannah opened the door and climbed inside. He moved closer to Wanda and said, "That grid record of hers . . . you're not really going to put that in the report, are you?"

Wanda smirked. "No, sir. I can't. It isn't—"

"That's what I figured," he said. "May I have it?"

When Wanda hesitated, he added, "If you don't mind. It would mean a lot to me."

Wanda looked over at Savannah, who was busy, studying the equipment in the cruiser. The woman slid her hand into her pocket, took out the paper, and discreetly slipped it to Manny, who put it into his.

"Thank you, and good luck here," he said. Then he reached for Stella's arm and started to lead her toward the cruiser. "Let's get going," he told her. "We've got people to interview this afternoon."

"*We?*"

"Unless you've got other, more important business to attend to," he said with a grin.

"Well . . . the mayor's wife and I were going to attend a matinee at the opera, but I reckon I could cancel it. After all, you bought me a burger."

He placed his hand on her back and gave her an affectionate pat. "And don't forget the fries and a shake."

"Not to mention all those quarters you provided for my grand-young'un."

"Naw. She worked those off laboring here at the dig site this afternoon. But you, you'll be a long time working off what *you* owe me."

For a moment, Stella laughed, and she felt happy and at peace for the first time since she and her grandchildren had made their terrible discovery the night before.

Manny Gilford had that effect on her, and something told her that she was a pleasant, calming influence on him, as well.

Once again, like many times before, she said a quick, silent prayer of thanksgiving for their special friendship.

Chapter 20

"I feel plumb guilty, asking you to wait in the truck while we talk to Elsie," Stella told Savannah when they and Manny climbed out of his cruiser in front of the Patterson mansion. "You were such a good girl back there at the dig, that I hate to leave you all by your lonesome."

Savannah slipped her hand into her grandmother's and looked up at her with understanding in her eyes. "I've got a library book in my backpack, so I won't get bored. Besides, it's what's best for Miss Dingle," she said. "When you talk to her, you want her to feel comfortable telling you anything that she's got on her mind. She might not want to discuss grown-up stuff in front of a little kid like me."

"You ain't that little, dumplin', I'm sorry to say, and you haven't been a kid for a long time now. You had to leave your childhood behind way sooner than you should have, and I feel mighty bad about that."

"You don't need to. I'm doing okay. It's just that other adults don't think of me as a grown-up. Not like the two of you do," Savannah added proudly.

Stella looked over at Manny, who was tucking his car keys into his pocket and trying to hide a smirk. "That's true," she told Savannah. "Most grown-ups don't know you as well as the sheriff and your grandma do."

"I have an idea," Manny said. "Instead of sitting in your grandma's truck, why don't you wait in my cruiser instead? It would actually help me out. That way, if the station house should try to call me on my radio, you can pick it up, find out what they want, and then come get me. Does that sound like something you might be interested in doing? I can show you how to operate the radio if you want."

Many times, Stella had seen her granddaughter do a little dance when told something she was pleased to hear. But until that moment, she had no idea that Savannah was capable of doing a most impressive, sprightly, Irish jig.

Manny laughed. "I figured you wouldn't put up too much of a fuss. Come on." He gave her a push back toward the cruiser. "I'll give you a quick lesson on how to answer a call, so's you don't sound like a civilian."

Stella and Manny were unable to locate Elsie in either her apartment or the mansion. The maid, who was mopping the main hallway, told them she hadn't seen her all day.

As they walked through the kitchen, heading for the back door, Stella said, "I wish we'd found Elsie, but I'm not sorry we avoided His Honor."

"Me either," Manny replied. "I think I'd be about as happy to see him as he would be to set eyes on me right now."

"I figure he's upstairs, stretched out on his bed, tryin' to recover what's left of his dignity and composure."

"Too late. After that vision of him on his hands and knees, surrendering his breakfast like that, I'll never see him quite the same way again."

"Yeah. None of us are at our best when we're tossin' our cookies. It's hard to project an image of bein' high and mighty when you're too weak to put a whuppin' on a gnat."

As they exited the back door, Manny looked beyond the pool area to the rear parking area and said, "Her red Mustang's here. I doubt she'd go far without it."

"I agree," Stella told him. "She's crazy about that car. It's her baby. If it's here, she's here."

"But where?" he asked. "Does she have a favorite spot? A place she goes when she's upset or doesn't want to be bothered?"

Instantly, Stella knew exactly where her friend was.

"Yes, she sure does," she told him. "It's a place us girls knew well when we were little. The best place in the world to be alone with your thoughts, commune with nature, or say a few prayers. Follow me."

One of the prettiest spots on the old plantation, at least as far as Stella was concerned, was the giant weeping willow that stood on the edge of the pond, far back from the main house. Its branches and leaves were so thick that if you were inside the lush, green curtain it provided, you could see no one, and more importantly, no one could see you.

In autumn, it was even lovelier, because the leaves turned a radiant shade of gold and the tree held on to its gilded beauty longer than most of the other deciduous trees.

Many years ago, someone had realized what a relaxing refuge it provided and placed a wrought iron, wraparound, tree bench about its trunk, so a visitor could sit and meditate in comfort.

More times than she could count, Stella and Elsie had hidden under that tree, sat on the bench, and spent precious, bonding time together. They talked about the mothers they'd lost, the boys they loved—or thought they did for two-week periods at a time—their life dreams, and greatest fears.

Sometimes, they talked of nothing at all, and the blissful silence was just as bonding as their conversations.

From time to time, they had sung together—the more popular songs of the day, old classic favorites, and hymns their moms had sung to them when trying to get the energetic girls to sleep.

"This is a pretty place," Manny commented as they approached the pond with its emerald water that reflected the crimson-, golden-, and coral-leafed trees lining its edge, mingled with the dark green pines. "I never knew this was back here."

"I don't recall you spending a lot of time on the plantation, when you were growing up," Stella said.

What she didn't add was, "Like us poor kids."

Throughout the history of McGill, or at least as long as Stella could remember, the population of the small community had been divided into two distinct social classes.

There had been the "town" folks and the "country" folks.

Out of compassion and good manners, it wasn't usually stated that those who lived in town tended to be considerably better off than those living in the country.

There were a few well-to-do people in the rural areas, wealthy farmers who owned large swaths of land. But most of those who dwelt outside the city limits worked for those few landowners and weren't paid particularly well for doing so.

The townsfolk, on the other hand, were mostly business owners, mixed with a few professionals.

Manny's father had owned the bank on the corner of Main Street and Oak. His mother was a schoolteacher. Manny was one of the few students in Stella's graduating class who had left the area, attended university, received a degree, and returned home to use it in service of his community.

When Stella, Elsie, Becky Dingle, and Stella's own mother, Gola Quinn, had been picking and chopping cotton there on the old Patterson estate and other farms in the area on sweltering summer days, Manny Gilford had been learning how to balance ledgers with his father in the back room of the air-conditioned bank.

That was part of why Stella had always wondered at Manny's interest in her. Since when did a banker's son carry a torch for a poor, country kid who picked cotton, whose family had worked the fields for as far back as anyone could remember?

The only answer she could come up with was that Manny Gilford didn't care about such things as whether someone lived in town or in the country. He didn't care who had money and who didn't, as long as they treated their neighbors with kindness and led halfway decent lives.

She blessed him for that.

If he had followed in his father's steps, as his dad had insisted to no avail, he would have, no doubt, made more money in his life. But like Savannah, Manny had decided early what he wanted to be when he grew up.

In spite of family pressures, he had taken his own path in life, protected, and served. He had the respect of his community. He had saved lives. He had kept good people safe from bad ones.

Stella was proud to call him her friend, and, if things had been a little bit different, they might have been far more than friends.

But there was Stella's Art, and Manny's Lucy, and Stella didn't believe that either she or Manny would have truly wanted to rewrite their life history, given the chance.

"There are plenty of pretty places on this old plantation," she told him, "if you look for 'em. Some ugly ones, too, where mighty evil things happened in times gone by. Even before the Civil War, let alone during."

"Like the hanging tree in the front yard?"

"That's one of the more infamous ones. But there's plenty of others, too." She thought of the woods near the corn maze. "Now there's another one to add to the list."

Manny looked around, as though getting his bearings. "Speaking of which, I don't think we're too far from it now. Should be right over that way, less than a quarter of a mile or so. Wonder how they're doing?"

"You would've liked to have stayed, huh?"

"Yes. But these interviews are as important as anything they're going to dig up out there. Let's hope your friend is under that willow, like you think she is."

It didn't take long for them to find out. They hadn't even reached the imposing, sixty-foot-tall willow with its golden boughs before they could hear Elsie singing.

"Whispering Hope," Stella told Manny, recognizing the old hymn right away as one of Becky's and her own mother's favorites.

Manny, whose parents hadn't been as regular in their church attendance as Becky and Gola, didn't know what she was talking about.

"I beg your pardon?" he asked.

"Her momma used to sing that all the time. Mine too," she explained. "Mostly when they needed to feel better about something, and that was pretty frequent."

When they reached the tree, Stella called softly, "Elsie? Sugar, it's me and the sheriff."

Instantly, the song ceased. A moment later, Elsie popped her head out, looking at them from a split in the lush, golden veil.

To her relief, Stella saw that she was wearing a smile. A tired one, perhaps, but a sweet one. Stella was also happy to see that her friend's eyes didn't look nearly as swollen as before.

"Good afternoon, Stella," Elsie said. "To you, too, Sheriff."

He took off his hat and gave her a regal nod. "I'm glad to see you, Miss Dingle. Though I wish it was under happier circumstances."

"Yes," Elsie said sadly. "Don't we all?" She pulled her willow "drapes" aside and waved her arm toward the inside of the canopy. "Would you two like to join me in here? It's real nice and shady and pretty as can be."

"I'll bet it is," Manny said. "We'd love to."

He stood back and allowed Stella to walk inside, then followed close behind her.

Elsie dropped the leafy branches back into place, and the three of them were standing in a glorious, small "room" of nature's creation.

"When we couldn't find you in your apartment or the big house, I knew you'd be here," Stella told her. She looked around at the leaves that glistened with a golden glow richer than any king's ransom. "I forgot how pretty this place is."

"Plus, people can't find you when you're in here," Elsie said. "Except the ones who love you and know you best, and that's okay."

Manny turned to Elsie and pointed to Stella. "I'm with her. Hate to disturb you, but I'm just doing what I'm told."

"I understand." Elsie waved toward the bench wrapped around the tree trunk. "Won't y'all have a seat and rest a spell? If I'd known I was going to have company, I'd have brought some cookies and hot apple cider."

"That's okay, sweetie," Stella said. "This ain't exactly a social call, I'm afraid."

"I didn't figure it was. I've seen more cheerful expressions than you two are wearin' on the faces of pickers in the middle of a cotton field at high noon on a blistering hot day."

The women sat down, but Manny continued to stand, his sharp eyes on an object that lay on the other side of the bench. "Were you doing a bit of reading?" he asked Elsie, nodding toward the book.

"I started to." She picked up the small volume and passed her hand over its cover slowly, lovingly. "But I didn't get far."

"How come?" Stella asked. "Slow reading, was it? Boring?"

"No. It was interesting enough. A bit *too* interesting, in fact. That was the problem."

Stella took it from her and looked over the cover. There was no title on either side. "What is it?"

"My momma's diary."

Stella and Manny exchanged quick glances. Stella felt her own heart rate rising.

"Your mother kept a diary?" Manny asked. Stella could hear the poorly hidden excitement in his voice.

"She did. Wrote in it every night, no matter how tired she was, about what happened that day."

"Now that you mention it," Stella said, "I remember her writing something every night after she read her Bible and said her prayers. I just thought she was making notes about what she'd read."

"No. Nothing quite so holy as that, I'm afraid."

"Oh?" Manny's eyes glistened with interest. "Anything in particular that I should know about?"

Elsie shrugged. "I'm not sure, Sheriff. It's tough stuff. I don't know if even I want to know about it. My momma had a rough life, you know. She tried her best, but things didn't always go so well for her." She looked down at her hands, which were folded in her lap. "But then I guess we know all about that now. I hate it that the story of her life ended like this. She deserved better."

"She sure did, Miss Dingle, and I'm doing everything I can to make sure she gets some justice, and whoever took her from you gets what's coming to him, too."

Stella was dying to open the journal and look inside, but she didn't dare do so without Elsie's blessing. "You say you couldn't bring yourself to read it all yet?" she said.

"No. I couldn't. I've started to a couple of times over the

years, but after a few pages, I just close it back up. It didn't feel right."

"Really personal stuff?"

Elsie nodded. "Very personal. Let's just say, when she was writing it, I'm pretty sure she wasn't intending for her daughter to read it someday. It feels like I'm violating her privacy, and heaven knows, she'd been violated enough already."

"That's for sure," Manny said, his voice soft and kind. "But do you reckon, if something written in those pages could guide us to her killer, it might be worth it?"

"That's pretty much what she said, when she dropped by to see me last night."

"She dropped by?" Manny asked. "Who? Your mother?"

Stella could see the incredulity, mixed with something that looked like a strange sort of hope, on his face.

"Yes." Elsie nodded emphatically. "She paid me another visit last night. She told me that she appreciated the fact that I hadn't read her diary out of respect, even though I've had it all these years. But she said it was time for me to take it out of the cedar chest and read every word of it. She said, 'It'll help you figure out what happened to all of us.'"

"*All* of us?" Manny asked.

His voice sounded as tight and tense as Stella felt.

"She didn't just say *her*?" Stella asked. "Or *both* of us? She said *all of us*?"

Elsie nodded. "That's what she said. I'm sure of it. She said *all*."

The three sat in silence for a few moments, absorbing what they had heard and what it might mean.

"If your momma told you the truth," Stella said, "and she was always a woman who leaned that direction, there's more victims than just her and my own mom."

Manny nodded solemnly. "That would indicate there's at least three, and you know what that means."

"What," Elsie said, "other than that it's a cryin', awful shame?"

"If your mother *did* visit you, and she was right about how many victims there's been . . . then we've got us a serial killer right here in little ol' McGill."

"That's a mighty disturbing thought, if ever I heard one," Stella said. "To think we might be rubbin' elbows with one of those heartless monsters, just walking up and down the rows of the grocery store, let alone sitting in the pews at church."

Elsie appeared scandalized. "Oh, I don't think serial killers go to church, Sister Stella! There must be some kinda rule against that, surely."

"You'd be surprised what serial killers do," Manny said, shaking his head. "Blending in with the rest of us is one of the things they do best. It's how they get away with their meanness and not get caught."

Stella looked down at the book in her hands and again, ran her fingers over its soft, leather cover. "I wouldn't ask this, Elsie, under any other circumstances. But this is a bad situation we're in. So, please find it in your heart to forgive me for my rudeness." She drew a deep breath. "Would you let me take your momma's diary home with me and read it? You know I loved her to pieces. Still do. She was a fine woman, who always did the best she could. I wouldn't judge her for a single word that's written in these pages."

When Elsie hesitated, Stella added, "I promise you I won't tell anybody anything I read—except the sheriff here, that is—and only then if I truly believe it has something to do with these killings."

It took Elsie a long time to decide. So long, in fact, that Stella thought she was going to refuse. And she wouldn't have blamed her.

But finally, Elsie looked at her with tears glistening in her eyes and said, "Okay, Stella. I'll let you read it, and you do whatever you feel is best with what you find. But it don't sit easy with me. Not one bit."

"Is there anything I can do, anything I can say, that would set your mind at ease?" Stella asked.

"I'm afraid not. Because, you see, it ain't just about my momma's privacy. It's about you, Stella. If you read what's in that book, it's gonna hurt you somethin' fierce. I can hardly stand the thought of that. You been hurt so much and so bad already in your life. I can't bear to add to your burden with the words in those pages."

"Why would I be hurt by what your momma wrote?" Stella asked, feeling a swell of apprehension rising in her spirit.

"Because some of it's about your daddy."

For a moment Stella felt a bit of relief. "Oh. Is that all? If that's what you're worried about, Elsie, don't fret. I know all too well that Finley Quinn and the ol' bogeyman himself were the very best of friends. Heck, everybody in town knew that. He didn't bother to keep it a secret."

"No," Elsie said. "But he had some other secrets."

"Like what?" Manny wanted to know.

Elsie's folded hands squeezed each other tightly as she said, "Stella, when I told you about the night my momma disappeared, I didn't tell you all I knew."

"Okay. Can you tell me now?"

"I think I'm gonna have to." Elsie closed her eyes, bit her lower lip, then spoke with quiet, gentle determination. "I told you that my daddy came home and caught her kissing another man."

"Yes, you did."

"Actually, she wasn't kissing that man. *He* was kissing *her*. He'd come by our house like he was stopping in for a visit. But after he talked to her for a minute or so he grabbed her and was forcing her against her will. When my daddy came in and saw what was going on, I guess he didn't realize that she was trying to fight the man off. Either that, or he didn't care. He wasn't the kind to check out all the facts before he administered a beatin'. Anyway, I told you that my dad chased the man away and then started to beat my momma up plumb awful."

"I remember every word you told me," Stella said. "To get away from him, she ran out into the cold night with no coat on."

"No shoes neither."

Stella glanced at Manny and saw the information register in his eyes.

"No shoes," she heard him whisper.

"What I didn't tell you, sugar," Elsie said to Stella as she reached for her hand and squeezed it, "is that I knew the man. He was no stranger. He was your daddy."

Stella said nothing as the ramifications of what she had just heard washed over her.

Becky Dingle had run out into the night to escape a man who was beating her. Had he run after her and finished the job? Or had she run right into the arms of the man who had attacked her only moments before?

Either way, it appeared that Elsie's father or her own could have killed Rebecca Dingle.

If Elsie's account of her mother's latest visitation was accurate, one of their fathers might even be a serial killer.

"When you read that diary," Elsie continued, "you're going to find out that your daddy was after my momma a long time before that awful night. Even before your own momma got killed. Worse yet, you're gonna find out that my momma thought he killed yours."

Stella felt as though time had somehow stopped. All of a sudden, she was aware of everything around her: the wind rustling the golden leaves of the willow tree's canopy; Elsie's breath, ragged and quick; the look on Manny's face—one of anger and sadness; and her own body trembling, as though she was standing, naked, in a snowstorm.

"I'm sorry," she heard Elsie whisper, as though from far away.

Stella turned, held out her arms to her friend, and a moment later was enveloped in one of the famous Elsie Dingle hugs.

"Don't worry about it, honey," Stella said as she held her close, soaking in the love and comfort the embrace afforded. "You ain't tellin' me nothin' that my heart ain't already said, years ago. I'm older now, and I just want to hear the truth. In the end, a pretty lie can make you happy for a season, but only the truth can give you peace."

Chapter 21

After supper was over, the dishes done, baths taken, a story told, and seven grandangels had been tucked into bed, kissed, and individually told they were the best kid alive on God's green earth, Stella sat in her avocado, leatherette recliner and read.

After the day she had experienced, she certainly couldn't go without her daily scripture reading and the strength it provided her weary spirit. But instead of her habitual dose of entertainment, in the form of the latest supermarket tabloid, Stella opened Becky Dingle's diary and began to read.

She thought that Elsie's warning had prepared her for what she would see on those pages. But to her surprise, it had not.

Nothing could.

To hear the details of the violence her father had visited upon her mother, written by her mother's best friend . . . It was almost more than Stella could bear.

Certainly, as a child, she had grown up hearing the blows on the other side of the wall of her bedroom. Countless times she had seen them administered firsthand. How often had she watched her mother trying to cover bruises with makeup in a futile attempt to hide the evidence of her husband's cruelty?

Far too many times.

But through it all, the young, naive Stella had thought their dark family shame was a secret to their friends and neighbors. Surely, no one knew but the three of them. Instinctively, Stella was aware that her mother believed their secrets were well hidden, as well.

Gola Quinn had to believe the lie in order to maintain her dignity, such as it was.

But the entries in Becky Dingle's diary showed all too clearly that Becky knew what was happening to her friend and was deeply concerned about it.

Stella read passages where Becky had poured her troubled thoughts onto paper, convinced that, eventually, her dearest friend would be murdered by her husband's hand.

The farther Stella read in the book, the more Becky's anxiety rose. Then, abruptly, her concern changed to grief and rage. Her beloved friend had been murdered, and Becky Dingle had absolutely no doubt whatsoever about who had committed the crime.

It touched Stella's heart deeply to see how worried Becky had been about Stella, a young child living with a man capable of such brutality.

On the pages of her book, Becky debated the pros and cons of taking what she suspected to the sheriff. It was well known in the town that Finley Quinn and the sheriff were close drinking buddies. Becky doubted anything worthwhile would come from her stepping forward. Quite the contrary, in fact.

She feared she would not only succeed in bringing Finley's wrath down upon herself personally, but possibly put Stella in an even worse situation than she was already in.

Finley lived his life angry, getting into trouble and hurting others at every turn. Drunk *and* enraged, who knew what he might do?

Finally, Stella could read no more. Both her heart and her eyes had seen more than they could bear for one sitting.

She went to bed, but lay there thinking of all she had seen and heard over the past day.

It felt like a wave of dark, black mud—like that which had covered the lower part of the body in the woods—sweeping over her, pulling her to the bottom of some putrid swamp.

"Art," she whispered. "Darlin', I'm scared."

As always, there was no response. Either she didn't have the sensitivity that Elsie did when it came to hearing and speaking with those who had passed over, or maybe her husband just wasn't as chatty as Elsie's mother.

But that never stopped Stella from talking to him.

"I told you about my mom, what happened to her, how I found her there in the house. . . . You helped me a lot that night, sweetheart. I was feeling particularly low because it was her birthday, and I was missing her so bad. The things you said about me being a brave kid and how much it must have helped her to have me there when she passed over, holding her, and telling her that everything was going to be okay—even though, of course, it wasn't . . . That was exactly what I needed to hear. Thank you."

Again, there was no response, and Stella didn't expect one. She had been talking to Art for over six years now with no answers. But then, even when he'd been alive, she'd done most of the talking.

It had been a comfortable arrangement, one that worked well for them.

Their marriage had been a good one, even if she had, from time to time, wondered, "What might have been?" if Manny Gilford had found the courage to step forward and propose to her before he had taken off for college. Before Art had popped the question.

There had been no point in wondering about it back then, and there was no point now.

Long ago, Stella had decided that life was a bit like a sweater, knitted with a highly intricate pattern of dark and light yarns. You couldn't pull out one thread here and another one there without destroying the entire garment.

She figured, if you truly loved your life and those in it, you had to leave everything as it was, even in your own imagination, or risk losing all you cherished.

But tonight, when she was so troubled and heavyhearted, she wished she had Art beside her, listening, his arms tight around her.

"It's a mess, baby," she told him. "I found out all kinds of unsettling stuff today. The worst of it is: my momma and Elsie's were probably killed by the same person. Can you even imagine such an awful thing?"

"Your momma was killed?"

The voice startled her, the words spoken nearly right in her ear.

She jumped and turned her head to see Savannah standing beside her bed, wearing her pink pajamas with black kittens and a look of horror on her face.

"What?" Stella said. She knew what the child had said but was stalling as she considered what her reply should be.

"Your mother, my great-grandma, was murdered, like Elsie's?"

Stella could see the girl was upset. Far more deeply than she had ever appeared to be while standing near the body that afternoon.

Murder, Stella remembered, was always an abstract concept, until it struck close to home.

She reached over and pulled the sheet and quilt back so Savannah could join her in the bed.

Wasting no time at all, the girl wriggled in beside her and snuggled close.

Stella kissed her forehead, squeezed her tightly, and said, "Yes, Savannah girl, my mother—your great-grandma—was killed."

"That's awful!"

"It most certainly was."

"How come I never heard about it?"

"You were just lucky, I reckon. I figured somebody would mention it to you or within your hearing sooner or later. I was hoping for later."

"How come? Didn't you think I could handle it?"

"Oh, I think you can handle a lot, love, or I never would have let you go out to that burial site the way I did today. But hearing things like your great-grandma was murdered, it changes a child into a grown-up. You've heard way too many things like that already. You didn't get to enjoy being a young'un as long as you should've."

"I don't mind. I like being a grown-up more than a kid. Kids don't have enough say-so when it comes to their own lives. It's nice to get older and decide for yourself what you'll put up with and what you won't."

"That's for sure."

They lay in quiet, companionable silence for a while. Stella stroked her granddaughter's hair and thought of Elsie's mother doing the same to her, both when she was a child and then in a spiritual visitation.

"Tell me about it," Savannah said.

"About what?" Stella asked, although she knew.

"About your momma getting killed."

"Are you sure you want to hear about it? Once you hear it, you can't unhear it. It'll be in your mind and heart for the rest of your life."

Savannah shrugged. "If it's true, I need to know. It's part of my family's story. It's important to know where you came from."

Stella laughed softly. "But where you're at right now and where you're goin' is a heap more important than where you came from. A lot of fine people come from ugly places, but they're beautiful all the same. Maybe even more so because they had a harder road to walk than most, climbin' outta the mire."

"Then tell me about the mire we climbed out of."

"Okay. I will. I always figured if a child is old enough to ask a question, they're old enough for an answer—of some sort anyway."

Stella turned onto her side, so that she could look directly into her granddaughter's face. "It happened when I was ten years old. I'd been over at our neighbors' house all day, helping out. Farmer Buskirk and his wife were real sick, and my momma volunteered me to go clean up their house to help 'em out."

"That was nice of you."

"I don't remember having a choice about it, but I'm sure they appreciated me doing it. They were fine folks, the Buskirks. Anyway, it was a far piece between our house and their farm. I didn't get home till after sundown.

"When I walked up to the house, I didn't think anybody was there. My daddy's truck was gone, and the lights were all off. Our old hound dog came running out to meet me in the road, and he was acting all funny, whinin' and such."

"He knew something was wrong and wanted to tell you?"

"Something like that, I suspect. I walked into the house and lit a candle."

"A candle? Didn't y'all have electricity?"

"Sometimes we did. Sometimes we didn't. Depended on whether or not we'd paid the bill. That time, we hadn't.

"I lit a candle, and that was when I saw her, layin' on the floor by the couch. She was breathing, but she wasn't movin'. She was wearing her Cherokee tear dress. It was yellow calico, as bright as the sun, with tiny blue flowers. She was so proud of that dress because it was made from a traditional Cherokee pattern."

"I'll bet it was pretty."

"It had been. But it was torn, and there was blood on it."

Savannah reached over and took Stella's hand between her two, squeezing it tightly.

"I could see her hands were bound in front of her."

Savannah perked up. "With a tie? A man's necktie?"

Stella nodded.

"Wow! Just like Miss Elsie's mom there in the woods."

"Yes. Exactly like that."

"Had she been hit on the head, too?"

Stella swallowed hard and nodded. "Yes. She had. Just like Miss Becky."

"What did you do?"

"There wasn't much I could do, honey. No grown-ups were there. I didn't have any brothers or sisters. I didn't own a bicycle, so I'd have had to walk, and that would've taken me a long, long time to run to another farm and get help."

"You didn't have a phone?"

"No, darlin'. A lot of people didn't have phones back in those days, and we were very poor."

Savannah laid her hand on Stella's cheek and patted it. "I'm sorry, Granny. I'm sorry y'all were so poor and that you found your momma that way."

"I'm sorry, too. But mostly for her."

"Then what *did* you do?"

"I just laid down on the floor next to her, put my arms around her, and held her while she passed on. It was gentle like, and it didn't take too long."

"Did she say anything to you?"

"No. I told her that I loved her a few times. She didn't say it back, but I could see in her eyes that she knew it was me and understood what I was saying. She seemed a lot more peaceful after I told her that."

"Wow." Savannah sniffed and wiped her tears onto her pajama sleeve. "You were such a brave kid! I'd have been screaming and crying and carrying on. I think most kids would've been. Grown-ups too. I'm *so* proud of you, Gran!"

The two of them hugged for a long time, their faces pressed close together, their tears mingling.

Finally, when Stella had composed herself enough to speak, she said, "Thank you, granddaughter. You'll never know what those words mean to me."

Savannah smiled. "No big deal, Granny. I just said what I was thinking."

"I know. But it *is* a big deal. A *very* big deal. They're the exact same words your Grandpa Art said to me when I told him about it, so many years ago. And just tonight, right before you came in here, I was wishing so hard that he was here to say them again."

"Really?"

"Really."

The light of pride shone on the girl's young face. "I'm glad I could help you, like he did. That's just so totally cool!"

"It's way better than *cool*, sweetie," she said, kissing her granddaughter's tear-wet cheek. "It's a miracle. Sometimes the good Lord sends us a special angel to minister to us, just when we need it most. And tonight, you were my angel."

"An angel? Really!?" The girl sighed, and Stella could feel her body relax softly against hers, the stress of the day leaving them both. "Wow. I got to be an honest-to-goodness police detective today and an angel tonight. You're right; being somebody's special angel is way better than cool."

Chapter 22

The next morning, Sheriff Gilford arrived just as a tornado was sweeping through Stella's little shotgun shack.

The twister consisted of seven grandchildren, who were in the process of gathering their books, sack lunches, coats, and milk money, while arguing about whose turn it was to wear the red hair ribbon.

"Marietta, it is Vidalia's turn to wear that danged doodad," Stella called from the kitchen in an attempt to quell the ever-escalating argument in the girls' bedroom.

"It don't matter whose turn it is," Marietta shouted back. "I'm the one wearing a red dress today, and she's got on her dumb ol' purple jumper. If she wears red with purple, she'll look downright stupid. Even stupider than she looks on a regular day, that is. Dumber than a box of hair."

"Marietta Reid! How many times do I have to tell you to watch that harsh language of yours? Do not speak of your sister— or anybody else, for that matter—in such an unkind way."

"I can't help it if she's dumb. I can't say she's smart, 'cause she ain't, and you'll get mad at me for lyin', 'cause you're death on lyin'."

Stella stifled a scream as she marched from the kitchen into the children's bedroom, just in time to see Marietta tear the ribbon, and a few strands of attached hair, from her sister's head.

The instant Vidalia saw Stella, she began to shriek like someone getting a wisdom tooth yanked without a drop of anesthetic.

Stella grabbed the ribbon from Marietta's hand and resisted the urge to smack her with it.

Turning to Vidalia, Stella said, "Stop that infernal caterwaulin', Vidalia, and I'll give it to you."

"It's *my* turn to wear it," Vidalia stated, bringing her hysteria under control with suspicious ease.

"I know it is," Stella said, using the calmest and most collected voice she could summon. "I've got it marked on my calendar whose day is whose to wear that hair ribbon, and today's your day."

"But I done told you," Marietta shouted, "she's wearing pur—"

Stella grabbed her second oldest grandchild by the shoulders, looked her squarely in the eye, and said, "Marietta Reid, you are dancin' on thin ice, girl."

"I thought it was *skatin' on thin ice*," the girl replied with a nasty smirk. "Nobody *dances* on thin ice, Granny."

Stella tightened her grip and pulled the child so close that they were practically nose to nose. "I am your grandmother, young lady. And if I say you're dancin', you are dancin'. Dancin' on my last nerve, that is. And if it snaps, heaven help you, girl."

Marietta pulled back a couple of inches and glanced over Stella's shoulder at something behind her. "Whatcha gonna do, Granny, when you snap?" she asked with a rudeness that was beyond even her usual level. "Huh, Granny? You gonna beat me to a frazzle right here in front of Sheriff Gilford? He'd have to arrest you for child abuse, and wouldn't that be a humdinger and a half?"

Stella whirled around and saw Manny standing in the bedroom doorway, a somewhat amused look on his face.

She was pretty sure she was going to die of embarrassment on the spot. However, that would have to wait, because she had a discipline issue to deal with before she could quietly move away, find the proverbial opening in the floor, and slither through it, into the crawl space below.

But before she could decide whether to restrict Marietta to the front swing for the rest of her natural life or take her out to the backyard and introduce her rear end to a hickory switch, Manny took charge.

Calmly, he walked over to the girl and knelt on one knee in front of her, so they were eye to eye.

"Are you aware, Miss Marietta," he began, "that in the fine state of Georgia, spanking little girls who smart off to their grannies isn't the least bit illegal?"

Stella noticed that in the face of true authority, backed up with a badge and various weapons, not to mention a well-practiced scowl, Marietta's bravado evaporated in an instant.

"No, sir," she said. "I wasn't aware of that."

"Well, now you are, and I want to tell you something else. The people I arrest all day long . . . the ones who get their backsides thrown into the rear of my vehicle and transported to jails— where there's nary a hair ribbon in sight—they all have one thing in common."

He waited and, eventually, she asked. "What?"

"When they were growing up, they were disrespectful to their elders. Almost every single one of them. So, when I hear a young lady say naughty things to the grandma who loves her and does so much for her, I tell myself, 'There's a little gal who'll be wearing a nasty orange prison uniform in just a few years and no bows at all.'"

Stella watched as her most troublesome grandchild practically melted on the spot. What she wouldn't give to have that same effect on the kid.

Of course, it didn't hurt that the sheriff was in uniform, was six foot three, had a deep voice, and an innate air of authority about him.

Stella cleared her throat and told the crowd of children who had gathered around to watch Marietta get her comeuppance, "Y'all better finish gettin' ready for school. No dillydallying around. That bus won't wait."

Only Savannah lingered behind and followed Stella and Manny as they made their way to the kitchen.

"Don't forget to tell the sheriff, Gran, about what you read in the diary this morning," she said as she grabbed her books and lunch sack off the table. "You know, about the Mexican lady."

Stella smiled. "I won't forget, honey. Skedaddle now and have a good day at school."

"I think it's really important," Savannah called over her shoulder as she disappeared out the back door. "I've just got a hunch about it, you know?"

"I know. I was fixin' to tell him about it first thing over a cup of coffee," Stella called out as the back door slammed closed, and the house went suddenly silent.

She grabbed a couple of mugs from the cupboard and headed to the stove where the coffeepot had just finished percolating. "I'm sorry you had to arrive just in time for that ruckus," she said. "I didn't realize you were on the premises, until I turned around and saw you there."

"I knocked, and Waycross let me in. Reckon I should have waited for you to invite me inside."

"Not at all. You can walk through my front door anytime you like, Manny Gilford. You know that. But when you do, I don't have to tell you, you're taking your life in your hands."

He laughed. "I've been in a few situations that were more

dangerous than your household and lived to tell about it. Takes more than the likes of Miss Marietta Reid to give me the shakes. Though she is a corker. I'll give you that."

"I often have a hard time believing those children are all from the same father."

Stella set the oversized mug of strong, black coffee on the table and motioned for him to have a seat. She added some sugar and a dash of evaporated milk to her own cup, then sat in the chair across from him.

"I didn't mean no disrespect to my daughter-in-law by saying that, Manny," she added. "I wasn't suggesting any misbehavior on her part. I was just making the point that they're so different."

"I know that, Stella May. I also know your daughter-in-law, and I'm not likely to take any offense on her part. I'm sure there are plenty of things that you could complain about, concerning her, and haven't."

"One or two, but we've got more important things to discuss."

"That's for sure. I didn't have any luck at all locating Edom Dingle. It's like he just dropped off the map."

"I was a wee bit surprised that Elsie had no idea whatsoever where her father was. I knew she didn't associate with him, but I figured she'd have an address or something. Some way of gettin' hold of him."

He nodded. "It's downright inconvenient for me, since I need to make sure he's notified and interview him. But I'm sure Elsie's life has been a lot more peaceful these past twenty or more years, not having him around."

"I'm sure it made a world of difference for her, not having him to contend with. Even a loving soul like Elsie would have a hard time putting up with the likes of him. I don't know about his current disposition, but back in his day, that man would argue with a fence post and win."

"It's a shame that some parents and their children spend their years apart like that. But sometimes it is for the better, to be sure."

"I know that my life's been a lot happier with my father gone than it would've been if I'd seen him regular like. Not that I welcomed what happened to him, how he met his end. But his passing did solve more than one problem, I'm ashamed and sorry to say."

"You've got nothing to be ashamed of, Stella. We don't choose who we're born to, otherwise a lot of people would go childless, for sure."

He took a long drink from the coffee mug, then set it down and gave her a searching look. "What's this earth-shattering discovery you made in the diary this morning, the one Savannah's got such a strong hunch about?"

"She's not the only one. I think it's important, too."

She reached for the diary, lying on the end of the table next to her purse. Thumbing through it, she said, "I've bookmarked it. I'll just read it to you."

She found the spot, took another sip of her coffee, and began to read, "'I saw Edom again today with one of his girlfriends. At least, I think she's one of his, though she's prettier than most of the ones he chooses. I've worked with her the last few weeks in the fields. She seems sweet enough. Young. I can see why he likes her. I know for sure that I'm not in love with my husband anymore, because seeing him walk down the street with another woman, talking to her the way he used to talk to me, all interested and laughing—it doesn't make me the least bit sad. I used to be so jealous. Back when I cared for him.'"

Stella looked up and saw that Manny was interested. Not fascinated.

But then, neither was she the first time she'd read it. Her interest had been roused by a subsequent entry.

"I know," Stella told him. "That's not a big deal. Everybody knew that Edom messed around. But listen to this."

She found the next bookmark and read, "'The pretty little Mexican girl, Woya Sanchez, hasn't been to work this week. We didn't know that anything was wrong until her mother came to the fields today, looking for her. Her mom told us that Woya walked down to the store one night to buy some bread for their supper and never came back home. I'm worried about the girl. I don't think she would scare her mother by being gone and not letting anybody know where she was. I think about Edom and the way he hurts me sometimes. I hope he hasn't hurt her, too.'"

"Wow! No wonder Savannah was excited! That's a good lead. Now I really want to talk to that guy. I want to talk to him *really hard*."

"You mean really bad?"

Manny's eyes narrowed. "Yeah, I want to talk to him really bad, and if he doesn't tell me anything worthwhile, I might need to talk to him really hard. If I can find him, that is."

"I might be able to help you with that, too," Stella said, tapping her finger on the diary. "A couple of times Miss Becky mentions that, after an especially bad fight, she'd go looking for Edom, so's she could apologize and make up."

"*She* would apologize to him after *he* beat her up?"

"I know, it's sick. I'm just telling you what she wrote."

"I'm sorry. Go ahead."

"Each time she went looking for him, she found him holed up in an old fishing cottage down by the river."

"My river? Pine River?"

"Yes, but on the opposite side from where you live. I got the idea it's one of the cabins in an old, abandoned fishing resort."

Manny thought about it for a moment, then nodded. "I think I know the place. It's been closed forever. Falling apart. But I suppose somebody could live there if they wanted or needed to badly enough. It's not like the landlord would come around with his hat out for the rent."

168

He pointed to her coffee cup. "Are you about done with your java there?"

She took the last sip. "I am. Why?"

"Because I'm on my way to see Herb Jameson at the funeral parlor. I want to know if he's got anything new for us on Mrs. Dingle. Would you like to come along with me, you know, for the ride? I'd appreciate your company."

Stella was touched by the look in his eye when he added that last bit. For a moment, the big, masculine, law enforcement official sitting across the table from her with his broad shoulders and his thick, silver hair reminded her of the little boy in her third-grade class who had passed her a homemade Valentine, with a big red heart, colored with crayons.

How could she say no?

She gave him a shy grin that matched his own and said, "I'd much rather stick around the house here and wash a ton of my grandchildren's dirty clothes, but since you asked so nice . . ."

Chapter 23

"Is Herb expecting us?" Stella asked Manny when he pulled the cruiser onto the circular, brick driveway in front of Jameson's Funeral Home and parked.

"He is. I told him I was going to stop by your house and pick you up, if you had a mind to come with me, and then we'd be over."

"He sure got the autopsy done fast."

"I think he worked on her all night long. I doubt he went to bed at all."

"Unlike you who hit the sheets and slept a solid eight."

As he removed the keys from the ignition, he glanced her way, as though to see if she was serious.

She gave him a playful wink. "I know you pretty well, Manny Gilford. You spent the night looking for Edom Dingle, huh?"

He laughed. "You do know me well, woman. I combed this town and the surrounding countryside looking for that no-good, wife-beating pinhead in every bar, pool hall, tattoo parlor, and gutter in the county. I hope this pans out, what you told me about the cabin on the river. Imagine, I'm searching for him all over Kingdom Come and he's practically my neighbor!"

They got out of the cruiser and walked up the steps of the massive colonial facade that was nearly as impressive as the Patterson mansion. Unless you looked beyond the white columns and elegant black shutters. The Patterson plantation was the real thing. Herb Jameson's funeral parlor was all about the "show." The pseudo-elegance of the place, contrived though it might have been, gave the impression that those who had their loved ones prepared and displayed here cared enough to give them an impressive send-off.

Although, it was a false assumption, since Jameson's Funeral Home was the only one in town, and therefore, everyone wound up here sooner or later, whether your family had money or barely enough to buy macaroni and potatoes.

Stella herself had last seen her precious husband within those walls.

She could never quite bring herself to forgive the place for that fact.

As Manny opened one of the large, double doors, and she stepped into the central hallway with its thick, navy blue carpeting and mahogany wainscoted walls, she remembered how much she hated it.

Or at least, she hated being here, and it seemed like the same thing.

They walked down the hall, their footsteps silent on the plush rug. When they reached the first door on the right, Manny knocked on it and said, "Herb? You in there? It's the sheriff. Flush those drugs, boy, and come out with your hands up."

A moment later, Herb opened the door, wearing a goofy, uneasy grin on his face.

As she had anticipated, he looked like he'd been "rode hard and put away wet."

His face was pale beneath his golf tan and there were dark circles under his red-rimmed eyes.

"Are we here too early?" Manny asked as they followed the undertaker into the office and settled into the comfortable chairs in front of his desk.

As before when she'd entered this room during the past six years, Stella felt a bit queasy and ill at ease. How could she ever forget sitting in that chair, making arrangements to bury her husband? Her husband whom she had thought she would be able to "have and to hold" another forty years or so?

"No, your timing's perfect," Herb told them. "I just finished up the paperwork ten minutes ago."

He reached into his desk drawer and pulled out a large, manila envelope, which he handed to Manny. "There you go. Signed, sealed, and now . . . delivered. Don't take this wrong, Sheriff, but I'm hoping that's the last one of those I have to do for you for a while."

"You and me both, Herb. I thought after we sewed up the Priscilla Carr homicide, you could, for all practical purposes, retire from your coroner job."

"One would certainly think so," Stella added. "In a town this tiny, you wouldn't think we'd have people turning up murdered every other day."

Manny opened the envelope, pulled out the paperwork, and studied each sheet carefully. "This all appears to be in good order, Herb. You did a great job, and I know this wasn't an easy one."

"The day I consider the investigation of a homicide an 'easy' job is the day I should go back to just being the town mortician."

"That's true," Manny said, still reading. "Reckon it's official now. 'Cause of Death: blunt force trauma to the head, resulting in fatal brain injury. Manner of Death: homicide.'"

"Doesn't get a lot plainer than that," Stella said. "Or more awful."

Manny held one of the pages up for Herb to see. "Sorry," he said, "but could you explain this to somebody who hasn't studied human anatomy since college?"

Herb took the paper, read it, and said, "Historical spiral fractures of the wrist. Evidence of antemortem naso-orbital fractures." He sighed. "Basically, it means that our victim was beaten repeatedly, and not just on the day of her death. Spiral fractures of the wrist are caused by someone having their arm twisted severely. It would've caused a lot of pain. More commonly you see it in child abuse cases, but it can happen in adult-on-adult violence, too. Her nose was broken more than once, as well, and not at the time of her death, because the fractures had healed."

Herb noticed that Stella's eyes were filling with tears. He paused and said, "I'm so sorry, Sister Stella. This must be mighty hard for you to hear."

"It is. But if she could endure it, the least I can do is hear about it. Go on. Tell us the rest."

"Okay. As we suspected at the scene, several of her toes were broken perimortem. Around the time of her death. Those were some of the few injuries that I think might have actually been accidental."

"Accidental?" Manny asked.

"Yes. I think she might have run out of the house barefoot to escape an attacker, and then later, at some point, she wound up running for her life through the dark fields and into the woods. It's pretty easy for anybody to break some toes that way. They're actually quite fragile, compared to other bones in the body and considering all the abuse they take."

Manny grimaced. "Don't I know that. I dropped a transmission on my foot one time. Broke three toes, and even though it hurt like the dickens, I didn't realize they were broken until the next day when I had trouble walking."

Stella tried to process what she had just heard, thinking more like an investigator than a friend who had just heard the terrible details of a loved one's final moments. "That sounds like she might have been killed there in the woods, right where we found her, rather than dragged there afterwards. The murderer might have chased her all the way to that spot and then hit her on the back of the head."

"But with what?" Manny asked. He turned to Herb. "After we left did the team find anything at the scene that might have been used as a murder weapon?"

"I saw that lady, Wanda, bag a couple of rocks that might have done the trick, assuming the killer didn't already have something with him to use."

"I'd rather think that he decided to kill her on the spur of the moment, in some kind of fit of anger," Stella said. "I guess it doesn't really matter. She's dead either way. But it would hurt more to think that he planned it to the point of bringing a weapon with him, intending to use it on her."

Manny tucked the remaining papers back into the manila envelope. "Believing that she ran across the fields to the woods and was murdered with a weapon of opportunity, or even one brought to the scene—unfortunately, that doesn't rule out either one of our top two suspects."

"You mean to tell me you already have some suspects in mind?" Herb looked pleased as well as surprised.

Manny nodded.

"Would you mind telling me who they are?" Herb asked. "I promise to keep it to myself. I'm good at that, you know. Us undertakers know a lot of interesting stuff about a lot of people, but we keep it to ourselves. You wouldn't believe half of it, even if we told you."

Manny chuckled. "I have no doubt that's true. Sure. I can tell the coroner who our suspects are. Not that we have anything solid on either one of them. The most obvious, of course, is the victim's husband."

"Ain't it always?" Stella said. "It's a sad state of affairs that, when a woman's murdered, most of the time it's somebody who held her close to his heart at night and told her he loved her."

"It certainly is sad. Infuriating too," Manny agreed. "Which is why my next job is going to be locating Edom Dingle and feeding him through a wringer, if necessary, to find out what he might have had to do with this."

"And if it wasn't Edom . . ." Stella said, feeling a heaviness in her heart that she hadn't felt for a long time. Not since she watched her father laid in his grave. "Then it might have been my dear ol' daddy who did the deed."

Herb gave a little gasp. "Really? Why would you think it was him? What did he have against Mrs. Dingle?"

"To put it plainly, Brother Herb," Stella said, "he had wicked designs on her. And he went to her house that night to see what he could get away with. Edom interrupted him just in time, so he didn't get away with much."

Manny added, "He might have chased after her out there in the fields with even worse evil on his mind."

"I'm sorry to hear that, Stella," Herb told her. "You've had a hard enough time already in this life without a burden like that added to your back."

"Thank you," she said, "but my life's had a lot of sunny days to go with the storms. I figure most lives run like that—the weather changing back and forth every little bit. We just hang on and do the best we can, don't we?"

She glanced back and forth between Manny and Herb, two men who had lost wives tragically, early in their lives. They were proof that Sorrow knocked on everybody's door, sooner or later.

"Yes, Stella May," Manny said. "That's exactly what we do." He tucked the envelope under his arm and said, "Herb, if that's all you've got for us, I reckon we'll be hitting the road."

"Actually, I do have one more thing before I let you go." Herb reached into his desk drawer once again and pulled out a brown, paper, evidence bag.

As he handed it to Manny, he said, "I have no idea if this has any significance at all. But it struck me as strange, and the searchers there at the site thought so, too."

Manny looked into the bag. "It's her dress," he said. "What's strange about it?"

Herb reached into his pocket and produced two pairs of surgical gloves. He handed one set to Manny, then put on his own.

Properly gloved, Herb reached into the bag and pulled the dress out.

"It's torn, Sheriff," he said. "There's a piece missing from the back of the skirt. Here, help me flip it over, and you'll see what I'm talking about. It's the strangest thing."

As they were stretching it out and turning it, Manny said, "It's not all that strange that her dress would be ripped, right? If she was running hard enough to break her toes, it doesn't seem like a tear in the dress would be that meaningful, does it?"

Stella felt something, like an icy hand clutching at her heart. Even before they had flipped the dress over to expose its back, she knew what they were going to see.

Worse yet, she knew what it meant.

"Look at that, Sheriff," she could hear Herb saying, though her thoughts were far away. "Just look at that, and tell me that ain't weird!"

There it was.

Not a rip. Not a tear.

It was a square.

A perfect square, about six by six inches, had been cut from Becky Dingle's skirt.

She felt Manny Gilford looking at her, his eyes boring into her.

She could swear that he was holding his breath, just as she was holding hers.

Herb seemed to sense that there was a significance to that square—one he wasn't privy to. But he said nothing, just stood, quietly staring at both of them.

Time seemed to slow for Stella. She was only vaguely aware of Manny pushing the dress into Herb's hands, taking off his own gloves, and tossing them onto the desktop.

Then he was pulling her into his arms and holding her tightly against his chest.

"I'm sorry, darlin'," he whispered. "I'm so, so sorry."

Chapter 24

"I apologize for falling apart on you back there," Stella told Manny as he drove away from the mortuary. "The idea was for me to come along and help you today. Not make a nuisance of myself."

He reached over, placed his hand on top of hers, and gave it a pat. "Don't say anything like that to me again, Stella May Reid. I don't want to hear it. You've never been a nuisance in your life. At least, not in *my* life. I'm grateful for every moment that I've had the pleasure of your company over the years."

"Quit that, Manny Gilford," she snapped, pulling her hand away from his. "Don't be nice to me right now. I can't take it. You say sweet stuff like that at a time like this, and I'll start bawling like an orphan calf."

He chuckled. "There's nothing wrong with crying, darlin'. Especially when the tears are called for."

She turned to stare out the passenger window at the autumn colors of the woods they were passing. Ordinarily this was her favorite time of year. The forests exploding in color. The gold, red, and orange leaves, signaling that the trees were about to begin their winter sleep. She loved the smell of smoke drifting on the cool breeze as she and her neighbors raked and burned those fallen leaves. Carved pumpkins and costumed munchkins everywhere. Apple cider, fresh baked, spicy pies, and the promise of the holidays ahead. They all warmed her heart and excited her spirit.

But now Stella wondered if autumn would ever be the same for her again.

"Me coming all unglued like that in Herb's office," she said, terribly ashamed, "that wasn't called for. I already knew that Momma and Miss Becky were probably killed by the same lowlife weasel. That square cut out of her dress, just like Momma's, it wasn't anything new. I don't know why seeing it got me all upset that way."

"It upset me, too, Stella. The man's necktie and the cause of death—those being the same in both cases—that was enough for us to suspect that one killer did both. But that square cut out of their clothes . . . Now we don't just *suspect*, we know *for sure*, and that's going to worry everybody in this town. Even those of us who didn't lose the two women who mothered us. You've got a right to be upset. Nobody's gonna judge you for that. And if they do, they'll have me to contend with."

Stella turned back to him and gave him a grateful smile. "You're a good man, Sheriff Manny Gilford, and a wonderful friend to me and mine. I don't know what I'd do without you."

"Same here."

"Aw, you'd do fine without me. Of course, when you got a hankering for apple pie, you'd have to finagle one out of Elsie. But it probably wouldn't be too hard, since she thinks the world of you, too."

She gave him a long look, up and down, taking in his hair, his dark tan, broad shoulders, and the decidedly masculine way he filled out his uniform. The friendly, mischievous gleam in his gray eyes didn't hurt either, suggesting that he was either up to something or thinking about it.

"On second thought," she said, "considering how good lookin' you are and how many single women there are in this town, you probably wouldn't get a chance to even work up an appetite. I'll bet that, most of the time, you're snowed under with baked goodies and such."

He laughed, looking a bit guilty. "I don't starve," he admitted. "If word gets around that I've got the sniffles, there's a virtual flood of homemade soup coming my way, sometimes biscuits, too. It doesn't hold a candle to your cooking, which is in a class all its own. But it's kinda nice. Makes a law enforcement officer feel appreciated."

"I'll bet it does. Especially when delivered by a sashayin' cutie with evil designs on you, like that waitress at the Burger Igloo."

"Not every gal who sashays is a cutie, Stella May, and not every cutie is my type." He gave her a look that warmed her heart . . . and other areas she preferred not to think about anymore.

She had grandchildren, seven of them, to consider. She had bills to pay, and laundry to wash, and peanut butter and jelly to buy. Not to mention hair ribbon wars to negotiate.

The last thing she needed to think about was a handsome sheriff with a twinkle in his silver eyes.

Then there was Arthur.

How could a woman even consider giving her love to another man, when her heart lay in the cemetery on the edge of town with her husband? The husband who left too quickly to even say, "Good-bye," or, "I love you."

No. Stella had decided that she wasn't fifteen anymore and didn't have room in her life for anything as all-consuming as romance. Or room in her brain either. A mind could only hold so much clutter.

They had come to the T at the end of the highway. A left turn would lead to her house, then, farther down the road, to town. To the right lay the river, where both Manny and, if they were lucky, Edom Dingle now lived.

To Stella's surprise, Manny turned left.

"Hey, did you forget?" she asked him. "We're going to the river to see if we can find Edom."

"I didn't forget," he replied. "I'm going to drop you home first. Didn't you tell me you've got a ton of laundry to do?"

"You know as well as I do that, with seven young'uns in the house, a ton of laundry's a daily occurrence, not a special occasion. You wanna be rid o' me, boy? Tired of my company, are you?"

"Never."

"Then why are you dumpin' me back home?"

"Stella, I'm going to go question my primary suspect in a murder case. I'm not taking any civilian, let alone you, with me to do that."

"Why the heck not?"

"It could be dangerous. I won't put you in harm's way."

"Dangerous? Edom Dingle?"

"He has a long-standing history of violence."

"He's a coward who used to beat up on his wife, 'cause she was a little, gentle thing, and he could. Have you ever heard a word about him fighting another man? Someone actually big enough to hit him back?"

"Not really. He used to get in a lot of shouting matches, but—"

"No buts. I ain't afraid of Edom Dingle, and if you are, then I'll protect you."

She knew that would get his goat. She was counting on it, in fact.

It did.

"I don't need *you* to protect me. Remember, *I'm* the one with the badge and the gun."

"That's right. Edom Dingle's a pip-squeak who's older than Egyptian dirt. What is he now? Eighty, if he's a day."

When Manny didn't slow down and turn the cruiser around, she decided to use honesty instead of goading.

"Someone took my mother from me, Manny, and another woman I loved dearly. I have to know who it was. I have to know if it was Edom Dingle. You're going to ask him if he did it, and I want to look into his eyes when you do it."

Manny continued to drive the cruiser down the road toward her house, but she could tell he was thinking, weighing, considering.

Finally, he pulled onto a dirt, farm road and turned the vehicle around.

"You've got to promise me that you'll do everything I tell you, Stella Reid," he said. "I mean it!"

"Sure I will, Sheriff Gilford," she replied with a self-satisfied grin. "Don't I always?"

"No. No, you most definitely do not. But promise me that this one time you'll make an exception."

"Okay, I promise."

"Really?"

"Yeah. Probably." She thought it over and added, "Depending on what you tell me to do . . . or not do."

He sighed. "Yeah. That's about what I figured."

Chapter 25

As Manny drove closer to the river, Stella noticed, not for the first time, how the woods were far thicker, the trees more dense, the closer they got to the water. The mighty slash pines with their dark green needles and their distinctive red bark provided a breathtaking contrast to the golden birches and red maples.

The air seemed colder here than in town. Perhaps, she thought, the added humidity in the area helped the chill to sink deeper into one's clothing and bite the skin.

Several minutes before, they had passed Manny's cabin, crossed a bridge, and they were now on the other side of Pine River. It was an area less developed, with fewer people and structures. Not a lot of building had occurred on this shore, and what few houses and cabins had been constructed long ago were now falling apart and basically uninhabitable, except by those who had no other resources or who wanted to remain invisible to society for one reason or another.

None of the cabins they passed could compare with the well-preserved, fully refurbished home where Manny lived.

Stella remembered, all too well, that his cabin had a lovely stone fireplace capable of keeping the small home cozy and warm, even on a cold night.

She had only visited Manny's cabin once since that terrible summer day when his wife, Lucy, had drowned in the river.

After that devastating tragedy, Stella had not been invited to his cabin, and she had respected his wishes to be left alone in it—until a winter evening, right before Christmas, when she had gone there to plead for help for her family and protection for her grandchildren.

She had brought her seemingly unsolvable problem to Manny, there in his home, and found comfort, as well as an answer to her dilemma. Stella would never forget that night. Not one moment or element of it. The comfortable, masculine, leather furniture. The knotty pine walls, covered with beautiful photographs of nature. The bright red, wool, Navajo blanket that he wrapped around her shoulders, as she shivered with fear and told him of the dangers that her grandchildren faced in their mother's home.

Dangers that Manny had eradicated, because she asked him to, because he cared about her and those she loved.

"Are you cold or nervous?" he asked, interrupting her reverie.

"I beg your pardon."

"You're shivering." He reached over and turned the car's heater up a few degrees.

Her natural inclination was to deny that she was either, but she decided to be honest. She might as well be. Manny had an uncanny ability to see right through most people, and certainly her. "Both, I reckon."

"I've got an extra sweater in the trunk. It would probably swallow you whole, but I'll pull over and fetch it for you, if you'd like."

"No. That's okay. Let's just get there, so's we can have this over with."

"Then it's mostly nervousness?"

"Probably. I'm gettin' myself all in a dither over nothing. It's been forty years or more since Miss Becky wrote that stuff in her diary. Edom's probably long gone from this area."

"Let's hope not. I want some answers from the old dirtbag. Even if he didn't do the killing, he might have seen or heard something."

"I don't remember nasty ol' Edom being all that cooperative or forthcoming even back then. If he's like most mean people I've known, he's perfected his art over the years and gotten worse. I can't see him helping you out of the goodness of his heart."

Manny grinned, but it wasn't a particularly warm smile. "Don't worry," he said. "I've got a way with people. They tend to open up to me . . . one way or the other."

Her eyes narrowed. "Hopefully it'll be 'the other.' I saw what that weasel did to Miss Becky, time and time again. I wouldn't mind watching you open him up nice and proper."

"Why, Mrs. Reid, I'm surprised. Are you advocating police brutality?"

"Not at all, Sheriff Gilford. But I *am* a firm believer that some-times justified force can lead to full compliance with the law."

"I agree and appreciate your support. But I hope I don't have to use any force, justified or otherwise, on ol' Edom or anybody else. That sort of thing can lead to the spilling of bodily fluids, and I just got this tie back from the dry cleaner. I want it to last at least a week."

They passed numerous cabins, but didn't bother to stop be-cause the structures were obviously insufficient to house even the most desperate of squatters. The windows had been knocked out, the doors ripped off, and the roofs were caving in.

"I don't think I'm going to move to this side of the river anytime soon," Manny said. "It's like a whole other world over here."

"Yeah. Sorta like the cheap, bad side of a Monopoly game board, only worse."

"Hey, look," he said, pointing to a row of small cabins, nearly hidden among the pines, close to the water. "Those aren't so bad. The best we've seen so far, anyway."

"True. Some of them even have windows and doors."

"Let's stop and look." He pulled the cruiser off the road and slowly drove down what had once been a wide road, but was now little more than a weed-strewn path.

"You sure you're okay with this?" he asked as he parked and turned off the engine. "If you're the least bit uneasy about it, just stay here in the vehicle with the doors locked."

"I'm more than okay with it," she said, throwing her door open. "Let's get her done."

"That's my girl."

For half a second, Stella almost said, "I wish I was." But she caught herself just in time and wondered at her own reaction.

Didn't she have enough on her mind already? Why did she have to add something like an attraction to a man to the mix?

Because you're a glutton for punishment, Stella Reid, she told herself. *Always have been. Always will be. Knock it off! He's just a man.*

An extremely good-looking man with a kindly way about him, another voice inside her head whispered. *One who thinks the world of you.*

Didn't you hear me? I done told you, "Knock it off!"

"Stella, are you okay?" Manny asked her as they approached the row of cabins.

She turned to see he was staring at her with a concerned look on his face—the same sort of expression he might wear if he was looking at someone who had recently lost their marbles. Every single one of them. The whole bagful.

Yes, that's me, all right, she thought.

"I'm just fine and dandy," she assured him, "and if Edom's

here, I'll be even better. I've waited for this day for many years, to tell that skunk a thing or two."

"Could you wait until I've had my say and listened to his before you clobber him with it?"

"Clobber him with what? I left my fryin' pan at home."

"This truth about his skunkedness that you've been holding back all these years."

"Oh, sure. I promised you before we came out here that I'd do whatever you said, remember?"

"Yes. And I remember all the qualifiers you tacked on, too. That's why I thought I'd better clarify my position."

"Sheriff Gilford, you have a suspicious nature. Has anybody ever told you that?"

"I think someone might've mentioned it a few years back."

"Yes, I'll bet they did."

Having reached the row of five cabins, they stopped and studied them, one by one.

Two were like the others they had seen along the road, ruined, unlivable, little more than heaps of decayed wood.

One was still standing upright, but the porch had rotted away, which would have made it difficult to enter and leave.

"Let's try those two," Manny said, "and you stay behind me. You hear?"

"I told you, I could take Edom myself right now if—"

"How are you with rabid raccoons, huh? A disgruntled bobcat? A cranky brown bear, who's decided to move in for his winter nap?"

She gave him a doubtful look. "Really, Manny? Heard of a lot of bears round here, takin' up residence in fishermen's cottages?"

"Get behind me and stay there, woman!"

"O-kay! Jeepers creepers, boy. Turns out you've got a bossy streak I never knowed about."

"Funny. I was always well aware of yours."

He walked to the door of the first shack. She did as she was told and trailed two steps directly behind him.

As she watched him pause in front of the door, put his ear against it, and listen for movement inside, she could feel her body tensing.

The last person on earth she wanted to see was Edom Dingle. Although she had lived in his home for nearly a year after her mother had died, she couldn't recall passing one single pleasant moment with the man.

His wife, Rebecca, had taken pity on her, and immediately after Gola's funeral, had brought the motherless child home with her, much to her husband's consternation.

"What do we need with another mouth to feed?" were his first words when seeing her standing outside his front door, tears running down her face and everything she owned crammed into a pillowcase. "She's too scrawny to work. Homely as a mule's rear end, too. Let her own father raise her."

"But he won't!" Becky insisted. "You know he drinks day and night. She's not safe with him. She needs a woman around. Here she'll have a mother and a sister. You know how well she and Elsie get along."

In the end, Stella stayed. She worked in the plantation's fields and handed every penny she was paid over to Edom, who promptly spent it on whiskey.

He complained about every bite she ate and included her in the Friday night beatings that he gave the other two females in his household when he was far too deep in his cups.

Eventually, the former Mrs. Patterson had observed Stella's plight and insisted that, if her own father was unfit to care for her, she should be housed in a foster home instead.

A week later, she was moved into the first of several such homes where she was temporarily housed until, still a teenager, she had married Arthur.

It was commonly believed that Mrs. Patterson had objected more to the fact that the Dingles were a black family than that Stella was being worked to death, starved, and beaten weekly. However, Mrs. Patterson's rationale didn't sit well with Stella, who would have been delighted to live with Mrs. Dingle and Elsie without Edom. But since Stella realized Finley was in no shape to care for her, she was grateful for the lifesaving gift of foster parents.

A month after she was removed from the Dingle household, Miss Becky disappeared.

Edom had spread the word far and wide that his "loose" wife with the morals of an alley cat in heat had run away with another man and that his ugly, worthless daughter was bound to follow in her mother's footsteps.

Since that day, Stella had worked very hard at not hating the man. Some days she succeeded, but most she did not.

As a result, when she saw Sheriff Gilford pound his fist on the old cabin's door and say in a loud, authoritative voice, "Sheriff's department. Open up!" she took a perverse pleasure in it.

Edom might not be guilty of killing his wife, but he had plenty of other crimes to atone for, even if the payment was nothing more than having the law call on him and scaring him half to death.

"Let him be here," she whispered. "Please, let him—"

Chapter 26

The door opened, and Stella was instantly disappointed. The decrepit old man who stuck his grizzled head outside bore no resemblance whatsoever to the younger, stronger, violent Edom Dingle or anyone Stella had ever met.

Looking one hundred years old at least, he peered at Manny with cataract-whitened eyes and mumbled through toothless gums, "Who're you? Whaddya want?"

"I'm Sheriff Gilford," Manny told him, tapping the badge pinned above his shirt pocket. "I'm looking for Edom Dingle. Is that you?"

"Might be."

"Mr. Dingle, this is no time to play games. I have something serious to discuss with you. May we come inside?"

"We? Who've you got there with you?"

Edom squinted, trying to see Stella, but she could tell from the look on his face he didn't recognize her. She wasn't surprised. Even with good vision, she would never have recognized him.

Looking at Edom Dingle now, she saw nothing remaining of the man who had regularly beaten her with his belt and seemed to thoroughly enjoy the experience. The old man standing before her couldn't have arm-wrestled a squirrel and won.

"This lady is a friend of mine," Manny told him. "She's just along for the ride. Pay her no mind. May we come inside?"

"Yeah, I guess."

The instant he opened the cabin door wider, a horrific odor escaped, so putrid that both Stella and Manny gagged. It smelled like a combination of rancid fish, urine, excrement, and stale whiskey.

"Great day in the morning!" Manny exclaimed, clapping his hand over his mouth and nose. "What in tarnation have you got in there?"

Stella pulled her sweater across her lower face and stepped back several paces. "Whatever it is, the smell alone would gag a maggot."

"My commode's backed up," Edom said.

"For how long?" Manny asked. "Since Moses tried to flush too much toilet paper down it?"

Edom flashed a toothless grin and added, "And I was cleaning some fish for my supper."

"There ain't enough fish in the Atlantic to smell that bad," Stella muttered.

"Why don't you just step outside?" Manny suggested. "We can talk out here in the fresh air."

"Yeah, okay. Lemme get my sweater."

He disappeared back inside for a few moments. They could hear him searching.

"When he comes out, be sure to stand upwind of him," Manny told her. "He's about as ripe as they come."

Stella didn't reply. She was thinking of how many times Edom had taken his belt to his wife, daughter, or Stella because the "lazy, good-for-nothin' womenfolk," as he called them, weren't keeping the house to his high expectations.

Apparently, since he was the one doing the cleaning now, his strict standards had slipped a bit.

Eventually, Dingle reappeared in the doorway. This time he was wearing a tattered sweater and a stocking cap.

With a great deal of difficulty, he maneuvered down the two steps from the door to the ground, then on wobbly legs, made his way to a sawed-off tree stump and plopped himself down on it.

Again, he attempted to focus on Stella. "What did you say your name is, honey?" he asked with something that sounded like a semi-flirty tone to Stella.

She found it more offensive than the odor.

"Like I told you," Manny shot back, before she could answer, "she's a friend of mine. Just along for the ride."

"What'd you want?" Edom asked Manny. "What's so serious that you gotta interrupt my fish cleaning?"

"It's about your wife, Rebecca," Manny replied as he watched him closely.

Stella scrutinized him, as well, trying to interpret every blink of his cloudy eyes, every twitch of his stained fingers.

"What about her?" was Dingle's offhanded response that told them nothing.

"Rebecca has been found," Manny told him.

"I don't care. As far as I'm concerned, she ain't my wife no more. She up and ran off with another guy. I stopped thinkin' about that bitch a long time ago. And that no-good, worthless daughter of mine, too. They're both dead to me. They better neither one show up here, lookin' for a handout. I'll kick both of their asses, if they even try it. They've gotten all they're ever gonna get outta Edom Dingle. I spoiled 'em rotten. Treated them way too good. Yep, that's where I went wrong."

Such words would have sent Stella into a fury, if she hadn't been dumbfounded by the man's totally warped sense of who he was, who his daughter had become, and what had gone wrong within his family.

In that moment, Stella realized, he wasn't just mean anymore. Edom Dingle was now both mean and insane.

Manny didn't react to Dingle's speech either. He donned a perfectly neutral face and said in an equally even tone, "I'm sorry to inform you of this, Mr. Dingle, but your wife's body was found in a small, wooded area on Judge Patterson's farm. Looks like she'd been there for a long, long time. Probably for as long as she's been missing."

At first, Dingle's face registered shock, which quickly faded to sadness. To Stella's surprise, she saw some moisture gather in his eyes, but he quickly passed his hands over them, then shook his head vigorously.

"No," he said. "Whoever you found, it can't be her. When she ran away and deserted me, she left these parts for good."

"Doesn't appear so," Manny argued. "The coroner examined her last night and determined she was murdered. Like I said, probably right after she ran from your house that night."

"No! That didn't happen!" he shouted, his face contorting with rage. "Those was lies that no-good Elsie told just to make me look bad. Becky didn't run away from me that night. She ran *to* another man. 'Cause she wanted to. 'Cause she was a two-bit slut. Not 'cause she had to!"

The fury on the old man's face stirred memories, bad ones, deep inside Stella. She could feel fear spring up in her like a frightened animal who was caught in the claws of a predator.

It wasn't logical, of course. She knew she was in no danger from this crippled old man. Especially with Manny standing by.

But every cell of her body remembered the terrible sting of this man's belt. The sense of utter helplessness as he had held her upper arm in a ruthless grip and struck the blows across her back, her buttocks and thighs that left red, raised welts and long, black bruises.

Edom Dingle had been young, strong, and much larger than her all those years ago. Subduing her was no problem for him . . . then.

Unlike now.

The temptation was strong for her to imagine how the tables could be turned now. So easily.

But some stronger, higher part of Stella reminded her of the advice she gave her own grandchildren almost daily. "We strive to treat people with kindness, not because they particularly deserve it, but so that we can like the person we see in the mirror every morning."

It was time for her to rise to her own teachings, not follow her baser instincts, which would encourage her to grab a switch off a nearby tree and give ol' Edom a taste of his own medicine.

Maybe later, she promised herself, *when Manny ain't around, holdin' me to a promise I made.*

Okay. So much for choosin' the higher spiritual ground, she added with a sigh.

"It was Rebecca that we found, Edom," she could hear Manny saying, through the fog of her memories and internal battles. "There's no doubt about it. She was wearing that pink and purple flowered dress that she liked so much. The one she wore to church."

"The one I bought her when we got married," he said, as though beginning to believe what he was hearing.

"She also had on her wedding ring and that leather barrette with the two crossed arrows carved into it, and the little silver and turquoise necklace that Elsie saved up and bought for her."

Yes, Stella decided. Those were definitely tears she saw in Edom's nearly blind eyes.

"It's *not* her, I tell you!" he shouted, jumping up off the stump with more vigor than Stella would have thought him capable of.

His hands clenched into fists, veins throbbing on his forehead, Dingle was literally spitting with fury when he continued to shout, "Somebody might've been wearing a dress and jewelry stuff that looked like hers! But my wife is gone! She is *gone*, I tell you! She's been gone all along! My wife didn't run out the door to get away from me and then get herself murdered! That did *not* happen! Don't you try to tell me that it did!"

Manny simply watched him, taking in every word, every movement as he spewed his venomous denial. When he finally stopped to take a breath, Manny spoke, his voice as peaceful as the other man's was agitated. "Okay then, Edom. Let's talk about something else. Somebody else."

"Who? Who the hell do you wanna talk to me about now?" Edom snapped, obviously still outraged.

"A young lady by the name of Woya Sanchez, from Mexico, I believe. I understand she was a friend of yours."

Dingle seemed almost as upset by this new line of questioning as he had been to hear the news of his wife, but more sad than livid.

At first, Stella thought he was going to deny any association, but at the last moment, he seemed to think better of it.

"Yes, I knew her," he reluctantly admitted. "She was a good kid. Worked there in the cotton fields with us for a while. A pretty little thing."

"We understand she disappeared. Nobody seems to know where she went."

"That's right. Her momma came to the farm looking for her, all worried and upset. But nobody had any idea what happened to her."

"No idea at all, Edom?" Manny asked. "Really?"

"No. None. One day she was there. The next she was gone. Poof."

"Did anybody go looking for her?"

"Old Judge Patterson did. Not the judge who's there now. His daddy. He was a judge, too. He came down into the fields whilst we was pickin' and asked if any of us had seen her. Said her momma was in his house, cryin' her eyes out, 'cause she thought something awful had happened to her daughter. But we weren't a bit of help to him."

"Then you have no idea what happened to her?" Manny asked. "None at all?"

"The only way I'd know for sure would be if I'd done away with her or something like that. Is that what you're gettin' at, Sheriff?"

"Just asking questions, Mr. Dingle. That's why they pay me the big bucks, you know."

"I didn't hurt her. That's all I know to tell you. I thought she was sweet. I tried to look out for her with the other men in the field."

"What other men?" Manny asked. "Who was after her?"

"Who wasn't? I told you, she was pretty, and she was nice. That's a lot more than you can say for most of the gals around here."

"Who in particular was hanging around her, Edom? Think hard."

Dingle scowled, making an effort. It occurred to Stella he might not do a lot of that these days.

"The judge hisself had an eye for good-lookin' women," Dingle said. "He was handsy with 'em, too. I don't know if he was after Woya in particular. But I'd say the one who just couldn't get enough of lookin' at her and talkin' to her was that no good Finley Quinn. He was always trying to finagle a pickin' place next to her, tryin' to get a look-see down her blouse. I was mighty glad to hear that white-trash peckerhead finally did the world a favor and kilt hisself."

Chapter 27

"Seems like, for the past twenty-four hours, all I've been doing is apologizing to you for the insensitive things folks have said in your presence," Manny told Stella as they left Edom and his cabin and drove back onto the blacktop. "I wish I could glue some of these people's mouths shut."

"In this town? Your glue bill would be sky high. You'd go broke in a week."

"Plus, if they couldn't gossip, their heads would explode."

"For sure."

They traveled along in silence for a while. She could tell he was thinking about something, and she had plenty to think about herself. . . . Like Edom Dingle, and why she hadn't told him off when she had a chance to do so. She didn't know if she was mad at herself or proud of her restraint.

Probably a bit of both.

As they approached the T in the road and headed on toward her house, Manny told her what was on his mind. "I'm going to call Social Services this afternoon," he said. "I can't just leave that man in his filth. Nobody should live like that."

"What would they do about it?" she asked.

"They could declare him incompetent, unable to properly care for himself."

"He seemed okay to me. Leastways, until he starts talking about his wife and daughter. Then he gets unhinged."

"No sane person lives like that, Stella. The man needs help."

Stella thought it over, trying to conjure some feeling of sympathy or concern for Edom Dingle, the way she would have any person or animal living in deprivation and squalor. But there was none in her heart to be found.

She wasn't proud of that.

"I know you're right," she told him, "and I admire you for your compassion. But if they clean up his place for him, it'll just be a mess in a week."

"They won't be able to clean it. The place is beyond cleaning. No amount of bleach and elbow grease would make that shack livable again. Plus, he has no running water or electricity. Those cabins need to be razed, so that squatters won't move into them like he's done."

"Where would he go?"

"I heard he's a veteran. I'm sure they'd find a home for him where he'd be fed and clean and looked after."

"They'd probably require him to stop drinking."

"Yes, and he won't like it, but they'll help him kick it with medical assistance and counseling. He deserves to live out the rest of his years in a clean, safe environment, healthy, with dignity, free of addiction, if he can manage it."

"That's true. I reckon. Though some might say he's reapin' what he sowed all those years ago."

"While we were talking to him, did you get the sense that he's the killer?"

"No," she admitted reluctantly. "He just has to hang on to the myth that his wife left him for another man. It's easier for him to accept that, than the truth. He beat her, she ran away to save her life, and was murdered as a result. That would haunt anybody with even a shred of conscience."

"I agree. And I don't think he's the one we're looking for either."

"I wish he was," Stella admitted reluctantly. "If it turns out that somebody I've known all my life is a serial killer, I'd just as soon it was him."

"Any particular reason why?"

"Yeah. I already hate him. At least, that way, I wouldn't have someone new to hate. You'd be surprised how much time I have to devote every day to prayer in order to keep all those mad, 'I'd-like-to-rip-your-head-off-and-shove-a-hive-of-wasps-in-your-neck-hole' feelings down to a minimum."

He gave her a long, blank stare, then said, "I'm glad to see you've got those feelings under control."

"I know, huh?"

He reached over and ran one finger down her cheek. "That man really hurt you, didn't he, darlin'?"

"Yes. But worse yet, he hurt Miss Becky, real bad, and Elsie. That's what I hold against him. I think I could forgive him a lot easier if it was just me that he harmed. They were both so innocent and kind. All they ever wanted was for him to love them."

"You're innocent and kind, too, honey. Always have been."

"You don't know me as well as you think you do, Manny Gilford, and that's probably a good thing."

"Now you're going to try to convince me what an awful person you are?"

"Yes. I'll prove it to you. You know that good turn you're going to do for ol' Edom, callin' in the Social Services to help him?"

"Yes?"

"I wouldn't do that. I'd just let him sit there and stew in his own soup of poop and rotten fish and whatever else he's got in that shack."

Manny pulled into her driveway, parked in front of the house, and cut the key. Turning to her, he said, "No, you wouldn't, Stella. You'd help him, too."

She thought about it long and hard. Finally, she shrugged and said, "Okay. I'd call 'em. Tell 'em he needs to be rescued from hisself. But I'd tell 'em to make sure that nice new home they put him in is situated in a Louisiana swamp where his neighbors are half-starved mosquitoes, rabid alligators, and rattlesnakes with poor dispositions."

When Stella entered her house, she found the light on the answering machine blinking along with a red number 2. She glanced up at the clock and realized she had only a few minutes before the children would be arriving home from school. She had told them to catch the bus that afternoon, anticipating she might be busier today than usual.

If neither of the callers were gabby Florence, she could probably retrieve the messages and return the calls before the gang came crashing through the front door.

To her relief, the first message was Elsie's dear voice, still cheerful, even under the circumstances. "Hi there, Sister Stella. I happen to have a coconut cake sitting here on my kitchen counter that needs a home. Would you like some company this afternoon? Or if you're busy, would you want a babysitter for a few hours? Let's just say, I've got some time on my hands, and I'd rather spend it at your house than mine, if you don't object."

Stella smiled. Most people in town would duck behind grocery store displays and hide in alleys to avoid Stella if they thought she might ask them to babysit. But Elsie would actually volunteer to watch the children for her several times a week.

When they were in Elsie's gentle care, they were far better behaved than anywhere else on earth. Stella hadn't decided if this wonder was due to Elsie's peaceful spirit or to the yummy goodies that she brought along to bribe them. It really didn't matter, since the end result was the same.

Stella pushed the button and played the second message. To her surprise, it was Savannah, and from her first spoken words, Stella could tell that she was up to something and a bit nervous about it.

"Hi, Granny. I hope you don't mind, but as soon as the school bell rang, I ran over to the library. Don't worry, I made sure the little ones were on the bus first. I've got something important I need to do here. Some research about the case. Real detective stuff. I'll find a way home later. Don't worry."

Experience had taught Stella that when her grandchildren said, "Don't worry," that was when she desperately needed to start worrying . . . with a vengeance. If her oldest grandchild told her in one brief message not to worry, twice, heaven only knew what calamity was about to befall her.

Stella picked up the phone and dialed Elsie. Her friend answered after the first ring, as though she had been waiting tensely for the call.

"Hello?" Even hearing that one word, Stella sensed Elsie's anxiety.

"It's me, honey," Stella said. "I hear you have a stray cake running around over there that needs a good home."

Elsie gave a nervous chuckle. "I do. It saw it hanging out by my back door this morning. It looked all forlorn. Got any ideas where I might take it?"

"I suppose you could bring it over here. We promise to pet it, and walk it, and brush it, and give it fresh water every day. Unless, of course, we gobble it down within the first hour it's here. No guarantees, mind you."

Elsie laughed again, and this time it seemed more genuine, a little more relaxed than before. "Thank you, Stella. I just need to be away from here for a little while. I know it's my home, but it's just a bit too close to, you know, where she . . . where *it* happened."

"I understand completely. We're happy to have you anytime. You know that. In fact, if you want to bring an overnight bag with you, you go right ahead. We ain't got a lot of room here, but we can squeeze you in somewheres, for sure."

"I'm on my way. As soon as I can get a leash around that cake's neck."

"Don't get bit in the process."

"I'll try not to. See you soon."

Stella smiled as she was hanging up the phone. What a dear person Elsie was, especially when one took in to consideration the man who had fathered her. Stella was so grateful that her friend hadn't seen Edom Dingle that day or heard the hateful things he had said.

Years ago, Edom had disowned Elsie, and Stella was convinced that his abandonment was a blessing from above. Experience had taught her that sometimes people walked away from you . . . and you should just let them go.

She placed her second phone call to the public library. She wasn't surprised when the person who answered was none other than her grandchild.

"McGill Public Library. This is Savannah Reid speaking. May I help you?"

Oh, she sounded so grown-up that it broke Stella's heart. She wanted her to stay a child forever, sweet, loving, kind.

But then Elsie was over fifty years old, and she was still all those things. Not everyone lost those virtues when they grew up. Hopefully, Savannah would retain hers.

"Hello there, Miss Savannah Reid. This is Mrs. Stella Reid

speaking. I see Miss Clingingsmith is allowing you to answer the phone today."

"It's her brother's birthday. She ran down to the bakery to get him his favorite chocolate cake. She figured since I was here anyway, I could answer the phone for her and check out books."

"What's this 'real detective stuff' that you're doing?"

"Oh, Gran. You're not gonna believe what I found. Is there any way you could come down here? I know the kids are going to be home any minute now, but you really need to see it with your own eyes!"

"As it turns out, Elsie's on her way over here this very minute with a coconut cake. I'm sure she wouldn't mind watching the young'uns for me a little while. I'll run over there, see what you've got up your sleeve, and then bring you home. How does that sound?"

"Real police work, Elsie's coconut cake, and a ride home so's I don't have to walk! Sounds pert nigh perfect to me."

Stella hung up the phone, and at that moment, the front door flew open. In an instant, her house was filled with giggles, running feet, schoolbooks, and papers flying in every which direction. What seemed like a thousand questions and statements bombarded her, each louder than the one before it.

"I got an A on my spelling test, Gran! You owe me an ice-cream cone, and this time I'm going to try that new peach flavor!"

"Granny, I *almost* got an A on my math test. Can I have a peach cone, too?"

"You didn't *almost* get an A. You got a D!"

"That's only three away from an A!"

"Mrs. Miller said that I was a precocious young lady today. I don't know if that's good or bad. I told her thank you anyway, just in case it was a compliment. Now she thinks I'm polite, too."

Then there was the scream from the girls' bedroom. Stella had no doubt that the bloodcurdling shriek had come from Marietta.

She was the only one of the batch who could holler with that degree of volume and hysteria.

Though Vidalia could score a close second when adequately riled.

"Granny! Granny, come quick! There's a frog in my underwear drawer! I swear! A real frog. An honest-to-goodness, green, warty, ugly frog! Granny, hurry! It's hoppin' around and everything! Eeew! I think it pooped on my new pink panties! It did! I've got frog crap on my panties!"

That was when she heard Waycross laugh hysterically.

Two seconds later, he howled in pain.

Stella sighed and sank onto one of the kitchen chairs.

Just another day in the Reid household.

Chapter 28

Stella found Savannah in the McGill Public Library, though it took a few minutes. The child wasn't where she usually was, cozied away in a lovely little alcove beneath the old Victorian house's curved staircase, reading a book by the light of a stained glass, dragonfly lamp.

Today, she was sitting at a desk in the office, her hands on a keyboard, her nose practically adhered to a screen in front of her as she stared at the black and white photos and printing displayed there.

She had the same look on her face that she had worn at the burial site—determination and focus, mixed with a strange, almost scary, sort of glee.

The girl didn't even notice Stella until she was directly over her shoulder.

"What are you doing there, child?" Stella asked. "Are you typing something or watching television?"

"Neither one, Granny." Savannah grinned up at her and wriggled in her chair as Stella had seen her do many times when she was overly excited. Or needed to use the restroom. "This here is a micro-fish machine! It's a wonder of the world!"

"Micro-*fish*?" She glanced over the machine. "I believe *micro* means 'little.' This contraption don't look like no guppy or minnow to me."

Savannah snickered. "I don't think it has anything to do with fish. Little ones or big ones. When I told Miss Rose what I was looking to do, she set it up for me. And it works real good, except that my eyeballs are fixin' to roll right out of their sockets because they're so tired."

Stella pulled up a chair and sat next to her. "Do you want me to help you with whatever you're doing there? Mine are pretty well rested, considering the pitiful amount of sleep I got last night."

"I don't think any of us detectives are going to get much sleep until we have this case solved," Savannah replied with all the seriousness of a well-seasoned, career-weary, homicide investigator.

Stella stifled a grin and pasted a look of pseudo-fascination on her face as she stared at the screen in front of them. It appeared to be a newspaper, or more accurately, pictures of newspaper pages.

"What is that you're lookin' at there? The *McGill Gazette*?"

"It is! From forty years ago!"

"Really? How can that be?"

"Miss Rose told me that some nice person with the patience of Job took pictures of every single page of every single newspaper the *Gazette* ever printed and put it on here so we can read it!"

Stella gasped. "Every page? Every paper?"

"It sure is. This one I'm looking at right here is from March 3, 1943. It says right there that one hundred and seventy-three people died when they all got crushed together in a tube in Bethnal Green in London, England."

"In a tube? What kind of tube? Must have been a big one!"

"They were trying to get into an underground tube station to get away from a bombing, it says. Isn't that sad?"

Stella nodded. "There was a heap o' sad and evil things going on in the world back then. But this is the first I've heard of folks gettin' mashed to death in tubes in London. Just goes to show, you learn somethin' every day."

She reached over and ran her fingers through the girl's mussed curls. Try as she might, Stella could never tame those wild locks. Heaven knew, she'd worked on them long enough over the years. But like their owner, they had a life and opinion of their own.

"Is that what you wanted to show me, honey?" she asked her granddaughter.

"Oh, no. That's not it at all." Savannah turned a dial and more pages flashed by on the screen. "It's something way more important to us right now. It's about that pretty Mexican girl who went missing, Woya Sanchez."

"You found something about her in the newspaper?"

Suddenly, Stella was as excited as Savannah.

"I don't know for sure that what I found was about her. But it might be, and if it is, then it's important."

Stella's head spun. "Okay," she said. "Why don't you just show me what you found, and maybe then I'll catch your meaning."

It took Savannah a while to locate the article, and as Stella waited, she began to realize how tired she was. The quiet, elegant ambiance of the old Victorian mansion, which had been donated to the town to be used as a library, had a calming influence that invited visitors to unwind and slip into a mental state of relaxation, far removed from the troubles of their day-to-day life.

The horrors of the past two days had drained her, physically, emotionally, and mentally. More than anything at that moment, she wanted to find a place on that soft carpet to curl up, maybe behind a bookshelf, where it was unlikely she'd be disturbed, and take a long nap.

"Here it is!"

Savannah's voice was so loud, it caused the nearly nodding Stella to jump and almost fall off her chair. "What?!" Stella asked. "What is it?"

"This article right here," Savannah said. "It was printed about a year after Mrs. Dingle disappeared. It says a woman's body was found at the edge of a woods on a farm up in Berniesville. They couldn't figure out who she was. They just called her Jane Doe. But the article says the coroner thinks she was from Central America."

"There's probably quite a few women in the surrounding counties who are from south of the border," Stella said. "But this could be Woya Sanchez, I reckon. I wonder if they ever figured out for sure who she was or if she's still listed as a Jane Doe."

"Why do you suppose they called her that?" Savannah asked, looking genuinely puzzled.

"That's just a name they give anybody whose real name ain't known," Stella explained. "If she'd been a man, they'd have called her John Doe."

"Where did something like that get started?"

"I have no idea. But in a world where over a hundred folks get squashed in a tube in London, about anything can happen."

"That's for sure."

"We should tell Manny about this. Maybe he can find out if this lady was ever identified or not."

"Yes, let's do," Savannah said. "It's an important lead."

Stella stifled another grin. "You think so, huh?"

"I *know* so. I haven't told you the best—well, the worst— parts yet."

"Okay, start talkin'."

"The coroner ruled this Jane Doe's death a homicide."

"Did he now? Based on what?"

"The fact that she'd been hit on the back of the head hard enough to fracture her skull. Bad. Real bad."

"That's terrible."

"Another thing is, her hands were tied. In front of her. With a man's necktie."

A chill swept through Stella and went deep into her spirit, where it burned like a large chunk of ice held against warm skin.

"Oh, no," Stella whispered.

"That's important, too!"

"Yes, I'm afraid it is."

"There were two other things that probably matter, too." Savannah leaned forward and pointed to a picture on the screen. It showed a couple of artists' sketches.

The first was a drawing of a barrette. The second was of the woman's skirt, and a neat square cut out of it.

Both frightened and upset Stella. Deeply.

But it was the picture of the barrette that bothered her most. The hair ornament was leather and had a short, pointed, wooden dowel thrust through it, to hold the hair in place.

"That's like the barrette that you've got that was your momma's. And it's like the one that Mrs. Dingle had in her hair, the one you gave her."

Savannah searched her grandmother's face eagerly. "That's got to be important, huh, Granny? For that much to all be the same?"

"Yes, sweetheart," Stella said. "I imagine it's mighty important. You done good, child. Real good."

"You figure Sheriff Gilford will think so, too?"

"I'm sure he'll be most grateful to you for finding this. It's the sort of thing that police like him are tickled pink to hear."

Savannah glowed. "It's a real lead in the case, huh, Gran?"

"'Bout as real as they get, my smart, wonderful girl. Yes, just as real as they come."

Chapter 29

Stella was surprised when Savannah asked if she could remain at the library a bit longer, rather than accompany her to the sheriff's station and report to Manny all she had discovered.

"Can I stay just a little while?" she begged. "There's something else I want to find. When I do, I'll run down to the station house and tell you and Sheriff Gilford all about it. Okay?"

Stella had agreed and left her granddaughter to continue working with her latest best friend, the library's newfangled machine.

When Stella entered the station house she wondered, not for the first time, if anyone would ever actually repair that hole in the screen door someday. The crisscross of cellophane tape had held up well for decades, but sooner or later, Stella reckoned it would peel off and hordes of angry, thirsty mosquitoes would come pouring through.

It was a well-known fact that Georgia mosquitoes held a grudge.

As she entered the reception area, she heard two male voices.

One was Manny, to be sure. The other, she didn't recognize. It was soft, quiet, with a strange monotone that Stella figured would put her to sleep in about two seconds, considering how tired she was.

Once she entered the room and could see Manny's visitor, she was no closer to recognizing his face than his voice.

He was an elderly man, probably as old as Edom Dingle—in his late seventies, possibly even eighties, but he was in far better shape than Dingle. Perhaps life had been kinder to him, or maybe he had just taken better care of himself. Other than some crow's feet lines around his eyes and a bit of arthritis that had misshapen the knuckles of his hands, he could have been taken for someone much younger.

"Stella!" Manny said when he saw her enter. "I wasn't expecting to see you again today. What a nice surprise. Come in and sit a spell."

The other man, who had been sitting on one of the folding chairs next to the sheriff's desk, stood along with Manny, to greet her. It wasn't until he took an awkward, halting step toward her that she realized he was either newly injured or disabled.

"Grady, this is Mrs. Stella Reid," Manny told the man. "Stella, I'd like to introduce you to Grady Tyrell. He used to be the overseer there on the Patterson estate many years ago. He heard what was going on over there and came in to offer some assistance with our case."

Grady gave Stella a friendly, warm smile and extended his hand to her. She shook his gently, knowing all too well the pain one could inflict on a person suffering from arthritis without intending to, even with a normal, gentle handshake.

Manny continued, "Mr. Tyrell, Mrs. Reid is one of my oldest and dearest friends. She and her family are doing everything they can to solve this awful crime along with us."

With a wave of his hand, Manny invited them both to sit.

As they did, Grady said, "I'm glad to make your acquaintance, ma'am. On behalf of the community, I thank you for your efforts. Once word of this awful thing gets out, everybody in the county's going to be worrying day and night about their loved ones. Can you imagine anything as horrible as a serial killer right here in our peaceful little McGill? It plain boggles the mind."

"It most certainly does," Stella agreed. "It's got me looking at everybody I know in a different way, wondering what they're up to, trying to figure out what they're capable of. It doesn't inspire trust and confidence in one's fellow man."

"You can say that again." Manny sank back down onto his chair and ran his fingers through his hair in an exasperated, exhausted gesture that Stella knew well.

Stella turned to Grady. "But then, there's nice folks who genuinely want to help out any way they can. They restore your faith in humanity. At least a little bit."

"Grady's been a lot of help," Manny said. "He's well acquainted with the lay of the land around the burial site. He can tell you what it was like even fifty years ago. He says there were no crops planted where that corn maze is now. The plantation's cotton fields didn't extend nearly that far."

"That's right," Grady agreed. "That was virgin land in those days. Rough, untilled, like the day it was first created by the good Lord himself."

Stella looked at Manny. "Then it's not such a surprise that somebody could injure themselves running through there at night with no shoes on."

"Is that what happened?" Grady asked. "You figure that poor girl actually ran from the monster that hurt her?"

Manny glanced away and cleared his throat.

It occurred to Stella that she might have spoken out of turn, revealed more than he would have liked her to.

She warned herself to watch everything she said from that

moment forward. The last thing she wanted to do was violate Manny's confidence or, heaven forbid, jeopardize his investigation in some way.

More than anything, she wanted to help Manny Gilford, not cause him harm. After all he had done for her and her family, she figured it was the very least she could do.

"What an awful, pitiful thought," Grady continued. "A woman running for her life like that, and then, still losing it in the end. What's this world coming to anyway?"

"It's a possibility that it happened that way," Manny said guardedly. "We don't know for sure yet. To be honest, we don't know much of anything at the moment. But there's one more thing I want to ask you before you leave, Mr. Tyrell."

"Of course, Sheriff. Ask me whatever you like. I'd consider it an honor to help you catch that brutal bastard." He gave Stella a quick glance. "Begging your pardon, ma'am, for the language."

"Pardon granted, Mr. Tyrell," Stella told him. "Believe me, I've called that cotton-pickin' bucket of horse puckey way worse than that behind closed doors. And I don't think the good Lord held it against me neither, considering."

"No, I'm sure you got a pass on that," Grady replied with an easy, open smile.

Manny laid his pencil on the desk and turned to face Grady squarely. "I'd like to ask you, Mr. Tyrell, if, in all the time you worked there on the plantation, you ever witnessed any sort of, shall we say, unwelcome advances visited upon either Mrs. Gola Quinn, or Mrs. Rebecca Dingle, or a little Mexican lady named Woya Sanchez?"

Instantly, Grady's demeanor changed from open and friendly to worried and guarded. He crossed his arms over his chest and stared down at the floor for such a long time that Stella shot Manny a questioning look.

Finally, he said, "I'm sorry, Sheriff, but I really can't say."

Manny thought that over for a moment, then replied, "You can't say because you didn't see anything, or you can't say for some other reason?"

Grady looked up at him with haunted eyes. "I already said something a long time ago, and believe me, it cost me dear. I promised myself I'd never make the same mistake again."

"What did it cost you?" Manny asked.

"A fine job that I loved. Then my wife, because she didn't cotton to bein' married to a man who didn't have two plug nickels to rub together. For the next twenty years I had to work, performing hard labor, and I'm a cripple today because of it."

"I'm sorry to hear that," Manny told him with a compassionate tone. "But that was back then. Is there anything you hold dear now that you're afraid you might lose if you speak up?"

Grady considered the question quite a while before he said, "No, now that you mention it . . . I guess I've already lost everything that I held dear. Reckon it don't matter anymore."

"Then let me ask you again, Mr. Tyrell. Did you ever see any inappropriate behavior done by any man on that farm toward any of those women I just mentioned? Anything? Anyone? The workers, the bosses, anybody?"

Grady nodded slowly. "I'm sorry to say, I did. One night, I walked into the barn to check on a wounded horse, and I saw that nice little Woya, getting her clothes torn right off her, then and there. She was screaming and crying, and I felt just awful for her."

"And . . . ?" Manny prompted him.

"And I put a stop to it. Even though it cost me my job. Right there. On the spot."

"You were the overseer at the time?" Manny asked.

Stella could tell Manny's mind was racing as hers was. Who would be high enough on the employee ladder to fire an overseer in an instant?

There was only one answer, which she figured out even before

Grady said it. "Yes. I was the overseer, and so proud of it, too. Took me years to work up to being the boss, instead of a grunt, giving orders instead of having to take them from people not nearly as qualified as I was."

Manny picked up a pencil and began to scribble on a piece of paper on his desk. Then he laid it down, looked Grady in the eye, and said, "Who fired you, Mr. Tyrell? Who was the one abusing that young woman?"

"It was old man Patterson, the current judge's daddy. Wasn't the first time he'd done that sort of thing either. He was famous for it. He reached out and grabbed every woman he wanted, and if they didn't reach back, they were in trouble. At the very least, they'd be fired. At worst, well, nobody was sure what that man's worst was. But we had our suspicions."

A while later, when Grady Tyrell left the sheriff's station, Stella had to admit she was a bit more hopeful and relieved than she had been when she'd first arrived at the station house.

Having glanced at Manny's open notebook on his desk, when she'd first arrived, she had seen her father's name scribbled in numerous places. She'd realized that Manny was, indeed, investigating her father thoroughly.

She hadn't been surprised. Now that they had pretty much ruled out Edom Dingle, her dad, Finley Quinn, had the dubious honor of being elevated to the status of Suspect Number One.

With Grady Tyrell gone, she was eager to share Savannah's news with Manny. Particularly in light of what the overseer had just revealed about the former Judge Patterson and Woya Sanchez.

If this case could be closed without indicting Stella's long dead father as a serial killer, she would be grateful. Not only would she be happy for herself, but for her grandchildren, who—with a murdered great-grandmother, their own mom in prison, and their father an absentee parent and prolific womanizer—had enough family skeletons rattling about in their closets already.

"I've got something to tell you, Manny," she said. "Something very interesting that Savannah found out."

"What's that?"

"I'll be glad to tell you, but first . . . I see you've made some notes there about Finley. Have you uncovered anything important about him that you'd like to tell me about?"

Manny hesitated, looked at his notebook on the desk, then reached down and closed it. "No, darlin'. I can't say that I have."

"Then you didn't find anything or you don't want to tell me about it?"

He gave her a sad, half smile. "That's right."

"Okay. I guess you'll tell me when you've a mind to."

"Reckon so. What's Savannah's interesting news?"

His answer about her father, or rather his *non*answer, left Stella with a sick feeling in her heart, but she could tell it would be pointless to press him any further.

Manny might think the world of her, but he had a mind of his own and wasn't one to budge once he was firmly planted.

"She's over at the library right now," Stella said, "where she's been since school let out. She's looking at that micro-fish machine they've got."

"Micro-*fish*?" He thought for a moment, then grinned. "Oh. Okay. Go on . . ."

"In particular, she's searching through old copies of the *McGill Gazette*. On March 3, 1943, they printed an article on—"

"All those people getting crushed in the London tube," he supplied.

"You knew about that?"

"Sure, it was a big deal. A lot of people died. A horrible thing."

"Boy, I wish I'd gone away to college, like you. I didn't know they taught you stuff like that there."

"I don't think you came here to tell me about the London tube tragedy, did you?"

"No, I did not. She found an article about a Jane Doe's body that had been discovered on the edge of a field, where it met a forest. She was small built, and they believed she might have been from Central America, or at least, Latin heritage."

Manny was instantly alert. "You think it was Woya Sanchez?"

"I figure it might've been. But there's more. Her hands were bound with a man's necktie. She was wearing a barrette just like the one I've got and like Miss Becky had in her hair. Not just that. Her skull was fractured in the back. And . . . a piece of fabric was cut out of her skirt, a perfect six-inch square just like the others."

"Wow! Whether the Jane Doe was Woya Sanchez or not, it's obviously the same killer," Manny said. "It has to be. That's a pretty unique signature he's got there."

"That's what we figured. It's a hard stretch to try to believe that three different maniacs thought of using their neckties on their victims, not to mention cutting a piece out of each dress like that. What do you reckon that's about?"

"I hate to say it, Stella, but the truth is, these serial killers like to take little souvenirs with them, something from each one of their victims." He cleared his throat. "To remember them by."

"That's sick. But then, somebody'd have to be mighty sick in their spirit to kill another human being like that in the first place. Cutting a little piece of fabric out of a skirt, that's the least of the sins they commit against the people they murder."

At that moment the front door of the station house flew open and Savannah rushed inside, her cheeks pink from running and the chill of the autumn afternoon.

She was waving several papers in her hand.

"I got it!" she shouted. "What I was looking for, Granny . . . why I stayed behind! It took me a while, but I found it, and Miss

Rose printed it out for me. She printed the article about the body being found, too."

With great ceremony, she plopped the papers down onto Manny's desk, right under his nose. "This is good stuff, Sheriff," she said, her eyes sparkling. "Even if I do say so myself. I think you should give me a deputy's badge for this."

"Savannah!" Stella exclaimed. "What have I told you about the quality of humility—what a precious thing it is?"

Savannah thought for a moment, then remembered. "That all the best people have at least a little bit of it and exercise it regularly?"

"Exactly. Let's just say that your humility ain't exactly front and center right now."

Stella expected the child to crumble or at least wilt a tiny bit beneath the criticism.

But instead, she gave her grandmother a saucy smirk and said, "Yes, but many's the time I've heard you say, 'It ain't braggin' if it's true.'"

Stella sighed, looked at Manny, and said, "What in tarnation am I gonna do with this girl?"

"I don't know what *you're* going to do with her, but *I'm* fixing to hire her." He turned to Savannah and motioned for her to sit on the extra chair that Grady Tyrell had vacated. He picked up the papers she had tossed onto his desk and started rifling through them. "Oh, yes . . ." he said, nodding as he read, "this *is* good stuff. Very good stuff, indeed. Well done, Detective Savannah Reid."

Chapter 30

Stella dropped by the house to take Savannah home and make sure that Elsie and the rest of the children were all doing well.

As she expected, the gang couldn't have been more happy, quiet, and contented.

Elsie was relaxing in Stella's favorite chair. The children sat in a circle at her feet, listening as she told them, for the umpteenth time, the story of *Jack and the Beanstalk.*

Stella interrupted the tale only long enough to ask if she could impose on the babysitter for another hour, while she visited an old friend.

The children cheered, Elsie laughed, and they all shooed Stella away so they could get back to the story, having left Jack in dire straits with the ogre about to grind his bones to make bread.

"Thank you, Lord, for Sister Elsie," Stella whispered as she left the house and got back into her truck. "Please stay close to her in her time of sorrow and bless her real, real good. Ain't nobody who deserves it more."

* * *

Once again, Stella headed back toward Pine River. Watching the horizon, she wished she had left earlier to make this journey into the past. *Her* past.

The sun would be down soon, the woods would be dark, and it had been so long since she had visited this area. Too long.

She hoped she could find her way.

This road, like most Memory Lanes, had some painful landmarks along the way, but they were still paths worth taking, at least from time to time. Stella had decided about an hour before that it was time for her to take this one.

The first ache in her heart came when she passed Manny's cabin. Certainly, it was charming, inviting, and well kept. But so much had happened there over the years.

Good memories had been made within that house when she and Arthur had visited Art's best friend, Manny, and his wife, Lucy. The four of them had played games into the morning hours, laughing, and sometimes singing while Manny accompanied them on his guitar. Wonderful barbecues that included a combination of Stella's and Lucy's best cooking with Manny's fine grilling. Art had supplied the arm power to crank the homemade ice cream.

But one day, when Manny was at work and Lucy alone, she put on her new red, white, and blue striped bathing suit that she had bought for a Fourth of July swim party, and she had gone for a dip in the river. They found her three weeks later, or what little remained of her.

Not only was her lovely spirit gone, but all the memories they had made, as well.

Stella liked to believe that, eventually, when she remembered Lucy, she would recall her life, rather than her passing. But it had been over two decades, and she still couldn't remember her friend without pain. She doubted that another twenty years would make much of a difference.

Having passed Manny's cottage, Stella followed the river another mile or so before she started looking for the log cabin where her old friend, Magi Red Crow, lived.

Stella felt as though she had known Magi her entire life, having been introduced to him as a small child by her mother. Gola had been born Cherokee, or as that First Nation called themselves, Tsalagi, which, translated into English, meant "The Principal People."

Stella knew that Gola and Magi had been close friends since childhood. Occasionally, he would drop by their small house—always when Finley was away—to give Gola news of their mutual friends. Gola always warned Stella not to mention Magi's visits to her father, explaining that Finley was jealous of the tall, strong man with the beautiful, bronzed skin.

One night, Gola and Magi had briefly been more than friends, and Stella had witnessed the tender exchange.

As Stella matured and learned the ways of men with women, she began to understand more about their relationship and why her father hated Magi Red Crow.

That evening, as Stella made her way to the old Cherokee's home, she remembered him, recalled his kindnesses toward her and her mother, and she looked forward to renewing their acquaintance, which, after her mother's passing, had all but disappeared like frost on windowpanes at the dawn of an autumn morning.

The moment she saw the log cabin, she knew it was his. She remembered the last time she had visited there. It was her tenth birthday and Magi had given her the barrette he had carved for her. The one with the crossed arrows. He had told her it was the Cherokee symbol for friendship, and it meant they would be forever bound by affection.

Pulling her truck into his driveway, Stella was anxious to see if he would notice that she was wearing her mother's barrette. He had carved it with a three-petaled squash flower, the Cherokee symbol of love.

She wondered if he would even know her now. She had been younger than Savannah the last time he had seen her.

That terrible last time.

She was somewhat surprised to feel her heart racing as she got out of the truck and walked up to the door of the small cabin. What if he had moved? What if, heaven forbid, he had died?

He's not dead, silly, she told herself. *You would've heard if he'd died*.

There were a few advantages to living in a small community. Few facts of a person's life could remain secret from fellow townsfolk, and that was both a blessing and a curse.

If you got sick, people would leave goodies on your door. But others would tell everyone they knew that you ate too many of those treats and broke the new diet you'd begun last week.

Stella knocked on the door, and it wasn't long until it was opened.

The moment she saw the tall, elegant man with the glistening copper skin filling the doorway, memories of him came flooding back. The first time she had seen him, when her mother had brought her here to meet "someone of our clan." The last time, he had come to their home, tried so desperately to rescue them, and failed.

Countless times, Stella had wondered how different their lives might have been, if only he had succeeded.

She stood on the porch, saying nothing, just smiling up at him.

He studied her for a moment—her face, her form, her hair. Then he grabbed her, pulled her into the cabin, and hugged her tightly. "Stella!" he said. "Look at you! My little Stella, so grown up!"

"I should hope I'm grown up by now, Magi," she said. "I'm a grandma now, for heaven's sake."

"A grandmother! Yes, I heard that you have *seven* fine grandchildren!"

She looked up into his face, seeing the handsome man who had so impressed her as a child.

In a town full of common, everyday folk, Magi Red Crow had stood out. Taller, more muscular, with shining black hair that reached to his shoulders, and a graceful, fluid gait that gave him a regal appearance. Now his hair was whiter than Manny's, and age had lined his face. But it hadn't bowed his back. He looked as powerful and vital as ever.

As a child, she recalled being oh-so-proud to be his friend.

"I also hear," he said, "that you care for those seven grandchildren, yourself alone."

Stella thought of Elsie sitting in her leatherette recliner at home, telling the story of *Jack and the Beanstalk* to fourteen eager ears. "Not exactly alone," she assured him. "I have more help than I'm entitled to from kindhearted friends."

He turned her halfway around so that he could see the leather barrette that was holding her salt and pepper curls in place at the nape of her neck. He looked puzzled. "You're wearing the one I made for your mother."

"I am. I wasn't allowed to wear the one you made for me, so I gave it to Miss Becky, Elsie Dingle's momma. I like to wear my own momma's. It makes me feel closer to her."

He looked sad as he walked away from her and over to the fireplace. Kneeling on the hearth, he stirred the flames with a poker. The logs sparked, then blazed higher.

"It's terrible what happened to Mrs. Dingle," he said. "I always assumed that her life had ended, some way or another, or she would have returned for her daughter. But to actually hear that she was found and it was a murder . . . It breaks the heart."

"Yes. It does. She was wearing my barrette when we found her."

"I heard you were the one who discovered her."

"My granddaughter, actually."

He replaced the poker in its stand, brushed off his palms, and said, "It's for the best, I'm sure, that she was found. It must have been dreadful for everyone who loved her, not knowing."

"It was. Elsie's actually relieved. Although, of course, now we all just want the killer to be caught."

"Of course."

He pulled a rustic, log rocking chair closer to the fire and motioned for her to sit down. When she did, he walked over to the small kitchen area, ladled something from a pan into two mugs, and brought her one.

She smelled the sweet fragrance of apple cider, cinnamon, cloves, and nutmeg as she held the hot mug with both hands and pressed it to her chest. The heat of it and the delicious smell was most comforting.

"Thank you," she said. "This smells wonderful."

"Apples are good for the heart," he said, "especially when one is grieving. I'm sorry for your loss of Mrs. Dingle. And her passing so similar to your mother's. You'll need a lot of apples and warm fires as you heal."

She took a deep breath, savoring the scents of the cider, the pine fire, coffee, and tobacco.

Although she had never seen him smoke a cigarette, Magi Red Crow always had the faint smell of tobacco about him.

He pulled up another rocking chair for himself and eased his long frame into it. "I'm glad you came to see me, Stella," he said. "So glad. I've carried a heavy burden on my heart since last I saw you. I was too ashamed to come and see you. But I've thought about you and your mother every single day since . . . since that last time. Having you come here tonight, it eases my burden of shame. At least a little."

"Shame?" She stared at him over the rim of the mug. "Whatever would you have to be ashamed of?"

He didn't reply. He just looked at her, and she saw the guilt in his eyes, the tight set of his jaw, the downturn of his mouth.

Then she remembered. "Oh," she said.

"I'm so sorry. I never meant for you to see that. I never meant for it to happen. It wasn't planned. Please believe me."

Stella thought back on that night. A nightmare had awakened her. She had left her bed and walked into the living room to find her mother.

She found her, standing near the door in the arms of Magi Red Crow.

The two were sharing a kiss that even one as young as Stella recognized as deeply passionate.

They didn't see the child, and when the embrace ended, Magi had pleaded with Gola, saying, "Please, my love, come with me. Tonight. I'll take you and Stella so far from here, you'll never have to worry about him again. You'll be beyond his reach. No one will ever strike you or her again for as long as you live. I won't allow it."

Her mother refused, obviously far too afraid of her violent husband to take the chance.

The conversation went back and forth several times, until finally, Magi acquiesced. He told her that if she ever changed her mind, to get word to him and he would come immediately.

Then he asked her for one final kiss to say good-bye.

In the middle of that sweet, gentle expression of affection, Finley Quinn walked into the house.

Finley struck Gola, a terrified Stella screamed, and a dreadful fight between the two men ensued.

Magi easily won. But in the end, he lost, because Gola chose to remain in her violent marriage.

A month later, she was dead.

"I can't even imagine," Magi said, his voice choked with emotion, "what that must have looked like to a young child. I've never forgiven myself for doing that to you. To your mother."

Stella set the mug on a nearby table, leaned toward him, and placed her hand on his. "Then it's high time you *did* forgive yourself, Magi Red Crow. You loved my mother and me dearly. That was obvious to me from the moment I met you. You wanted to save us from him. You came to our house that night to try to persuade her to escape, to leave the darkness behind and walk into the light with you. If she had, I believe she'd be alive today. But who knows why people do what they do? Especially a woman in that situation."

He shrugged. "It was simple enough. She loved him more than she did me."

"No. I don't understand why she stayed, but that wasn't the reason. She feared him, but she didn't love him. She cried when she was with him. Her eyes shone with happiness when she was with you."

He thought a long time, staring into the fire. Then he turned to her and said, "Really? Do you truly believe that, Stella?"

"With all my heart."

He squeezed her hand and said softly, "Thank you. You'll never know the healing your words just worked in me."

She smiled. "Better than apple cider?"

Nodding, he laughed. "Yes. Even better than apples, smoke from the old tobacco, and a dozen eagle feathers."

Their moods lifted, especially Magi's. He seemed lighter somehow, as though an enormous burden had left him as they chatted about her grandchildren and their antics.

But eventually, the conversation came back to the recent discovery of Mrs. Dingle and the investigation.

"I have a question to ask you, Magi," she said. "About the wonderful barrettes you make."

"Would you like another one? Perhaps for your brave, smart granddaughter?"

"Another time, I'd love it. But I was wondering if you ever made another just like the one you gave me, with the crossed arrows, the symbol of friendship."

"I did. For a little girl who reminded me of you. She lived down the road with her family. She had a pet burro who loved apples, and I let her come pick some off my trees to give to him when she got home from school each day."

"What was her name?" Stella asked, anticipating the inevitable reply.

"Her name was Woya Sanchez." His face grew dark, and he turned to stare into the fire.

"Do you know what happened to her?"

"I know she disappeared one day, and no one ever saw her again."

"She was Mexican, right?"

"Her mother, Ama, was Cherokee. Her father, Manuel Sanchez, was from Monclova, Mexico. He left them when Woya was only five. She had no father to look after her, to keep her safe."

"From what?"

"From men who told her that she was beautiful and that they loved her when they had no love or even respect for her. I tried to help. I chased some of them away, told them, if they came back, I would hurt them. I tried to protect her. I was afraid something bad would happen to her. I tried to warn her and Ama. But . . ."

"People only hear what they want to hear," Stella said. "To tell them anything else is pretty much a waste of breath."

"Yes, but we have to warn the ones we love. How can we not tell them when we see danger ahead for them?"

"That's true. We do."

He turned and looked at her long and hard. After a few moments, the intensity of his gaze began to make her uncomfortable.

"What is it, Magi?" she finally said. "Why are you—"

He jumped up from his chair, set his mug on the table next to hers, and rushed over to a workbench in the corner of the room. After searching in a drawer for a minute, he found what he was looking for and hurried back to her, carrying it in his hand.

"This is for you," he said, placing a round disc of leather into her palm. "You must keep this close to you at all times. For a while. I don't know how long."

She looked down at it, studied the pattern he had cut into it, just as he had carved the barrettes. There was a circle and, in the center, a small dot. Two arrows pointed to the dot, one on each side of it.

"What's this?" she asked, upset by the urgency of his words and actions. "Why are you giving it to me?"

"It's for protection," he told her. "I see a darkness around you, my little Stella, a powerful, evil spirit that means you harm. Promise me that you'll keep this with you, day and night, until the danger passes."

"Okay. I promise. But how will I know when the danger's passed?"

"You will know. Your enemy will be revealed, and then all will be well. But until then, be very careful. This dark spirit feeds on the light of those he destroys. He seeks those whose light is brightest, the better to satisfy his hunger. But his hunger is ravenous and will never, never be satisfied."

Chapter 31

When Stella arrived back home after visiting Magi Red Crow, she was surprised to find that all the grandkids were already in bed asleep, and Elsie was sitting on the porch swing in the semidarkness.

"Them children was more tired than usual," Elsie told her. "Or maybe it was me who was draggin' my tracks out. Either way, they seemed happy enough to go down for the night."

Stella sat beside her on the swing. By the dim light of the porch lamp, Stella could see that Elsie was crying, and the sight nearly broke Stella's heart.

In all the years the two had known each other, Stella had seldom seen the sunshine of Elsie's smile dim even for a moment, let alone witnessed her crying. But it was to be expected, considering the circumstances.

Some storms were so mighty they could challenge even the strongest ship.

Surely, finding out your mother had been murdered was such a tempest.

Stella reached for Elsie's hand and squeezed it between her

own. "I'm sorry, sugar," she said. "It's all gettin' the best of you, at least for the moment, huh?"

Elsie nodded. "When I was telling the kids that story, I got to remembering when my momma told it to me. It was one of my favorites. I liked hearing her do the mean, old ogre's voice."

Stella chuckled. "She was mighty good at doin' that giant's voice. I remember it myself."

"She throwed herself into the performance, to be sure. When it came to you or me, and taking care of us, she throwed herself into everything she did for us."

"That's for sure. I'll always remember her for that, and bless her name."

"Anyway," Elsie said, "I was telling the story, and it was like I could hear her voice coming out of my mouth. It got me thinking about her, and the thinking got me all choked up. Then, as soon as the kids were all asleep, I came out here to have myself a little cry."

"Does a body good sometimes," Stella said. "Cleanses the soul like a good spring housecleaning."

Elsie nodded thoughtfully, sniffed, and said, "How did your visit with Magi Red Crow go?"

Stella looked at her with astonishment. "For heaven's sake, Sister Elsie. Since when did you become a psychic? You're starting to spook me a bit with all of this supernatural knowledge of yours."

Elsie giggled. "I hate to disappoint you, but in this case, it's just plain old nosy detective skills. Nothing supernatural about it. When we was stuffing our faces with cake earlier—and by the way, we saved you a big ol' piece—Savannah told me how she found the newspaper story about the little girl in Berniesville turning up dead. You know, the same way as our mommas. She told me about the girl's barrette. So, I figured that would send you straight to Magi's door. I was right, huh?"

"Aren't you always?" Stella put her hand into her jacket pocket and felt the circle of leather the old Cherokee shaman had given her for protection.

She thought of the dark presence he had sensed lurking about her. But Stella decided not to mention it to Elsie. Her friend's plate was full to overflowing as it was. Considering how seriously Elsie took her "haunts," she didn't need to hear about an evil, dark presence, hovering above her best friend's head.

"Mostly," Stella said, "we talked about a young woman named Woya, half Mexican and half Cherokee, who disappeared. Magi was a friend of hers; he gave her a barrette with the crossed arrows symbol, like he gave me."

"And Savannah said that body they found in Berniesville was wearing one like that. So, the dead woman was most likely her?"

"Seems so." Stella pushed the swing with her feet, taking comfort in the rhythmic motion, as she had all her life. "We also talked about Finley."

No matter how many times Stella called her father by his first name, rather than addressing him as "Father" or "Daddy," she would feel a twinge of shame at her own disrespect of the man who had brought her into the world and cared for her, however badly, for at least the early part of her childhood.

She tried to tell herself that he had done so out of paternal love and devotion.

But she had been there, experienced every minute of it, and she couldn't lie to herself. Finley Quinn had provided sustenance for his daughter because he had to. Thankfully, society monitored and enforced such things, and he would have been shamed, or worse, if he had neglected to do so.

While his wife was living, he provided the girl with the barest of essentials necessary to keep her body and soul together. But once his wife was gone, Finley Quinn ceased to do even that.

The whole town considered him a wife killer. Who cared if they were upset that he spent his meager monies on whiskey instead of bread and jam?

Stella couldn't bring herself to call him "Father" or any other term of endearment. It felt dishonest. Wrong. Even worse than the disrespect of referring to him by his name.

"Mr. Crow never was a fan of your daddy's," Elsie said. "Everybody in town knew that."

"Not hard to see why," Stella added. "Finley being a horse's backside and Magi being in love with my momma."

"I wasn't gonna say that, but I think pretty much everybody in town knew that, too. He didn't exactly go outta his way to hide his feelings for her."

"He's still in love with her, Elsie. I could tell by the look in his eyes every time he spoke of her. He's never gotten over her."

Elsie nodded thoughtfully. "I've never been truly in love myself. But I'd imagine, if it's the real thing, it's not something a body just gets over."

"No, you don't. It sticks with you for life."

"Okay, but it seems to me a person should work at trying to keep that grief in its proper place, in the past, where it doesn't muddy up the present and ruin any chances of happiness in the future."

"Uh-oh. I can tell where this conversation is headed. In a minute you'll be preaching to me about Manny Gilford and how I'm throwing my chance for happiness right out the front window with both hands."

"Sooner or later, I probably would've worked my way around to that topic, all sneaky like."

"You ain't near as sneaky as you think you are, Elsie Dingle. You're about as subtle as a Cotton Belt freight train, chuggin' through the middle of town at midnight. You'd have gotten onto the topic sooner rather than later, and I ain't in the mood. I got enough weighin' down my mind right now as it is."

Elsie nodded solemnly. "Yes, I can see how thoughts of Sheriff Gilford might be distracting. How nice he looks in that freshly pressed uniform of his, muscles bulging here and there, strainin' at the seams. That big bright smile, especially when he looks at you that special way. I can understand how that might clutter a gal's brain something fierce. I'd avoid it like the plague if I was you."

"Smart aleck."

"That's me. Just keeping you honest, Sister Stella."

"Gee, thanks."

"You're welcome. My pleasure."

"Well, it ain't *my* pleasure, so knock it off!"

Stella felt Elsie nudge her in the ribs with her elbow. Just a friendly little poke. Not like one of Florence's painful gouges.

They laughed, their voices blending in a warm, companionable way.

But the lighthearted moment was short-lived.

Stella thought of what Magi had said about her father and the old fear and anger rose inside her, like a pot of hot water, boiling over on the stove.

"Elsie, I hate to say this," she began, squeezing her friend's hand tightly. "But . . ."

"Just spit it out, Stella. I figure I know what it is anyway."

"I hate to even think it, let alone say it to you, but I'm afraid Finley might've killed your momma and mine. Maybe that little gal, Woya, too."

"Part of it makes sense. He always was hurtin' Miss Gola. It was just a matter of time until he beat her real bad or worse. But why would he go after my momma?"

"Who knows? There's a couple of reasons that come to mind. You saw him trying to kiss her and her rebuffing him. Maybe it was as simple as him wanting her and her not bein' interested. A lot of women have been killed for that reason since the dawn of time."

"Sad but true."

"Or, maybe your momma accused him of killing mine. We know from her diary that she was convinced he did it."

"Momma did think that. I heard her tell my daddy so, more times than I could count. She might've said it to somebody else, too. Word might've gotten back to Finley."

"For all we know, she might have said it right to his face! One of the things I loved most about Miss Becky was how she spoke her mind. She had the courage of a bobcat. Didn't hold back."

"Maybe Finley killed my momma to keep her from spreading word of her suspicions about him killing yours."

"That would make more sense than anything anybody's come up with yet."

"But what about that little gal, Woya? The same person must have done all three murders. Did your daddy know her?"

"He had his eye on her, or so the old overseer Grady Tyrell says. He claims old Judge Patterson did, too. Grady stopped him from assaulting her one time and lost his job for his troubles."

"Don't surprise me much. I've heard plenty about the former judge whispered around the house. Consensus is—he was chummy with the old Horned One hisself."

"That's pretty much what Grady said. But whoever it was that done these killings, I'm startin' to believe we'll catch him." Stella could hear the note of hopefulness in her own voice. "Our resourceful little Savannah also found Woya's mother's address . . . or, at least, one that's more recent than any Manny had turned up. Savannah gave it to him this afternoon, and he said he was going out there to talk to Mrs. Sanchez right away. I'm sure that, among his other questions, he'll ask her if her daughter had any personal interactions that she's aware of with the judge and Finley."

"Good. Sheriff's got a talent for squeezin' information outta people and them not even figuring out they been squoze. It'll be interesting to see what he comes up with."

The women were quiet a while, swinging, breathing in the crisp autumn air, scented with pine logs in fireplaces and burning leaves. Stella looked at the jack-o-lantern next to the door on her porch and was pleased to see that one of the children or Elsie had lit the candle inside. Its smile was more cheerful than fierce, and tonight she was grateful for that.

But a hard, cold question was sitting heavy on her heart. She didn't want to speak it to her friend, but she felt she had to.

"What are we gonna do, Elsie, if it turns out that my daddy killed, not just my momma, but yours, too? How is our friendship gonna stand that? How are *we* gonna stand it?"

Elsie scooched closer to Stella on the swing and slid her arm around her shoulders. Hugging her tightly to her side, she said, "We're just gonna. We'll stand it because we won't have any other choice."

Stella laid her head on Elsie's soft, cushy shoulder, enjoying her warmth and love.

"You're right," Stella said. "We'll bear what we must, and we'll lean on the Lord and each other."

"We'll be mommas to each other. The mommas we ain't got no more."

"We will. I'll mother you, and you'll mother me, and if the other one ain't around at some particular moment of need, we'll just mother ourselves. 'Cause ever'body needs a momma to get through somethin' as hard as this."

"Then that's exactly what we'll do, you and me. I promise."

"Me too."

Chapter 32

Elsie spent the night at the Reid house. Stella refused to let her go back to her lonely apartment that was far too close to a piece of land that bore terrible significance for Elsie now and would, no doubt, forever.

Maybe someday Elsie would feel the Patterson plantation was her "home" once again. Stella hoped so, because living there and being a part of the grand old place as a free woman had been important to Elsie. But Stella was sure it would take a long time before Elsie would feel that way again.

As soon as the children had run out the door the next morning, heading for the school bus, Stella and Elsie settled down in the living room to finish their final cups of coffee before tackling the day and all the challenges it might bring. Stella was lounging in her recliner, and Elsie on the sofa, her lap covered with one of Stella's cozy, crocheted throws.

"I reckon I should get along home," Elsie said. "If I don't show up pretty soon to fix the judge's breakfast, he's bound to start looking for another cook."

"I understand," Stella said, "but he also knows what side his bread is buttered on, so to speak, so I reckon he's aware of how hard it would be to replace the likes of you. He can make allowances for you to grieve a bit before you start flippin' his flapjacks again."

"Maybe I'll just drop by the church instead and offer to help arrange Sunday's flowers. Mrs. O'Reilly always appreciates it when I help her with the altar sprays, and I get a kick outta doin' it."

"Sounds perfect," Stella told her.

"What've you got on your agenda?"

Stella wondered if she should answer that question. She was afraid Elsie might think she was a bit daft if she did.

But that was what friends and stand-in mothers were supposed to do. Love you even when you weren't at your smartest.

"I'm going to drive down to the river," she said.

"To visit Magi again?"

"No. To the spot near the dock where Finley drove hisself into the water."

"Oh. I wasn't expectin' to hear you say *that*!"

"I wasn't expectin' to do it when I got up this morning."

"Then why the hankerin' to go out there now?"

Stella shrugged and said, "Oh, I don't know. I got to thinking about how your momma contacted you the other night. Even though I can't imagine that Finley would bother to reach out to me the way she did you—or that I would even want him to, for that matter—I thought maybe if I went there, I might get some sort of sense of him."

"Something that might tell you whether he's the killer or not?"

"Something like that."

"I think it's a good idea. Don't let me hold you back. If you wanna get goin', I'll make sure the stove's turned off, and the place is locked up tight when I leave. I won't be stickin' around long myself, once this cup of coffee's gone."

* * *

Stella did as she was bid and left the house within minutes.

All night she had lain on the sofa, since she had insisted Elsie take her bed, and wrestled with the notion that her father might have been a far worse man than even she had imagined.

Her mind simply couldn't come to terms with the thought that he had actually killed, not one, but several women. It didn't seem possible.

But then, she reminded herself that the thoughts she was having, the denials, were probably exactly what most serial killers' families thought when confronted with the evidence of their relatives' dark deeds.

Even serial murderers had mothers, fathers, siblings, spouses, and yes . . . daughters.

She got into the old Mercury and headed for the river bend just north of town where Finley Quinn had met his end.

His truck had been found, submerged, a few feet from the riverbank, near a public dock. Inside was Finley. His troubled life finished, his deeds, good and not-so-good, ended.

Some said it was a blessing. Stella couldn't recall one single person at the brief funeral who had seemed to be genuinely grieving his abrupt passing.

Including herself.

She would forever feel at least a bit guilty about that.

Within ten minutes, she had arrived at the spot, and she was relieved to see there was no one else present, fishing at the dock, boating in the river, or eating at the nearby picnic tables.

She parked the truck and sat there for a moment before getting out, whispering a fervent prayer. "Lord, I need help right now, real bad. This is tearing me up inside. The wondering, that is. I think I'll be able to bear it—with your help and Elsie's and Manny's and those who love me—if it turns out that Finley did all this evil mess. Though, I'd like to think that what I already witnessed was the worst of his orneriness. But I ask you for answers. Right now, if you please, Lord. I don't wanna leave this place without knowing, one way or the other. I'm begging you to enlighten me."

She got out of the truck and strolled down the well-worn path to the riverbank.

Although she had expected to feel some sort of horror, knowing her own flesh and blood had met a violent end here, the only sensations she experienced were gentle ones provided by nature.

The sound of the water rushing by seemed more relaxing than sinister. The colors of the fall leaves floating by delighted her eyes. Autumn was surely her favorite season. Every year, the beauty of its ever-changing hues thrilled her to the core of her spirit and reminded her that the cycle of deep rest followed by renewal was necessary and good.

The chill in the air invigorated her, and she could feel the blood rising in her cheeks as the cold swept over her skin.

Standing on the dock, drinking in the sweet, fresh air and the glorious sights, Stella felt only life. Nothing of death.

She looked across the water to the exact place his car had crashed. Although, as a child, she hadn't been allowed to see the actual accident with her own eyes, she had caught a glimpse of a newspaper the next day and its front-page photo.

She knew where the vehicle had landed. Just there on the other side of that large rock that rose, higher than the rest above the water's roiling surface.

Turning, she looked back at the road that she had taken down to the dock and tried to imagine how it had looked that night. It had been late, after midnight, so it was quite dark, no doubt. There were no man-made lights installed here to illuminate the area after sunset.

Could he have simply missed that curve and driven into the water by accident?

Had he, overcome by the sorrows and troubles of his life, deliberately sought the oblivion he hoped death would give him?

Had someone caused him to leave the road and enter the water, by accident or—considering Finley's troublesome nature and the long list of enemies it had created—by design?

"Did you have an accident, Daddy?" she whispered into the cold, autumn breeze.

Although she didn't really know how, she tried to open her spirit to receive the answer.

But none was forthcoming.

"Or did you deliberately end your life yourself?" she asked, her voice so low she could barely hear her own words above the burbling of the river.

Her heart could hear even less.

Silence. Profound and deep.

Then she heard an unspoken question rising from deep inside her, and this time the voice was strong and clear.

Does it matter?

Taken aback, she tried to imagine how her father would have answered. But then she realized, the question had been addressed to her, not him.

She knew it was a life-changing question, one she had to answer with all the honesty she could summon.

Finally, she whispered, "Not really."

She held up one hand, her palm toward the place where her father had left this earth, and she said to him, "It doesn't matter if you drove here deliberately or if it was a drunken error. You were killing the life inside you every day that I knew you. Suicide isn't always committed in one desperate act. Sometimes it's a series of life decisions."

Dropping her hand, she closed her eyes and allowed the power of her newfound truth to wash over her, cleansing and empowering her.

It was a sad truth, to be sure. But truth strengthened, even as lies weakened.

She recalled the conversation she and Manny had shared earlier about how life wasn't a merry-go-round. You couldn't just jump off when you had a mind to. Not more than once, anyway.

"Maybe you jumped that night," she told her absent, silent father. "Or maybe you were easing over that way a little bit at a time for years. Amounts to the same thing in the end. So, it doesn't really matter. What's done is done and can never be undone."

She took one more deep breath of the river air, filling her lungs, heart, and mind with its healing peace, and turned to walk back to her truck.

That was when she saw Manny coming toward her. Without her noticing, he had parked his cruiser next to her vehicle and gotten out. He raised one hand and waved to her.

She hurried to meet him halfway.

"Good mornin', Sheriff," she said. "What're you doing here?"

"I dropped by your house and ran into Elsie, who was leaving. She said you were down here." He glanced quickly toward the dock, then the spot in the water by the big rock. "I hope I'm not interrupting anything."

"No. I just finished."

"You okay?" he asked, searching her face.

"As good as can be expected. Maybe even a bit better."

"I like hearing that."

"Why were you looking for me?"

"I have some news," he said. "I've also got some fresh donuts and two extra big cups of coffee in my vehicle. Care to join me?"

I'd love to join you, Manny Gilford, anytime, anywhere, for anything! her heart shouted.

"Yeah, okay," she said. "Sounds nice."

Chapter 33

Once Stella and Manny were settled inside his cruiser, donuts and coffee in hand, he began to share his news with her.

"I followed up on Savannah's newspaper leads. I drove to Berniesville, talked to the police chief there, and he showed me the file on their Jane Doe."

"Is it Woya Sanchez?" Stella asked around a bite of apple fritter.

"We're all but certain it is. They'll confirm it with dental records. But the chief and I went out to the nursing home where Ama Sanchez is now, showed her some pictures of the clothing and personal effects on the body, and she identified them."

"That must have been awful for her."

"It was. She'd been holding out hope that her daughter would be found, safe and sound, someday."

"That's a hope that'd be hard to give up."

"It is." His voice caught in his throat. "Until you know for sure."

A few heavy and awkward moments of silence passed between them as they thought of Lucy, remembering those agonizing three weeks between her disappearance and the discovery of her body downriver.

Manny had kept hoping.

They all had.

There was nothing else to do, just search, pray, and hope.

"Did Ama have anything else to say?" Stella asked after a respectful amount of time had passed for Manny to compose himself. "Anything helpful?"

"As a matter of fact, yes. She admitted that Woya had a lot of lovers. Not like she was a loose girl with no morals. More like she was sad, missing her father . . . or the idea of having one . . . and was vulnerable when it came to male attention."

"Even if those males were skunks, weasels, and rattlesnakes?"

"Males of all sorts, apparently." He paused, then added, "Including Finley, I'm afraid."

Stella's throat constricted, and for a moment, she thought she might choke on the bite of donut she was trying to swallow.

"Really? Oh. That's bad news," she said. "That means he had a connection to all three of them. Makes him look all the more guilty. And here I was hoping maybe he wasn't the one who . . ."

Manny set his coffee and donut on the dash and reached for her hand. "Don't think that, darlin'. You haven't heard all I've got to say yet."

"There's more?"

"There sure is. Ama told me that the night your mother died, Finley was with Woya. The whole night."

Stella felt a glimmer of hope, but she didn't dare fully embrace it. "Are you sure, Manny?"

"She was sure. Very sure. Apparently, she allowed Finley to stay there at her house, in Woya's bedroom. Said she preferred that because at least then she knew where her daughter was and that she was safe."

"How can she be so sure it was that night?"

"Because he was there, sleeping in her daughter's bedroom, when the sheriff came to the door and told him his wife had just been found dead in their living room. The sheriff told Finley his daughter needed him, and he had to go home right away."

"But he didn't. He went to a bar."

"I know, sweetie."

"Miss Becky came to get me."

"Bless her heart."

Stella felt hot tears well up in her eyes. She wasn't sure if they were from the pain of remembering or the realization that her father had an alibi for at least one of the three killings.

"Then Finley didn't kill my mother."

"He didn't, darlin', and that means he didn't kill the other two either. The police never released the information about a square being cut from your mom's dress. Nothing was said about the necktie either. The first time those facts were released to the public was after they found the Jane Doe, who it turns out is Woya."

A relief of unexpected intensity washed over Stella. Until that moment, she didn't realize how upset she had been to think her father had been the killer. Knowing that he wasn't filled her with a happiness that she could hardly contain.

She began to sob so hard that it was difficult for her to breathe. Once again, Manny was there, arms around her, rocking and comforting her.

"It's all right now, honey," he said. "You don't have to worry about it being him anymore. I'm sorry you ever had a moment's worry about that. It's all over. Everything's all right now."

He handed her a bunch of tissues and waited until she had wiped her eyes, blown her nose, and partially recollected her senses.

"If you can stand it," he said, "I've got a little more news for you."

"Good or bad."

"Good, I think."

"Okay, but I'm such a tender buttercup these days that I might fall to pieces again, either way. So, just ignore me."

He smiled. "I could never do that, Stella May. But I have plenty of tissues, so you can blubber to your heart's content."

"Okay, lay it on me."

"Before I had the chance to talk to Mrs. Sanchez, I was thinking about Finley, wondering if he'd committed suicide, rather than had an accident. I was debating—if his wreck was deliberate, whether that had anything to do with the murders or not."

"Like him being overcome with guilt or afraid he was about to be caught or whatever?"

"Exactly. I talked to some of the old-timer bartenders who were active around here back then. I managed to find the last guy who served your dad his last drink before closing time."

"A double scotch, straight up?"

"Yes. Exactly. As it turns out, he'd been downing those all night long. His blood alcohol level must have been sky high. Anyway, this old bartender told me that Finley had been chatting up this one gal there in the tavern all evening, trying to talk her into taking him home with her after the place closed."

"Sounds like Finley, smooth-talkin' charmer that he was."

"Right before Finley and the woman left, the bartender heard her tell him to come on over to her place. The guy said Finley was happier than a hog in a mud bath when he boogied out the door, looking forward to the rest of the night."

"Then he was drunk as a skunk swimmin' in a beer barrel?"

"He was."

"And happy as a puppy rollin' in a cow pie at the prospect of gettin' lucky within minutes?"

"That's right."

"Drinking himself comatose and fooling around with the

ladies, preferably one he'd never been with before, were his two favorite things in life. I'm thinking there's no way he'd end himself on a night like that one. Not deliberately, anyway."

"Does that make you feel any better, Stella?" Manny asked, when he saw a trace of a smile cross her face.

"A little. But then, I'd already decided before you showed up that it didn't really matter much. He'd been courtin' death, in one fashion or another, for most of his adult life. It was bound to come to a head. If not that night, another one."

"I think that's quite true." He pushed a lock of her hair out of her eyes, and said, "With all that in mind, how's my girl doing right now?"

She took stock, then nodded. "Not so bad. Much better, actually. Except for one thing."

He rolled his eyes. "It's always something with you females. What is it now?"

"As long as we thought it was Finley, we didn't have to catch the guy and bring him to justice. Plus, we didn't have to worry about him committing any more murders."

Stella reached into her jacket pocket and felt the leather circle that Magi had given her. She added, "If it wasn't Finley, the killer could still be out there."

"Well, yeah," Manny said with a sigh. "There *is* that."

Chapter 34

Stella wasted no time accepting Manny's invitation to accompany him to the Patterson estate. The thought of seeing the judge squirm about anything from his father's misbehavior to overly snug underwear gave her more satisfaction than she cared to admit, even to herself.

Considering the good Patterson had done her family, Stella figured she should entertain nothing but the kindest thoughts about him and harbor nothing but the gentlest of feelings.

Too bad he was such a low-down skunk of a guy, who made it so hard for her to reach that virtuous standard.

Some people were just contrary, she'd decided long ago. Judge Patterson was one of those—the kind who could make a preacher spit nails and cuss a streak.

Most of the time she just tried to avoid contentious folks, who delighted in spreading mayhem wherever they went and making everyone around them miserable. But it wasn't easy. There were just too many of them in the world, it seemed, and new ones coming of age every minute.

As she and the sheriff pulled in front of the mansion, Manny seemed to be thinking the same thing, because he said, "Don't be surprised if the judge tosses us both out on our ears. I passed him on Main Street last night, and he gave me a look . . . whooo-eee! Madder than the snake that married a garden hose."

"What's he got to be mad about?"

"He's a judge and rich to boot. He doesn't need a reason."

"Doesn't he have to talk to you, by law?"

"Nope. He can throw me off his property like I was a vacuum cleaner salesman with bad breath and the measles."

"And me?"

"Even quicker."

"Boy, howdy." She sighed. "Somethin' to look forward to."

A few minutes later, once they had gotten past the butler, the housekeeper, several red-tick hounds, and Mrs. Patterson, still wearing the same negligee, they walked down the hallway toward the judge's office.

The door was open, so Manny motioned for Stella to get behind him, and he stepped into the room.

Patterson sat at his desk, scribbling in some ledgers.

The instant he saw Manny, he slammed the book shut, then crammed it into the nearest desk drawer.

"What do *you* want?" he asked, more than a little cranky. "I told you, Gilford, you and I have had our last little chat about this dead body situation. You got anything else to say, you can tell it to my lawyer."

"You've actually got a lawyer of your own?" Manny asked, grinning. "Really? I didn't think a judge would have need of one. I mean, you're the final word on what's lawful and what's—"

"What's *she* doing here?" Patterson said, his eyes boring into Stella's. "She is *not* welcome in my home from this day forward!"

"What did Mrs. Reid ever do to you, Your Honor?" Manny asked.

"She burnt my eggs!"

"Hardly a felony," Manny replied.

"She did it on purpose!"

"Okay, First Degree, Premeditated Burning of a Judge's Breakfast. Still sounds like a misdemeanor at best, sir." Manny shrugged and pulled Stella around to stand beside him. "She was with me, running an errand," he said. "I didn't have time to drop her off elsewhere, and I didn't think a fine son of the South like yourself would expect me to leave a lady outside in a cold car, while I conducted a short, pleasant interview with a gentleman."

Patterson sighed, leaned far back in his leather chair, his arms crossed over his chest, and said, "What? Tell me what you want and then get outta my hair. I got things to do. Important things."

"Yesterday afternoon, someone dropped by the station house. He wanted to assist us in this case of the lady buried on your property."

"I don't think it's been established yet that she was a lady, but go on. . . ."

"The gentleman offering assistance was once the overseer here. One Grady Tyrell."

The look on Patterson's face was shocking in its change from annoyed to something far more intense. For a moment, Stella was sure it was fear.

But fear of what?

She glanced at Manny and saw that the judge's expression had his full attention, too.

"So? What about Tyrell?" Patterson snapped.

"He made some rather unsettling accusations."

"*He* made accusations? *Tyrell?*" The judge laughed, but it came out as a dry bark rather than good-hearted laughter. "That's a joke."

"Shall I tell you who they were against?"

"No. You don't need to tell me anything that son-of-a-mange-infested-hound said. He's a liar and far, far worse."

Manny took a step closer to the desk and said, "He told me that he saved a woman from being raped in your barn."

"Saved? Saved? From rape?" Again, Patterson laughed, and the sound was bitter and sarcastic. "That's the funniest thing I've heard in ages."

Manny didn't look at all amused. "I fail to see how any accusation of a sexual attack against a woman could be considered funny."

"Of course, a woman being raped isn't funny. But to hear that it was a former rapist making the accusation, now that is *hysterical*—in an ironic sort of way."

"Former rapist?" Manny said. "What are you telling me, Judge?"

Stella felt a tightening in her belly that could have been horror, excitement, or a combination of both.

If this was true . . .

"I'm telling you," Patterson said, "that Grady Tyrell served seven years for aggravated sexual assault in Florida. Of course, my father didn't know he had a record when he hired him. It wasn't until after, well, until there was a problem that it came to light."

"How did it become a 'problem'?"

"When my father walked into the barn and caught Tyrell in the act of raping a young woman."

Manny's eyes narrowed. "Her name wouldn't have been Woya Sanchez, would it?"

Patterson seemed taken aback. "It was. How do you know that?"

"I've been working on this case night and day since the body was found, sir. I've learned a bit along the way. You might be surprised at what I've learned."

Manny backed out of the room, glanced up and down the hallway, then reentered, shutting the door behind him.

"I've learned that systematic sexual abuse of women—mainly young, pretty, minority women—was rampant here on the farm back in the day. I don't just mean pre–Civil War days either."

"Because Grady Tyrell was engaging in it himself and overlooking it in others," the judge stated.

"It's been said that your father did the same."

"He did not! And if you say those words again to anyone, anywhere, ever again, I'll have your badge. Just see if I don't. I'll not have my daddy's good name slandered by the likes of that filthy pig, Grady Tyrell."

The two men stared at each other in silence for several long, tense moments. Finally, Manny said, far more calmly, "Judge, I mean no disrespect, but you know I can check Grady Tyrell's record, if he has one. I understand you wanting to protect your father's good reputation, but if you're being less than truthful—"

"Shut up, Gilford! You just shut your mouth and wait one minute."

Patterson picked up the telephone receiver, punched some numbers, and waited. When his party answered, he said, "Judge Patterson here. I want you to pull up one Grady Tyrell's Florida prison record. That's T-Y-R-E-L-L. Yes, I can wait, but make it snappy."

He sat, drumming his fingers on the desktop, listening to the phone, grinning at Manny.

Finally, he said, "Okay. Thank you. I'm going to put Sheriff Maniford Gilford on the phone right now, and I want you to read him exactly what you just read to me."

Stella's heart beat faster still, as Manny walked over to the desk, took the phone from Patterson, put it to his ear, and said, "Gilford here. Yes, if you please."

He listened for what felt like ages to Stella. Then he asked,

"How old was the prisoner when he began serving that sentence?"

Oh, Lord! It's true! she thought, remembering how benign Grady had looked last afternoon as he sat in the sheriff station and acted the part of the perfect southern gentleman, so willing to help with the case, so deeply concerned about the welfare of mistreated women far and wide.

"Did he serve his full term?" Manny asked. "And one more question, if I may, ma'am. When was he released?"

Patterson leaned back in his chair once more, tipping it onto its rear legs. He had an ugly, terribly self-satisfied smirk on his face.

"Okay, thank you very much," Manny said. "And to you, too."

Manny hung up the phone and faced Patterson squarely.

"Okay," he said. "I beg your pardon, Your Honor, for doubting your statement about Tyrell's record. But now I have to ask you one more question and please don't take offense."

"That's what people usually say right before they say something they should be shot for," the judge replied.

"Maybe so, but it's my job to ask it anyway, so I hope you'll demonstrate restraint."

"Go on."

"We know now that Grady Tyrell was a no-good sack of mule droppings, but what sort of fellow was your father when it came to the members of the fairer sex?"

"My daddy was a horse's rear end when it came to women. He chased every one of them within his reach and proposed more indecent acts than you can beat with a stick. That's why my mother, may she rest in peace, divorced his ass. But he never in his life forced any woman to do anything. And he sure as hell never raped one."

"I understand, sir," Manny replied.

"One more thing," Patterson added. "The day—the very instant—that my father caught Tyrell attacking that young woman there in the barn, he fired him and had him and his belongings thrown off the property. He's never been back, because my daddy told him that if he ever set foot on this plantation, he'd shoot him, and everybody knew he meant it."

"I see."

"That still holds. I swear to God, if he sullied this land by setting one foot on it, I'd shoot him right where he stood and enjoy doing it."

"I believe you."

"Good. Then get outta here!"

"We're leaving, Your Honor. In fact, just consider us already gone."

Manny reached for Stella, took her arm, and they headed for the door, smiling all the way.

Chapter 35

"I know. It's intriguing and even promising, but it isn't proof of murder," Manny told Stella as they drove away from Patterson's mansion. "I doubt I could even get a search warrant, let alone arrest Grady. We have nothing but his former crime, which he served his time for and was released, and a 'hearsay' story about how a guy, who's long dead, saw another guy attacking a woman."

"We could at least go talk to Grady," Stella argued. "See how he reacts when he hears the accusations against him."

"I'll question him again, but I'd like to have a few more cards up my sleeve than just this one when I do. Maybe if I talk to Woya's mother again, she might remember if she ever saw Grady come around Woya."

"Magi," Stella said. "When I talked to Magi Red Crow last night, he said he ran a lot of different guys off, men who were hanging around, trying to take advantage of Woya. I got the idea he might have actually gotten into fights with some of them."

"If one was Grady Tyrell, he'd probably remember it."

"Have you got a picture of Grady?"

"His DMV shot."

"Good enough. Let's go."

When Stella and Manny pulled off the highway that paralleled Pine River and onto Magi Red Crow's property, they saw him down by the water's edge. He was holding something in his hand that was obviously burning because it was releasing clouds of white smoke.

He stood for a moment, holding the object as high as he could, allowing the smoke to rise into the air. Then he rotated clockwise a quarter turn, lifted the burning object far above his head, and once again, allowed the smoke to ascend.

"What's he doing there?" Manny asked, watching the ritual with keen interest.

"He's praying," Stella replied.

"Really?"

She chuckled. "Not exactly the way Baptists pray over the morning offering or for their missionaries aboard, but yes."

"Okay. If you say so."

"He's turning north, east, south, then west. The Cherokee believe that fire connects us with the spiritual world. The tobacco he's burning is old tobacco."

"Old?"

"Wild. It grows in nature. Not like that stuff they make cigarettes out of."

"What's with the smoke?"

"The smoke is lifting his words—his prayer, if you please—up to the spirits who live in the four directions."

"What's he praying for?"

"I don't know. You can ask him if you want."

"No. That's okay. To tell you the truth, Stella May, I've always been a little scared of Magi Red Crow."

"I'll bet you watched too many western TV shows and movies, where the Native Americans are always the bad guys."

"More like I just don't know diddley squat about them. We all tend to be leery of things we don't understand. He's a little bit creepy, in a cool sort of way, if you know what I mean."

"Yes. I think I do. But he's my friend, and I love him dearly, so if you call him 'creepy,' it had *better* be in a cool sorta way."

They got out of the cruiser, and Stella started to walk down to the riverbank to join Magi.

Manny lagged behind. "Isn't he going to get mad if we interrupt his prayers? We don't want to irk him while he's sending up smoke signals to the gods. He might order up a plague of locusts or whatever for us."

"You shouldn't worry about it. He's not that touchy about these things, I promise you."

Manny said nothing, but he didn't follow her down the path to the river.

She stopped, turned, and laughed at him. "Why, Manny Gilford. This is the first time I've ever noticed a streak of timidity in you, boy. The man's as old as Edom Dingle, and you're scared of him?"

"Edom Dingle doesn't blow smoke in all four directions and sing chants and communicate with spirits from the other side. I told you, that sort of thing sends a shiver up my spine."

Stella shook her head and shrugged. "Okay, then we'll wait in the car until he's done praying."

"Hello?" called a voice from the river.

Stella turned to see Magi gathering up his pipe and tobacco, then walking toward them with a bright smile.

"I just asked the spirits to send you to me again," he said when he reached them. "See how quickly you came? This is good *tsolagayvli*."

"What's that? Marijuana?" Manny whispered.

"No. It's that ancient tobacco I told you about. It's hard to find. Strong stuff! Not meant to be smoked recreationally. It's mostly for sacred rituals."

"If burning it can cause you to show up in a jiffy," Manny said, "I'll have to get me some."

A few minutes later, the three of them were sitting on the log cabin's porch, overlooking the river and sipping mugs of freshly brewed spicebush tea. The aroma reminded Stella of allspice and sassafras and brought back memories of her childhood when both Magi and her mother had made it for her.

Down a short hill, the river flowed, and the sound of its rushing waters soothed her, as they had before at the dock.

Someday, she thought, *I'd like to live by the water. Either a river or lake or . . . maybe even the ocean.* Though she couldn't imagine how lovely it would be to even stand beside the sea, let alone live near it.

"So, there's no doubt now?" Magi asked Manny. "The woman who was found, she is Woya for sure?"

"I just heard that they've compared the dental records and the identification is official," Manny said. "I'm sorry. Stella told me that you and she were good friends."

Magi nodded and looked sad when he said, "We were. I'll always remember her gathering those wormy old apples and taking them down the road to feed her burro. Fortunately, he wasn't picky. She was a sweet child, who grew up to be a nice woman. Too nice. To the wrong people."

"That's what I want to ask you about," Manny told him. "I mean no disrespect to your friend. But I understand you helped her from time to time by, shall we say, suggesting to certain fellows that they not hang around her house."

Magi's old eyes blazed with anger. "I told some of them that I'd kill them if I saw them with her again. In special, painful ways that only my people know. Is that what you mean?"

"Yes, sir. That's exactly what I mean." Manny gave Stella a quick, nervous look that almost made her laugh.

"Don't worry, Sheriff," Magi said. "We have no ways that are more painful than yours. I just lied to scare them."

"That's good to know. Thank you for the clarification there, Mr. Red Crow."

Briefly, the men laughed together, but the lightness soon faded as Magi's face darkened.

"For as long as any of us can remember," he said, "other men have used our women. Our women are desirable in the eyes of the others. The others want them, but only for the beauty of their faces and their bodies. Not for their strength, their wisdom, their kindness, their endurance. They want to use them when they are young, then throw them away. For as long as any of us can remember, this has happened."

The rage in Magi's face was frightening to see, although Stella could understand it completely. The proud man had seen too many women he loved so used and a certain amount of resentment, even hate, was to be expected.

"I never killed any of them, as I said I would," he continued. "Like I said, I lied to scare them. Some of them believed me and stayed away. Some did not."

Manny reached into his pocket and pulled out a photocopy of Grady Tyrell's driver's license photo. He held it out to Magi and said, "Did you ever see this man bothering her? Did you ever have to warn him away?"

Magi took the picture, looked at it for less than two seconds, then wadded it up and threw it to the ground. "I warned that one many times. Woya didn't want him. One time she willingly accepted him. From that first time, even she, whose eyes looked only for good in people, knew he was evil. He hurt her. Worse, he enjoyed hurting her. She told him, 'Never again,' but he came back to her house and forced her. He would look for her in the town and on the roads, and when he found her, he would force her. Afterwards, she would tell her mother and her mother would tell me. Then I would go find him and warn him to stay away. The last time, I was tired of warning him. I was afraid he would kill her. So, I challenged him, and we fought. It was a very, very bad fight."

Magi pulled down the collar of his shirt and showed an ugly scar that looked like a deep knife wound from above his collarbone, extending downward at least six inches. "That man and I, we nearly killed each other."

He closed his eyes, and when he opened them, they were filled with tears. "Then Woya disappeared."

"Did you report it to the police?" Stella asked.

"And tell them what? That I hunted a man, challenged him to a fight, and almost killed him? No. But I looked for him. I've never stopped looking for him." He pointed to the crumpled paper at his feet. "That is the first time I've seen his face since the night we fought."

Stella rose, set her cup aside, and walked over to stand behind Magi's chair. She leaned down and wrapped her arms around his neck. Putting her head beside his, her cheek against his, she said, "You did all you could, Magi. You risked your life for Woya. Nearly lost it in her defense. No man could have done more."

He shook his head and leaned forward to escape her embrace. "No! It wasn't enough. I loved Woya like a daughter, and I couldn't protect her from the men who said they loved her, but only wanted to use her. I loved your mother more than I've ever loved any person on this earth and I couldn't save her from that evil man who called her 'wife,' but treated her worse than an old, toothless dog. I couldn't save you from him either, my little friend."

"But Stella's safe now, Mr. Red Crow," Manny told him. "You showed her what it was to be loved by a man. A good man. Like a father. She values herself and requires those around her, men and women, to value her. She wouldn't be strong like she is, if she hadn't felt loved and valued by people like you and her mother and Mrs. Dingle. We can't save them all. But if we can save even one, that's everything."

Stella walked around to the front of Magi's chair, dropped to her knees before him, and cradled his face in her hands. "He's right, Magi. When you made me that barrette and gave it to me, it meant the world to me. And this one, the one I'm wearing now . . . my mother told me she would never be able to wear it because of my father. But she asked me to keep it safe for her, no matter what might happen to her, for the rest of my life. And I will."

She leaned forward and kissed him tenderly on his forehead. She hugged him tightly, breathing in the scent of him—the smoke of old, sacred tobacco, spicebush tea, and apple cider, and she said, "You've done more good for the women you've loved than you'll ever know, Magi Red Crow. Far more."

Chapter 36

"Let's go arrest Tyrell's hind end, right now!" Stella said, the moment she and Manny were back in his cruiser, before he'd even had a chance to put his key in the ignition.

Manny said nothing until he had the vehicle on the main road, and when he did, Stella didn't like what she heard.

"There are a couple of things wrong with what you just said, Stella May," he told her. "Probably more than two, but a couple in particular spring to mind."

"I can't think of one single reason that son of the Devil, Grady Tyrell, shouldn't be behind bars inside of an hour! He's been running around free, spreading death and destruction for decades, and getting away with it. Now that we know who he is, his time has come!"

"First of all, we may know he's our killer, but knowing it and proving it are very different things."

"But Judge Patterson and Magi both said—"

"I know what they said, sugar. I was right there when they said it. But as sure as we are that he's the one, we have to find some solid evidence for the prosecutor to make a case with."

"Don't go using your 'patient' voice with me, Manny Gilford . . . the one you use to calm down crazy folks. I ain't crazy. Just excited."

"I know. I don't blame you for being excited. I am, too. But—"

"Don't 'but' me either. I've been waiting for this over forty years, Manny. Forty years! Ever since I found my momma. . . ." She paused to catch her breath, then said, "I want, I *need* that man locked up."

"I know you do. I know how important it is to you, and that's one of the main reasons why I'm going to make sure it's done right. We'll get him. But we have to find some evidence. Solid evidence."

"Then get a search warrant."

"I sincerely doubt I could get one with no more than I have."

"Then what's next? What *can* we do?"

Manny pulled the cruiser off the road onto a broad shoulder, then he turned to her and said, "Stella, listen to me. *We* aren't going to do anything else. *I* am going to take it from here."

"What? Why? I'm helping you! Even Savannah's been helping you!"

"Yes! You have. She has, and I'm very grateful. Really, I am. But now we know who this killer is. He's still alive, and he's still a threat. I won't have you getting anywhere close to him!"

"But—!"

"No buts! You stop and think about it for a minute. You were inches away from a serial killer. Right there in the station house, we both chatted with him like we were at a church picnic, and we had no idea what he was. If you can stand it, think about what he did to those poor women. He enjoyed that, Stella! These monsters love what they do. That's why they keep doing it. We have no idea how many victims he's had. You shook the hand of a man who would kill you in a heartbeat if he got a chance."

Stella hadn't realized that she had slid her hand into her jacket pocket, until her fingers closed around the leather circle Magi had given her, the protective talisman. Her friend had warned her of a dark, malevolent spirit that was dangerously close to her.

Now Manny, another beloved friend, was doing the same. She would be a fool not to listen.

"Okay," she said. "I understand that you know way more about the law than I'll ever know. I know you want to keep me safe, and I love you for it."

For the space of a few heartbeats, Stella was aware that both she and Manny had registered her last words and were surprised by them. But she let the moment pass, rushing ahead to make her point.

"But hear me out before you close your ears to me. Okay? I'm not a stupid woman, Manny, and I might have something to say that's worth hearing."

She could sense him calming down, regrouping, and preparing himself.

"Okay," he said. "Make your case."

"You say you can't get a warrant. His victims are dead, so they can't talk. Old Judge Patterson is gone, so he can't testify to the attack he saw in the barn. Magi didn't actually see Grady attack Woya. Woya told Magi and her mother that it happened, but anything they know would be hearsay. Right?"

"That's right."

"So, we . . . I mean, you . . . need some sort of solid evidence to nail him."

"Physical evidence is always the best. But by the time the bodies were found, things like fingerprints, bodily fluids he might have left behind, they've all degraded or disappeared entirely."

"What sort of thing do you need then? The murder weapon?"

"That would be great, but it's a lot to ask for."

"What else then? If you had a search warrant in your hand, what would you look for?"

"Searching for evidence is a funny thing, Stella. You don't usually know exactly what you're looking for until you find it. If you're lucky, when you're searching a place, it sorta jumps out at you. Something unusual, out of place, similar to something you saw at a crime scene. I'm sorry, honey, but it's hard to explain."

She grinned. "Actually, I think you're doin' pretty well. I feel like I just took a class in Crime Solving 101."

Manny sighed and leaned his forearms on his steering wheel. Stella could tell he was exhausted. "I need to see him again," he said. "He was eager to talk to me, milk me for information, find out how close I might be getting to him. You know that's why he came into the station, don't you?"

"I figured. He's a sly one."

"He's probably not as sly as he thinks he is. They usually aren't."

"Then go and talk to him. Make up some reason to drop in on him for a friendly chat. He said he wants to help you with the case. Give him a job to do."

Manny considered the suggestion, nodded thoughtfully, then shook his head. "I don't want to tip him off that I know it's him. His antennae will be out, feeling for that."

"Yeah. A cop just drops in on you out of the blue to have a cup of tea and chitter-chat about the weather. That would make him suspicious."

"Yes. I'm afraid so."

"Unless you had a woman friend with you."

"No."

"He'd never dream you'd bring a female to a guy's house if you had the slightest inkling that he was a serial killer."

"I said no."

"I can be disarmingly charming when I've a mind to be."

"And stubborn as a blue-nosed mule, but it's still no!"

"You showed Magi Grady's driver's license photo, and if you've got his picture, you've got his address."

"I have his address, Stella May. So, what?"

"Say he lives in Berniesville—"

"He doesn't."

"Just say he did . . . you could call the police there in Berniesville and explain the situation to them. You and this unnamed, mysterious woman friend of yours could go to see him at his house or place of work."

"They're one and the same."

"Even better, and the police could stay a little way down the block, out of sight, and if there was a problem you could signal them, fire a shot, or your lady friend could run outside screaming and—"

"Stella Reid, that is the stupidest plan ever hatched in the history of law enforcement."

"I sincerely doubt that. Somebody, somewhere must've done worse."

"Well,"—he shrugged—"it's in the top ten."

"Then you come up with something better, Mr. Sheriff Smarty Pants."

"We bring our own deputies along. Merv's an idiot, but Augustus thinks on his feet. They'll be dressed in utility workers' uniforms, sitting in a white van right out front."

She didn't dare smile, just in case he hadn't figured out that he was giving in. She just sat there quietly as he continued to formulate his plan.

"He lives in the same building as his small appliance repair shop. We'll knock on the door a couple of minutes before closing time, that way it's less likely we'll be interrupted by any customers he might have."

"Good thinkin'. Go on . . ."

"But what's the ruse? Why are we supposed to be there?"

"We've got a super exciting lead on a suspect. A drifter, who committed a murder somewhere else, was passing through here around the time that Woya disappeared. We show him a picture of the guy and—"

"Of who?"

"Heck, I don't know, Manny. Do I have to think of ever'thing? Herb's brother from Cleveland? Just somebody Grady's never seen. Then we ask him if that guy ever worked there on the farm, or came by looking for employment or whatever."

"Not bad. Not bad at all." He nodded slowly, rubbed his palm over his two-day stubble, and thought out loud. "While we're there, we mostly just prompt him to talk. He's a bit of a blabber-mouth. Let him blabber. He might let something slip."

"We look around, too. See if there's anything that's out of place, strange. You never know. We might luck out."

Manny put the engine in drive and pulled back onto the road.

Stella sat still, almost afraid to breathe, unable to believe her luck. What a turnaround! She wasn't even sure what she'd said to convince him, but rather than question this gift, she'd just take it and run.

"There's one thing that we have to get straight, Miss Stella," he said, eyes trained on the road ahead.

"What's that?"

"I don't want you to think for one minute that you outsmarted me back there. I have absolutely no wool whatsoever pulled over my eyes. Understand?"

"Of course. I came up with a plan, then you came up with a better one because you're a man and you fellows are so-o-o much smarter than us silly females."

She poked him in the ribs, and when he turned to look at her, she gave him a wink and a grin.

He said nothing. Just growled.

Chapter 37

By the time Stella and Manny pulled up in front of the lack-luster shop with the sloppily painted sign GRADY'S APPLIANCE REPAIR above the front door, a white utility van was parked across the street. Inside, Deputies Augustus Faber and Mervin Jarvis were already in position, dressed in generic green uniforms with fast-food bags and milkshake cups on their dash, signifying to the world it was supper time for city workers.

Ordinarily, Stella would have found them humorous as they made a great show of rifling through the contents of the bags and slurping the shakes. But considering the task in front of her and Manny, it was hard to muster a smile, let alone any laughter.

"Are you okay?" Manny asked before they got out of the cruiser. "Are you sure you want to do this?"

"Yes, I'm okay, and I absolutely want to do it. How are you?"

"I'll be glad when it's over, but I'm okay. We're just going in to scope him out. That's all this is. All right?"

Stella nodded. "Whatever you say, boss."

They got out of the cruiser and casually strolled up the broken sidewalk to the ramshackle house with its cracked, dirty windows. Displayed inside were older model vacuum cleaners, a mixer, hair dryer, typewriter, and sewing machine.

When they entered, a tiny bell chimed, and a moment later, Grady Tyrell walked out of the back room, a sandwich in his hand and a surprised look on his face.

"Sheriff!" he said. "And . . . Stella, was it?"

"Great memory, Grady!" she replied brightly, as though she was about to nominate him for a Nobel Peace Prize. She glanced around the shop at all the boxes filled with dusty bits and pieces of household appliances. It looked like a place that toasters went to die. "Nice shop. I'll bet you can fix *anything*!"

"If the customer hasn't already tried to fix it first!" He pealed with laughter at his own joke. Stella did the same and even Manny joined in.

Stella fought her revulsion when he reached across the counter that separated them and slapped her on the arm.

She looked down at his hand, thought of how he had used those hands, and instantly cast the thoughts from her mind. If she allowed herself to think those things, the thoughts would show on her face, and give them away.

She had to convince this vicious animal that she thought he was the funniest, most interesting male she had met in a long time.

"Boy, you'd be mighty handy to have around the house with your talents," she said, waving a hand from one side of the shop to the other. I'll bet you could even fix that old Victrola my Aunt Jenny left me in her will."

He beamed, soaking in the attention. "You bring it by sometime and I'll fix 'er right up."

"I sure will! Maybe I'll bring you some of my pecan fudge when I do."

She glanced over at Manny and saw he was watching her with a mixture of something that looked like amazement and alarm in his eyes. But he must have decided to play along because he said, "There's an offer you can't refuse. Her fudge is out of this world!"

"I can't wait to try it."

"I'll tell you what . . ." Manny reached into his pocket and pulled out a photo of Deputy Merv's cousin, Billy. "You said you'd like to help us with this case. If you can answer a question for me, I'll make sure she brings you some of that fantastic fudge of hers. Real soon, too."

"Hey, you got a deal! What can I do ya for?"

Stella watched him carefully, trying to read his face. He seemed jovial enough, but she sensed that their lighthearted banter was as much an act for him as it was for them. Just beneath his down-home smile, she sensed his stress, his suspicions.

Manny held the photo out to him. "We've got a break in the case. We think we might have our guy."

Grady searched the sheriff's face intently, then took the picture and looked at it. "Really?" he asked doubtfully. "How exciting. Is this him?"

"Might be. He's a drifter, charged with a murder recently in Arizona. Similar MO. It was a cold case, a killing that happened in the sixties. The cops in Phoenix told us they think he might have lived here about forty years ago. That's when you were overseer there at the Patterson place."

"Okay," Grady said, studying the picture.

"Does he look familiar? Could he have worked there on the farm, or come by asking about a job?"

Grady looked at the picture for a long time. Stella could practically hear his gears turning in his head. She sensed that he suspected it was a setup, but wasn't sure of the best way to respond.

Finally, he laid his sandwich on the dirty counter, handed the picture back, and said, "He does look familiar. I'm pretty sure he worked for me there a little while."

"Can you remember when?" Manny asked.

"Um, I'm not sure."

"You don't recall what name he used, do you?"

"No. I don't remember what he said his name was. Sorry."

"Hey, don't be sorry," Stella said. "That's more than the sheriff had before we got here."

"I wish I could be more help. I hate it that you drove all the way here for that."

"It *is* a pretty far piece," Stella said, tittering, trying to conjure an "embarrassed" look onto her face. "And it's a far piece back, too. I hate to ask, but do you happen to have a little girl's room I could use before we leave? I don't think I can make it all the way home."

Again, he gave her a searching look that made her wonder if he was buying any of this act at all. Then he said with quite a casual air, "Sure. It's not a little girls' room. More like a big boys', so I don't know how clean it is."

"Hey, beggars can't be choosers."

"Okay. You were warned." He pointed to the doorway in the back that he had entered through. "Right through there and down the hall. Second door on the left."

"Thank you," she said, scurrying past him, trying to look like one of the grandchildren on the verge of doing a pee-pee dance. "I'll just be a minute."

She headed down the depressing hallway with its dark, fake, wood paneling and threadbare carpet that stank of mold and pet urine. She looked around, trying to memorize everything she could see. Some faded nature pictures on the walls, more boxes of machine parts littering the floor on either side of the passageway, making it hard to navigate through it.

"Look for anything unusual," she recalled Manny saying. "Anything that stands out, that doesn't belong."

She saw several boxes of pornography: magazines, VCR tapes,

and DVDs. From what she could see, walking quickly past them, they appeared to be primarily bondage themes. Amidst the collection she spotted a pair of handcuffs and something that looked like leg restraints.

Kinky, maybe, but not incriminating, she thought.

Aware that she had to hurry, that Grady was probably anxious and counting the seconds she was gone, Stella didn't have the time to focus on anything in particular, and it frustrated her.

Just calm down and do what you can, gal, she told herself. *Take it easy. All will be well.*

It was when she passed the first door on the left that she realized this was his living quarters. The door was open to what was a terribly dirty, cluttered bedroom.

This is where his secrets are, a voice in her head told her. *He keeps them close. Private and close.*

Did she dare to step inside? What would she say if he came down the hall and found her there?

"I'm so sorry, Grady. I thought you said the first door on the right. Ha-ha. Silly me."

It would do in a pinch.

She looked around the room, at the filth and the clutter. Dark, drab, faded fabrics in piles. More porn. Windows too dirty to let in the light. Nothing bright or cheerful.

Except.

"Something that stands out. That doesn't belong."

The one spot of color in the otherwise depressing room was a quilt that, unlike the piles of things thrown on the floor and spilling out of the closet, was hanging neatly on a nice quilt rack beside the bed.

The instant Stella saw it, she knew, and she felt something like an electric shock go through her brain, then her body, to her fingers and toes.

The sewing machine in the window, she thought. *You have to know how to sew at least a little to repair a sewing machine.*

In the lonely years since Art's passing, she had made a few quilts herself. This was a simple one, a small lap quilt, with a wide border around the edge and inside sixteen basic squares, sewn together in rows of four.

Men can sew, too, she thought. *Sixteen squares.*

Sixteen.

No! Dear Lord in heaven! Sixteen!

She moved woodenly across the room and stood next to it.

Pick it up? Leave it here?

She paused, listening. She could still hear the two men conversing in the other room.

Take it? Leave it? Decide now!

You're wasting time, Stella. You know you aren't leaving this room without that quilt.

She snatched it off the rack, and forced herself to look at the squares.

The second square of the top row . . . pink and purple flowers, still so colorful, still lovely.

The next to the last square on the bottom . . . a yellow calico print, as bright as the sun, with tiny blue flowers.

Sixteen squares.

Looking at one after another, Stella thought her heart would truly break and stop beating, then and there.

Clutching the quilt to her chest, she stumbled out of the room, through the dark hallway, and into the workshop.

Manny was standing near the door, where she had left him. Grady was on the other side of the room, beside an old television set with a cardboard box sitting on its top. He was facing Manny, his back to her.

Stella wasn't sure what to do, what to say. She held up the quilt so Manny could see it, and simply said, "The squares."

Grady whirled around. Saw her. Saw the quilt. He thrust his hand inside the cardboard box.

"Manny!" she cried out.

But Sheriff Gilford had seen the movement. His Smith & Wesson was already drawn and aimed.

Grady lifted his hand out of the box. He was holding a large butcher knife.

Instinctively, Stella rushed over to Manny and stood near him.

"Drop the knife, Grady!" Manny told him. "Drop it now!"

Stella watched the fear, the indecision, the rage on Grady's face. But instead of releasing the weapon, he clutched it even tighter.

"Drop the knife or I *will* shoot you!" Manny shouted. "Drop the knife!"

Without taking his eyes off Grady, Manny said, "Stella, is that—?"

"Yes. The squares from their clothes. They're here."

"Your mother's? Elsie's mom's?"

"Yes."

"We've got you, Grady," Manny told him. "There's no way out of this, except to drop that knife and serve your time."

"No," Grady replied. "I'm not going back to jail. You're going to have to kill me."

"I don't want to kill you, but I will if I have to. Put it down!"

Grady looked at Stella, then down at the quilt. Then back to Manny. "If you knew what's in that quilt, you would," he said. "Stella, tell him what else is in that quilt."

"No!" Stella said, hugging it even tighter against her chest. "Do what he says. Put down your weapon."

"Ask her what's on the quilt, Gilford," Grady said with a horrible, taunting tone. "Go on. Ask her."

Manny hesitated, then said, "What's he talking about, Stella?"

"Nothing. Don't listen to him."

"There's another square on that quilt that might interest you, Sheriff," Grady said.

"Shut up!" Stella shouted.

"It's one of those in the middle, Sheriff," Grady continued. "A pretty one with red, white, and blue stripes."

Grady waited and so did Stella for Manny to absorb what he'd just been told.

She could see his eyes glaze over and his fist tighten around his weapon so hard that his fingers turned white.

"She was one of my favorites," Grady was saying. "Out there swimming in the river all by herself."

Slowly, stiffly, like a man sleepwalking, Manny took a step toward Grady.

In doing so, he had stepped away from the door, and Stella was able to walk behind him and open it. She stuck her head out and yelled, "Get in here!" to the deputies in the van.

Then she pulled back into the shop and saw that Manny was even closer to Grady, less than six feet away.

"Put the knife down," he said in a strangely calm voice.

"I didn't actually have much fun with her though," Grady was saying. "She got all weirded out and tried to swim away from me. She wasn't much of a swimmer. Sunk like a rock."

Stella watched in horror as Manny took yet another step closer. She thought of the long scar on Magi Red Crow's neck and how he'd told them that he and Grady Tyrell had nearly killed each other.

"Manny, please stay back," she pleaded.

But Manny took one more step, and in a movement so quick that neither she nor Grady saw it coming, Manny struck out with his weapon and knocked the knife from Grady's hand.

In the same instant, the deputies charged through the door, nearly running Stella down.

Manny pushed Grady backward against the television set and leaned over him, pressing the barrel of his revolver to his temple.

"Go on, kill me," Grady said, half taunting, half pleading.

"Manny, don't," Stella said, moving closer to them. "That's what he wants. Don't do it, please. If you do, you'll never get over it."

"Sir," Augustus said softly as he thrust a pair of handcuffs at Manny. "Would you like to cuff him or would you like me to?"

When Manny didn't accept the manacles, Stella lifted the quilt and said, "If you kill him, there are thirteen more squares here, thirteen more families who will never know the truth. Let him go, Manny. Not because he doesn't deserve to die. He does. But let him go because that's who *you* are."

She knew when her words had reached his heart. He turned and looked at her, as though seeing her for the first time after a long absence. Lowering his weapon, he turned to Augustus and said, "You cuff him. Then gag him and put him in my cage."

"Gag him, sir?"

"Yes, I don't want him to talk me into killing him on the way to the station."

Stella and Manny stood aside so that the two deputies could do as they had been instructed. The look Grady gave Manny, then Stella, as he was led away was one of pure hatred.

Stella reached into her pocket with one hand and touched the talisman, thinking how Magi had said her enemy would be exposed and then the danger would be past.

With only the two of them left in the room, Manny turned to Stella and, with shaking hands, reached for the quilt.

She watched, her heart aching as he ran his hand over the striped square, then pressed it to his cheek.

"Oh, Manny," she said. "I'm so sorry. I can't imagine how you must feel."

Slowly, he lowered the quilt and looked at her with tear-filled eyes. "Yes, you can," he said as he leaned forward and kissed her, slowly and tenderly on the forehead. "If there's anyone on this earth who knows how I feel right now, Stella, my darlin', it's you."

Chapter 38

"I've been to parties that were way funner than this one," Waycross said.

"Wouldn't take much," Marietta replied. "Grown-ups don't know nothin' about throwin' a good party. Sittin' around talkin' don't cut it."

"Yeah," Cordelia joined in. "Somebody could've brought one little piñata. A pin the tail on the donkey game maybe?"

"Heck," Vidalia said, "I'd settle for a round or two of bingo if there were prizes."

"We've got Elsie's coconut cake, Granny's apple pie, and all those pizzas that the sheriff ordered. At least we won't starve to death," Savannah observed.

The children sat on the front porch, watching the adults who had built a bonfire in the side yard and were getting ready to roast marshmallows. Jesup and Alma had already fallen asleep in the porch swing.

Stella sat nearby with Elsie, threading marshmallows onto twigs and unwrapping chocolate bars for the s'mores. She could hear her grandchildren complaining nearby, and she smiled, thinking how quickly their moods would change once the warm, gooey, chocolatey treats were being served.

Elsie pulled out a box of graham crackers and began to unwrap them as well. She glanced over toward the bonfire and nodded at Manny, who was watching Magi add even more twigs and branches to the already impressive flames.

"How's your sheriff doing these days?" Elsie asked. "I know he was mighty depressed there for a while. Can't blame him, poor man. What an awful shock that must've been."

"It was," Stella said. "I had my doubts there for a while that he was gonna recover from it. I think it was as bad for him as losing her the first time around. Maybe even worse."

"An accident's a lot easier to come to peace with than a killing," Elsie said. "You might be able to talk yourself into believing an accident was meant to be. But a killing . . . no way, no how."

"I'm sure that having the trial behind him will help. That jury coming back with a guilty-of-first-degree-homicide verdict didn't bring back the women we lost, but it helped a bit."

"It did." Elsie nodded. "Justice is a sweet thing. Just ask anybody who's been denied theirs. They'll tell ya."

Stella watched Manny as he said something to Magi and both men laughed. She enjoyed seeing that. She loved them both, and she hoped they would become good friends. They each deserved a good friend.

She looked at Elsie, carefully unwrapping the crackers, making sure she wasn't breaking any of them. Stella couldn't imagine what she'd ever done to deserve a friend like Elsie, but she was grateful for her, every day of her life.

"Manny's gonna be okay," Elsie said. "He just needs some of that mothering you and me promised each other that night on the porch. He needs a woman to be strong for him when he's not feelin' so strong hisself and to tell him everything's gonna be okay in the end."

"If it ain't okay, then it ain't the end."

"Exactly. Did I show you what your friend Mr. Red Crow gave to me?"

"No. What?"

Elsie reached into her pocket and pulled out a leather barrette. She placed it into Stella's hand and said, "He told me that symbol there is a cactus flower. He said it's the Cherokee symbol of mothers, because mommas have to endure the cold and all the other harsh things that come along. They refresh and restore people, like the cactus does when it stores up life-giving water."

"What a beautiful thing, Elsie. I'm so pleased he gave you this. It's perfect for you."

Elsie's face flushed with joy. "I told him I wasn't a momma, so I couldn't wear it. But he told me I'm one of the best mommas around. He said you don't have to bear a child to mother one. He said I take care of every child within miles of me, ones from nine days old to ninety years old. I thought that was real sweet of him to tell me that."

"So do I," Stella said. "I couldn't agree with him more. You wear that barrette as a badge of honor. A mother's honor!"

Stella glanced over toward the fire and saw that Manny was looking her way. Magi had joined the children on the porch, showing them how to carve a bird from a block of wood.

Manny alone. Stella couldn't bear to see him alone. Not now. He still had a lot of healing to do.

She stood and said, "Would you excuse me, Sister Elsie? I think our sheriff needs a bit of that mother love we've been talking about. Reckon I'll go give him some."

"Well," Elsie said, as Stella walked away. "That probably ain't his first choice when it comes to types of lovin', but if that's what you've got to offer . . ."

Stella walked across the damp grass, breathed in the smell of the fire, and felt the first bite of winter wind on her cheeks.

"Hey, you," she said, when she reached him. "Whatcha doin' over here all by yourself?"

"Hoping you'd join me."

"Really?"

"Yep. Magi gave me some of that special, ancient tobacco of his. I threw a little bit of it in the fire here, made a wish . . . and poof, here you are."

He slipped his arm around her shoulders. She put hers around his waist, and between the heat of his body and warmth of his affection, Stella no longer felt the winter's chill.